THIMBLERIG'S ARK

BY NATE FLEMING

Web: www.thimblerigsark.com
Blog: thimblerigsark.wordpress.com
Facebook: /thimblerigsark
Twitter: @RNFleming

Nate Fleming
July 2013

For more information, contact author Nate Fleming at info@thimblerigsark.com.

ISBN 978-0-615-98489-6

Copyright © 2014 by Nate Fleming
Cover Illustration © 2014 by Burton Booz

12 11 10 9 8 7 6 5 4   14 15 16 17 18/0
Printed in the United States of America

Fourth printing, July 2014

To Koolyash,
who was there when the idea was conceived.

To Joshua and Asena,
who watched the idea develop and grow
as they developed and grew.

To Noah Abai,
who helped the idea be completed
through the simple act of being born.

PROLOGUE

CHAPTER 1
THIMBLERIG'S DREAM

CHAPTER 2
GETTING THE RIGHT SPOT

CHAPTER 3
RUNNING FROM THE RHINO

CHAPTER 4
A CON IS BORN

CHAPTER 5
THE PROBLEM WITH BELIEVERS

CHAPTER 6
THE SEARCH FOR SUCKERS

CHAPTER 7
THE COMPANY OF ANIMALS

CHAPTER 8
MAKING PREPARATIONS

CHAPTER 9
OFF TO A ROUGH START

CHAPTER 10
DEALING WITH KID DUFFY

CHAPTER 11
A SURPRISING REVELATION

CHAPTER 12
THE HUNT BEGINS

CHAPTER 13
THE UNICORN'S SPRING

CHAPTER 14
A RATHER LARGE ADDITION

CHAPTER 15
CONNING THE CONS

CHAPTER 16
THIMBLERIG'S DREAM, PART TWO

CHAPTER 17
THE AMBUSH

CHAPTER 18
OUT OF THE DARKNESS

CHAPTER 19
COSTLY FREEDOM

CHAPTER 20
ESCAPE TO THE EDGE

CHAPTER 21
UNEXPECTED HELP

CHAPTER 22
THE ARK

CHAPTER 23
A SURPRISING ALLY

CHAPTER 24
THE BATTLE FOR THE ARK

CHAPTER 25
THE MOUND OF DRY BONES

CHAPTER 26
FLOOD

CHAPTER 27
THE THIN PLACE

CHAPTER 28
HOME

A long time ago, when the Earth was green,
There was more kinds of animals than you've ever seen.
And they'd run around free when the Earth was being born,
And the loveliest of 'em all was the unicorn.
Shel Silverstein, "The Unicorn"

~

"So the Lord said, "I will wipe from the face of the earth the
human race I have created—and with them the animals, the birds
and the creatures that move along the ground—for I regret that I
have made them."
Genesis 6:7

~

Downpour on my soul
Splashing in the ocean, I'm losing control
Dark sky all around
I can't feel my feet touching the ground
Jars of Clay, "Flood"

4

PROLOGUE

The colossal fig tree towered over the lush, green forest like a massive guardian. So enormous she could be seen from one corner of the forest to the other, the fig tree offered a place of coolness and shelter for all the forest's creatures.

The animals called her "Asarata", which meant "she who provides" in the old language, and after the spring rains she would sprout plump, juicy figs that would fill all their bellies. It was festival time for the animals of the forest, when they came together to enjoy the delicious fruit in peace and safety. The apes and birds enjoyed the first choice of fruit high up in Asarata's branches and the animals on the ground treasured the figs that fell to the forest floor. Everyone had plenty, and according to ancient forest law, no animal could harm another while under Asarata's branches.

"Who made the forest law?" the tiny young groundhog asked the older groundhog leading him through the crowds. They were on their way to the base of the big fig tree to see how many figs they could collect. Last festival they'd made a personal best record of six figs, a record they fully intended to beat.

"Nobody remembers who made forest law, Thimblerig," the older groundhog answered patiently, dodging a lumbering hippopotamus, and swiftly pulling the younger groundhog back before he could be crushed. It was just another question in a long string of questions her curious groundson asked, and since she knew that one only learned by asking, she didn't discourage him. "But you remember who kept the law and guarded us all, don't you?"

5

"The unicorns!" he shouted enthusiastically, hopping up in front of his groundmother, oblivious to the animals around him. He loved hearing the stories about the unicorns, those noble animals who had once been the guardians of the forest. "I want to see a unicorn, groundmother!"

"Of course you do," she answered. She glanced nervously at a pair of badgers who'd looked their way when Thimblerig had shouted.

"Look at me!" he called, pointing a claw out from his forehead and galloping around. "I'm a unicorn! I'm Tannier Isa, the king of the unicorns!"

At that, Thimblerig's groundmother grabbed him and pulled him into the shadow of an enormous ficus plant. Taking a quick look back, she saw that the badgers had continued on, apparently not caring about Thimblerig's display. Realizing that she was holding her breath, she exhaled. "Sometimes it's good to be a groundhog," she muttered. "Nobody cares about what a groundhog does."

"Did I do something wrong?" Thimblerig asked with a quivering tone to his voice. Had she really been so rough when she'd grabbed him? She looked down at Thimblerig and smiled.

"You did nothing wrong, cub," she said reassuringly. "We just have to be careful that we don't talk too loudly about the unicorns."

"Because of the wild dogs?" Thimblerig whispered.

"Because of the wild dogs," his groundmother whispered back, hating that the child had to be so fearful. But how else would he survive if he didn't fear the wild dogs? They had ears everywhere these days, and you couldn't be too careful.

Sighing, she pulled back the big leaves of the ficus plant and saw that the crowd was moving normally, a variety of animals – big and little, predator and prey – all heading for the base of the big tree. Everyone appeared excited about the festival, but the older groundhog could also sense the tension and anxiety that was always there with all animals, just under the surface.

6

All because of the wild dogs.

"I wish the unicorns would come back."

Thimblerig had poked his head out underneath her own, and also looked out at the crowds. Realizing that she'd succeeded in frightening her young charge, she closed the leaves and took Thimblerig up in her arms, hugging him tightly.

"Don't you doubt it, Thimblerig. The unicorns are going to come back any day now and set the whole forest straight," she ruffled the fur on the top of his head, and set him back down. Since his parents died when he was a newborn, she'd raised him on her own. She'd been sharing the old stories with him since he was old enough to understand, and she hoped against hope that the stories would stick. The way things were going in the forest these days, it was a long shot, but she'd be faithful in loving her groundson, and faithful in the telling. At the end of the day that's the best she could do for him. But she reminded herself that he was also still a cub, and while he was, she needed to let him be a cub.

"Now why don't you hop on my back and let's get a move on to Asarata before all the good figs are taken?"

Thimblerig smiled and nodded up at his groundmother. He climbed onto her back, and held on tight as they set out into the crowd. As they entered the steadily moving stream of animals heading for the big tree, the young groundhog quietly put his paw up to his forehead, stuck out a single claw, and imagined the forest again full of unicorns.

CHAPTER 1
THIMBLERIG'S DREAM

Thimblerig lay sprawled out on his belly on the floor of his subterranean home with a sizable pool of spittle under his face. Half-eaten figs surrounded him, along with leftover bits of some sort of possibly edible leaf, shells, and peas of various sizes. Having unwisely overdone it the night before with rotten figs, Thimblerig was snoring loud enough that animals passing aboveground would think a small earthquake was rattling the forest.

Physically, Thimblerig was a typical adult male groundhog. He was about a foot long, and covered from head to toe in coarse, brown fur. With big buckteeth and small beady eyes, there was absolutely nothing that distinguished him from any others of his species. He used this to his advantage on a daily basis in his particular line of work, which involved quite a bit of cheating, a healthy dose of deceit, and a near-constant need to blend into the crowd. He was a grifter, a con-artist, a hustler, a swindler, and a crook, with two simple goals in life: first, to separate other animals from their figs; and second, to do so without getting caught.

At the moment, Thimblerig was so out of it that he didn't notice the breeze that began to blow through his ratty little burrow. It ruffled Thimblerig's fur, and had he been awake, he might have asked himself what a breeze was doing ruffling his fur in his underground burrow. But he was so comatose, just a step or two above being a corpse, that nothing short of a trumpet blast from an elephant's trunk would have even begun to wake him.

That, or a few drops of cold water.

Just such a drop of cold water plopped onto the face of the snoring groundhog, but it didn't faze him. Eating half-rotten figs way past their date of expiration is always a good way to ensure that a groundhog is not easily roused.

A second, more insistent drop of water spattered on the groundhog's face from the raincloud that formed near the ceiling of the dry groundhog burrow, but had the same effect.

And then a third drop fell.

And then a fourth.

Finally, the fifth raindrop stirred Thimblerig enough that he groggily wiped a paw across his now moist whiskers. As if encouraged by his slight movement, more rain began to fall, making little puffing sounds as it struck the dry ground around him.

"It's too early. I'm not ready to get up..." Thimblerig muttered, turning over on his side. Even more drops fell, and what started out as a gentle shower turned quickly into a pouring rain, like a flash summer storm.

In the groundhog's burrow.

Thimblerig's eyes shot open as the downpour soaked him and everything else in his nice dry burrow. He sat up, shocked by the clouds that had formed over the low ceiling, and put his paws down on the floor to steady himself. But the floor had taken on a definite unfloorish feel to it and rather than the comforting dusty feel of tightly packed dirt, he felt wood. Looking down he saw that it looked like wood, too. Not just wood, but more specifically, a tree branch.

"That's just nuts," Thimblerig muttered, fighting to find his way out of the fog of sleep. "Why am I sleeping on a tree branch?"

A bolt of blinding light flashed across the burrow, illuminating briefly that Thimblerig was no longer in his burrow at all. He was, for some inconceivable reason, sitting in the darkness on a tree branch, with rain crashing down around him in a furious thunderstorm. Yelping at the top of his lungs, Thimblerig started to slip off the branch and just managed to grab hold. It took all his strength and effort to pull up where he could cling to the branch like a cub to his mother.

9

Thimblerig braved a fearful glance up and saw rolling, swirling, and ominously dark clouds like he'd never seen before. Looking down, there was pretty much nothing *but* down as far as the eye could see, and the groundhog immediately regretted looking.

"Groundmother!" he cried, grasping the wet tree branch even tighter.

As if in response, the wind gusted harder and howled through the branches of the tree. The falling rain added to the chaos and made it even more intense and frightening.

Then, in the middle of the madness, Thimblerig heard his name, and it made his soaking wet fur stand on end.

"Thimblerig…"

It came as a whisper in the middle of the storm, and Thimblerig shouldn't have been able to hear it against the booming thunder and crashing rain. "Who is it?" he called out. "Who's there?'

Lightning flashed again, followed quickly by a crack of thunder, the growing howl of the wind, and another whisper.

"It's coming soon, Thimblerig. You need to be ready."

The whisperer was right behind him now, but whipping his head around, Thimblerig didn't see anyone. He was alone, in the middle of a rainstorm, high up in a tree, hearing a disembodied, whispery voice. This wasn't good. Either he was going nuts, having a particularly vivid nightmare, or he was the subject of an elaborate and cruel practical joke. Either way, playing along seemed to be the quickest way back to sanity.

"What's that?" he called out to the darkness. "What's coming?"

Lightning flashed again and illuminated something in the distance. At first Thimblerig imagined it to be the dark outline of the Edge, the mountain chain located to the north three or four days walk away. But as he watched, the outline of the mountains changed, and he could tell the mountains were moving back and forth, growing larger by the moment as if they weren't mountains at all, but a huge wall of water.

A huge wall of water rushing his way.

This was too much for the groundhog, and he started scrambling on the branch trying to find a way down from the tree, trying to avoid slipping and falling, but there was no way down. The terrible sound of trees being snapped and crushed in the distance stopped him in his tracks. One quick glance showed him that the massive waves were growing closer, quickly and destructively, like a stampeding herd of freakishly large wildebeests.

I should have paid better attention when my groundmother was teaching me how to swim, he thought as he clung to the branches of his tree, paralyzed with fear. The wave grew closer and larger, and Thimblerig gasped as it crashed into his shelter, which shuddered but held fast. Before he knew it, a sea of heaving, churning water surrounded him.

But the water was several feet below! It looked like the tree, which he'd been so terrified to find himself sleeping on, was going to be his salvation!

The tree… only one tree in the forest was big enough that it would survive a direct hit by a wave of that size. Only one tree towered over all the other trees of the forest like this one.

That one tree was the great fig tree, Asarata.

He was trapped on a branch on the crown of the queen of the forest in the middle of a raging flood?

Flood.

The word transported Thimblerig back in time and deep under the earth to his long-dead groundmother's burrow, where he saw himself as a young cub, sitting on the dry dirt floor, listening to her tell her stories. It had been so many years since he'd been able to sit at her feet, but it was as real as the storm and the tree and the flood, and seeing her again made him catch his breath.

"Things are bad, boy, and they're just going to get worse," Thimblerig's groundmother said, sitting on her haunches and

11

chewing on a branburry root. She continued, pointing the root at Thimblerig to emphasize her point. "But you just wait and see, the unicorn won't let that happen forever. One day he's just going to clean house and start over fresh."

"What do you mean?" young Thimblerig asked, eyes wide with fascination. "How could he do that?"

"Don't you know?" she replied. "It's in the old stories. It's going to be a clean start. What makes things clean?"

"Water!" he shouted enthusiastically.

His groundmother reached down and touched the tip of his nose with her root, nodding.

"Not just water, little 'Rig. But lots and lots of water," she whispered. "A whole flood of water."

A sudden flash of lightning forced Thimblerig to close his eyes for a moment, and when he opened them, he was back in the branches of Asarata. How much time had passed? He looked down to try and see if there was any change in the water level below, and could just make out the surface of the water, which had risen considerably since before. With no help from the voice he'd heard earlier, he knew that there was no scheming that would save him from the waters when they finally reached him.

A wave crashed just under his feet, soaking his feet as it shuddered his branch again, as well as the remainder of Thimblerig's confidence. He was cold, exhausted, drenched to the bone, and losing his grip. So it was no surprise when a monster wave rose from the darkness and crashed over him, pulling him away from his safe branch, and sweeping him into the deep.

The current sucked him beneath the water's surface and he clawed his paws into the darkness grasping madly for anything to keep him from staying under. He knocked his head up against something solid, and he quickly grasped the object, which turned out to be a log. He pulled himself up and held on for dear life, sputtering.

It was probably the end, he realized. Even if he could keep holding onto the log, there was nobody to help him, and the storm showed no signs of abating. This was it. He was going to drown and die.

"Help!" he gasped in desperation, to the disembodied whispery voice that was out there somewhere.

"Thimblerig…"

It was back! "Who's there? I can't swim!"

"Thimblerig," the whisper repeated, as calm as a quiet breeze. "I need you to lead my children."

Thimblerig nearly lost hold of the log as an animal begin to materialize out of the mist a fig's throw away. It was big and dark, and stood on the water like on dry land. As the shape became recognizable, Thimblerig stopped struggling as he saw the single brilliant golden horn jutting from the animal's forehead, shining out in the darkness of the storm as if on fire. Then, the groundhog looked into the new animal's eyes, and they were so big and dark that they threatened to suck him in like a whirlpool.

It couldn't be. It was impossible. The animal standing before him appeared out of the mists of the stories of his childhood, and it was impossible that it could be there, and yet there it was.

It was a unicorn.

"Thimblerig," the jet-black unicorn was much too calm considering the circumstances. "This is coming, and I want you to lead my children to safety."

"You're not real," Thimblerig muttered. There hadn't been unicorns since well before he was born. What had been in those figs he'd eaten? "You can't be…"

The unicorn ignored his protestations. "Lead them to the Edge. That's where they will find the place of safety."

Lightning flashed again and Thimblerig shielded his eyes. When he opened them, the unicorn was gone, and all that was left was the madness of the storm; dark, wet, tedious madness. Before he could try to call out again, a wave slammed into him, prying him away from the log and tossed him into the waters.

13

Thimblerig struggled for his life as the water attacked him from all sides; the rain hammering from above, the waves tossing him from side to side, the current sucking him down. The raging waters that were destroying the world were going to destroy him too, and send him to the forests beyond. But Thimblerig was too tired to care.

Finally, overwhelmed with fatigue, the groundhog gave up. With the unicorn's words echoing through his mind, he stopped fighting and allowed himself to be pulled under, and he was overcome with watery darkness.

CHAPTER 2
GETTING THE RIGHT SPOT

Thimblerig slammed onto the dry, dusty floor with such force that it knocked the air from his lungs. Eyes closed, he curled up, wheezing, wondering that the forests beyond were dry and dusty like a groundhog burrow.

But at least they were dry.

Thimblerig opened his eyes. He wasn't in the forests beyond after all, but in his own burrow. He ran his paw over the floor and found that there wasn't a drop of water to be seen or felt. Pushing up to a sitting position, he wondered if it was possible that it could have all been a dream. It was so real!

"It couldn't have been a dream," he said to the empty walls of his burrow, but he had to see for himself.

Leaping to his feet he scampered up the dark, narrow tunnel that led to the surface. He poked his head out of his hole and saw that everything topside was normal; there were no giant waves, the morning sky above Asarata was typical cobalt blue with vast white puffy clouds, and most importantly there were no jet-black unicorns. The normal cast of shady characters were hanging about, munching figs, and shooting the breeze.

"Hey bud," he called to a wombat scurrying past. "Has it been raining?"

"Raining?" the little bear-like animal scoffed, not stopping as he scurried. "This time of year? And you call yourself a groundhog?"

Grumbling about groundhog stereotypes, Thimblerig turned and went back down to the base of the tunnel, where he stopped and peered cautiously into his lair. A skylight tunnel allowed a single shaft of light to enter the small room, and provided the groundhog with enough illumination to see shells and leaves scattered all over the floor, half-eaten rotten figs from the night before still lying on his bed of grass, and the regular layer of general griminess that had obviously not been cleaned away by a flood of water.

"Everything's normal," Thimblerig muttered. He collapsed on the bed of grass and absentmindedly picked up one of the offending figs from the night before. "It must have been the figs."

He grimaced as he sniffed the fig, and then tossed it aside with disgust. He'd heard all kinds of stories of bad figs inducing all-night vomiting, endless trips to the toilet bush, bellyaches that floored a yak, and then there was that time Lenny the aardvark had eaten a couple of bad ones and tried climbing *in* an anthill. But vivid hallucinations like the one he'd had? That was a first.

It had all seemed so real; from the wetness of the water to the rough bark of Asarata.

"Asarata?" Thimblerig sat up quickly. "I'm going to be late!"

He jumped up, grabbed his pack of fake figs lying in the corner, and then tore back up the tunnel to the forest above.

Scurrying on all fours with his pack slung over his shoulder, Thimblerig dodged the suckers scrambling for figs. The festival of Asarata was always his most profitable time, and this year he wasn't going to lose his favorite spot on the eastern side of the colossal fig tree.

The key was getting to the spot early. He'd learned that valuable lesson last festival when he'd wasted time loitering around a booth run by a shifty-eyed marmot. He'd gotten so caught up haggling over the price of a warthog tooth necklace that he'd been beat to his favorite spot, and he'd been relegated to the only open spot left: beside the toilet bushes.

Ugh. The toilet bushes. The stench of those bushes still lingered in Thimblerig's nostrils a year later, and he was determined that it would not happen again. And yet, here he was scrambling, again, thanks to that disturbing dream that had made him oversleep.

The groundhog entered the clearing near his favorite spot, and was pushing and elbowing his way through the morning crowd when he saw something across the clearing that made his heart plummet: Mullins, the gazelle con-wannabe from the year before, the one who had stolen his spot, also heading in the same direction.

His favorite spot.

Again.

Not this year, Thimblerig thought bitterly. Picking up his pace but not watching where he was going, Thimblerig slammed into an old armadillo grandma and bounced off her leathery old shell.

He struggled to keep on his feet, even as she tumbled over on her side. Having missed a very important beat, he took off again. "Watch where you're going, grandma!" he spat back at her.

"You scum sucking pig! You dirty stinking rat!" The enraged armadillo screamed at the groundhog, shaking her tiny little fist at his backside as he disappeared into the crowd.

The gazelle had become a real burr in the groundhog's fur since the previous festival, apparently having made it his mission in life to horn in on Thimblerig's territory. Every time Thimblerig would set up shop, he'd turn around to find the gazelle grinning that idiot grin of his, begging him to partner up, and blowing it for just about every mark that walked by.

But the gazelle was fast, Thimblerig had to give him that. And so with furious determination that one might not expect from a groundhog, he closed his eyes and dove, rolling to a stop with his back against the base of the big tree, dead center on his favorite spot.

"Made it," Thimblerig said victoriously, panting hard. He reached behind to pat Asarata, but she wasn't hard and rough. She was soft and fuzzy. Maybe it was just a patch of moss growing on her great trunk? He took a look, and was peeved to see that he was actually leaning against the gazelle.

17

"You okay, Thimblerig?" Mullins asked. How could such a naïve gazelle sound so snarky? The fact that he didn't mean to irritate made it that much more irritating.

"Can it, Mullins," Thimblerig shot back. He picked himself up from the ground with extreme effort. "This is my spot, and you know it. You knew it last year, too. Go find someplace else to stink up!"

Mullins shook his head mournfully. "C'mon, where's your festival spirit?"

"On this spot," Thimblerig replied, gesturing to the place where Mullins was standing.

"This really is a prime location," Mullins said as he looked at the masses of animals passing by. Suddenly, he turned back to the groundhog. "I've got an idea! Let's work it together! With my good looks and your experience, we'll take these suckers for every fig!"

"I've told you before," Thimblerig grumbled. "I don't work with partners."

"Come on, Thimblerig, twice the team, twice the profits!" Mullins replied.

"I'll just find another spot," Thimblerig said. He lifted his pack from the ground and smacked it a few times to remove the dust.

"This time of day, you'll be lucky to get the toilet bushes," Mullins called as Thimblerig shuffled away. "If you change your mind, the offer stands!"

"There'll be a thunderstorm in my burrow before I change my mind," Thimblerig muttered, and he went in search of a decent place to set up for the day.

The rhinoceros stared hard at the figs sitting on the stone table in front of him. He'd just won them playing a simple shell game with a groundhog where he tried to guess which shell hid a pea. It wasn't hard, and the groundhog was pretty bad at it, which

18

meant the rhinoceros could clean up, if he played it smart. Finally, he made a decision.

"I'll bet both figs," the big beast rumbled.

"Going double or nothing?" Thimblerig asked, turning to the crowd. "Ladies and gentlemen, we have a real player here! He's going double or nothing!"

The only open spot Thimblerig had been able to find after leaving Mullins had been the dreaded toilet bushes. So, he'd stubbornly set up his shell game and started trying to attract suckers. Unfortunately, just thirty minutes before, a hippopotamus suffering from a severe gastrointestinal virus had descended on the toilet bushes with a vengeance, and it had been all Thimblerig could do to not pass out, even standing upwind. He'd had no choice, and so he'd packed up his gear and his pride and made his way back to the gazelle.

"Yes! Partners!" Mullins had shouted, jumping up and down like he'd just won the annual fig lottery.

"Just this once!" Thimblerig had barked back. "And let's get this straight: I run the operation and you are my shill. When it's done we divide the take seventy-thirty, and then this partnership is done. You got it?"

"Seventy-thirty? Who gets the seventy?" Mullins had asked, no longer jumping.

"I do, of course," Thimblerig said calmly.

"You've got to be kidding! It's my spot we're working, remember? It needs to be fifty-fifty."

"Fifty-fifty, eh?" Thimblerig sighed with relief. It was like taking figs from a cub, as if Thimblerig had written the lines himself. "To be honest, I was hoping you'd say that."

"You were?" Mullins' eyebrow arched suspiciously. "Why?"

"Because that way, if the wild dogs show and decide to bust up the game, you get half of the blame, too. Otherwise, if you'd accepted the thirty percent, I would have to pretend like I don't know you, and then I would have to take all the blame myself. Fifty-fifty is much better. But I had to negotiate, you know."

Now, Mullins stood in the middle of a huge crowd of animals, happily talking up Thimblerig's game like a good shill, and probably imagining what he would do with his thirty percent of the take.

Thimblerig's heart pounded as he covered up the pea once more and started shuffling and sliding the shells. "Hey diddle-diddle, the pea's in the middle! One fig'll get you two, two will get you four. Play and play and you'll win some more!"

In the zone, Thimblerig was doing what he was created to do. The shells moved back and forth on the table so fast that he wouldn't have been surprised if they'd burst into flames. Finally, he stopped, and looked up at the rhinoceros's blank face. His right ear was twitching so much that Thimblerig thought it might twitch off his head and go running into the forest. He'd have to keep an eye on that twitching ear.

"Time to earn some figs, my friend," Thimblerig said. "Where's the pea?"

The rhinoceros glared at the shells like that would help him see through to the pea underneath. And as eager as he was to seal the deal, Thimblerig sat patiently and waited for the big predictable sucker to make his choice. The entire crowd leaned in to see what the rhinoceros would do.

"The middle. It's under the middle shell."

"Hey diddle-diddle, is the pea under the middle?" Thimblerig called out as he started to lift the shell. But before he'd completely raised the shell, he stopped, and looked up at the rhinoceros, alarmed.

"I'm so sorry about this... I don't know what happened..."

The rhinoceros scrunched up his face as he prepared to hear the worst.

"I'm afraid to tell you..."

The crowd held its collective breath.

"...that you won! Again!" Thimblerig yanked up the middle shell to show the little pea sitting faithfully where the rhinoceros had predicted. The crowd went ballistic and the resulting sounds of celebration were deafening.

But a single voice carried over the noise, and it whispered the groundhog's name.

"Thimblerig."

Again? The whisper from his dream? Thimblerig looked around but couldn't see anything out of the ordinary, just the suckers celebrating. Connecting with Mullins, he saw that the gazelle was gesturing at the rhinoceros, who had stepped up to take his juicy winnings.

Forgetting the whisper, Thimblerig moved his tiny furry paws over the figs and got back into the game.

"How about we give it another go, Mr. Rhinoceros?"

"I think I'll quit while I'm ahead," the rhinoceros laughed.

"I thought you might say that," Thimblerig said, hopping onto the rocky table and gesturing to the sack of figs hanging around the rhinoceros's neck. "How many figs would you say you have in that nice sack of yours?"

"Dunno. Maybe fifteen?"

Thimblerig nodded his head and patted the rhinoceros's horn, which the groundhog noticed seemed to be a bit bent. He hopped back down on the ground and reached under the stone table. Huffing with apparent exertion, he pulled out a bag half as large as himself and heaved the bag onto the table.

In most ways the bag was the typical plain brown festival bag woven from dogbane fibers; the kind everyone carried around. It was also noticeably bursting at the seams with what appeared to be figs, but what was, in actuality, balls of tightly packed leaves and dirt.

"What we have here, my friend, is my savings account," Thimblerig said, breathless. "It's about forty figs, give or take. Good plump ones, too."

The rhinoceros's eyes grew wide at the sight of the huge bag of figs. The bag was bulging, ready to burst. "That's a lot of figs," he rumbled.

"That's the understatement of the festival," Thimblerig replied proudly. "I've been saving them up for my kids. But I tell you what I'm going to do. I'll put up my forty against your fifteen. Whaddaya say? That's nearly three to one odds in your favor!"

The animals in the crowd shuffled and stamped with nervous energy at the seriousness of the wager. Fifty-five figs in one place was an impressive amount, and while not a fortune, it was more than your typical animal saw during the festival.

"Oh, wow!" the gazelle exclaimed, doing his job, hopping up to the rhinoceros's side. "You gotta do this! Look at the size of that sack!"

"It's a big sack," the rhinoceros agreed. "But what if I lose…"

The excited gazelle bounced around the rhinoceros, chanting, "Do it! Do it! Do it!" The other animals, wanting to see someone win big and someone else lose, joined in the chant. Soon, the echoes of the crowd's chanting resounded across the base of the enormous tree. Thimblerig stood still with a serene grin on his face. He was extremely confident what the mark would choose to do.

The rhinoceros, meanwhile, looked the polar opposite of serene. His twitchy ear had gone eerily still, but his eyes were bugging out and looked as if they might explode from his head. At just the right moment Thimblerig hopped up on the table again and raised his hands to quiet the crowd. He turned to the rhinoceros.

"What's it going to be, superstar? You in or out?"

The rhinoceros looked down at the tiny groundhog as if really seeing him for the first time. For a moment, Thimblerig thought that he might have misjudged the beast and was rapidly starting to think of a plan B when he heard what he'd been waiting to hear.

"I'm in."

"We got us a player!" Thimblerig cried out, answered by the roars, yelps, barks, and caws of the crowd. The gazelle bounded madly between the watching animals, hooping and hollering louder than any.

The rhinoceros dropped his bag of figs on the table and smiled at the crowd as they patted him on the back, shouting words of encouragement. The gazelle was especially excited, and all the activity distracted the rhinoceros and kept him from from noticing that Thimblerig had hopped off the table and quickly switched the rhinoceros's bag with a similar looking bag pulled from underneath.

"Let's clear the table!" Thimblerig shouted, getting the rhinoceros's attention again. He grabbed the bags from the table and set them on the ground beside. "You ready, friend?"

The rhinoceros nodded confidently. He'd won twice already, so he knew he could do it again. He could just imagine the fig high he'd have after eating fifty-five figs...

"We're playing for the big figs now!" Thimblerig said loudly, as he started shuffling the shells around the tabletop.

The animals crowding the table were leaping up and down, patting the rhinoceros on the back, as enthusiastic as any crowd he'd seen at any festival. If he shifted his shells right, he could walk away from this with enough figs to pay back the wild dogs and disappear into his burrow for the rest of the festival.

"Time is running out, Thimblerig..."

The whisper was back, loud and clear, and Thimblerig could easily hear it over the noise of the crowd. He glanced back and forth among the animals to see who might have spoken, and then he saw him.

Standing behind the rhinoceros, staring directly at him, golden horn gleaming in the morning light, apparently unnoticed by everyone else, was the black unicorn from his dream.

"Let's go, groundhog!" the rhinoceros shoved his enormous leathery face into Thimblerig's line of sight, blocking his view of the unicorn. Thimblerig jumped up, but couldn't make out anything with all of the animals leaping back and forth again.

"Move it, you big galumph!"

Before Thimblerig could say anything more, a panicked voice cried out from the edge of the crowd, "The wild dogs! The wild dogs!"

Already? Why had Mullins sounded the alarm so early? What had happened to the unicorn? Had he imagined it? But there was no time for going insane. Thimblerig had a con to finish.

"Wild dogs?" Thimblerig cried out theatrically, falling back into his routine. "Everyone scatter before they catch us!"

The simple mention of the wild dogs was enough to strike terror into the hearts of anyone in the forest; such was the sway that the pack held. The unnerved animals started pushing and shoving and running in every direction in an attempt to vacate the area around the illegal shell game. Thimblerig jumped in front of the confused rhinoceros, holding up his bag.

"Hey mate, don't forget your figs!" He tossed it around the rhinoceros's neck, chunked him a military-style salute, and hoisted his own bag onto his shoulder. "Stay safe, Mr. Rhino! We'll have to continue the game at another time!"

With that, Thimblerig disappeared into the rapidly dispersing crowd like a puff of smoke on a windy day. The big beast was left standing quite alone in the now quiet and empty spot under Asarata.

"Where'd everyone go?" the rhinoceros asked the empty spot.

As if in response, a solitary fig plopped to the ground, fallen from the branches high above.

CHAPTER 3
RUNNING FROM THE RHINO

Under a shelter of foliage, safe from the nosy eyes of prying animals, Mullins the gazelle lay on his side, breathing hard from leaping back and forth among the "stiffs", and causing general mayhem. He didn't move when Thimblerig, lugging the rhinoceros's bag, broke through the safe canopy of musky leaves and branches and collapsed on the forest floor beside Mullins, and lay gasping for breath.

"Finally!" Mullins said. "I was starting to think you'd skipped out on me!"

"I gave it serious consideration," Thimblerig wheezed, his head lying on the cool mossy ground, eyes closed.

"Fig me," Mullins said.

Grumbling, Thimblerig sat up and reached into the bag, pulled out two figs, and tossed one to Mullins. He hesitated, but he had to find out if anyone else had seen the unicorn. "Hey, Mullins, did you see anything strange out there?"

"Strange?"

"Yeah, like anyone out of the ordinary?"

"Oh yeah," Mullins replied, laughing. "That guy's horn!"

"You saw that?" Thimblerig asked, relieved. Maybe he wasn't insane after all. "I thought I imagined it! What was that all about?"

"I know! How does a rhino get a bent horn?" Mullins asked, examining his fig carefully.

"Rhino?" Thimblerig replied.

"Yeah, the way that rhino's horn was bent. He must have caught in a rock when he was little. Are rhinos ever little?"

Thimblerig shook his head back and forth. It was exhaustion. He'd been working too hard, and eating too many fermented figs at night. He'd have to slow down on that. Meanwhile, it was time to change the subject. "Why'd you cry 'dog' so early? I could have taken that crowd for another fifty, easy!"

"You gave the cue," Mullins answered, more interested in munching on the fig then debriefing the con they'd just run.

"What do you think the cue was supposed to be?"

"You were jumping up and down," Mullins answered, with mouth full of fig. "That was the cue."

Thimblerig pulled his ears in frustration. "That wasn't the cue, Mullins. We only went over this a dozen times."

"Then why were you jumping up and down?" Mullins asked, fig juice running down from his mouth.

"Never mind that," Thimblerig groaned. "The point is, the cue was 'eenie meenie', as in, 'eenie, meenie, money, me, now you have to find the pea'."

"You've got to be kidding me. That's way too complicated," Mullins said, matter-of-fact. He was a simple gazelle, concerned primarily with two things: finding his next meal and staying alive. He didn't have time for such complex cues. "A cue should be something simple, like jumping up and down. Or a buzz word."

"A buzz word?" Thimblerig asked.

"That's right, something easy to remember," Mullins answered. Absentmindedly, he watched a fly buzzing around his head, attracted by the scent of the fig. "How about 'razzamataz'?"

"Razzamataz?" Thimblerig repeated.

"Yeah, razzamataz!" Mullins perked up with excitement. He didn't usually come up with such good ideas.

"That has to be the worst cue I've ever heard!" Thimblerig griped. "How the heck am I supposed to use "razzamataz" naturally during a con?"

The two grifters were so wrapped up in their conversation that they didn't notice that the light inside their undergrowth sanctuary had dimmed, as if a cloud had passed over the sun.

"It's easy! You just look at your mark, like that sucker rhino back there, and you say, 'it's like razzamataz!' when you're doing your thing with the shells. It's gold, Thimblerig!"

"You're right, Mullins, it's brilliant," Thimblerig replied sarcastically. "But I have an even better idea. Why don't I just look him in his brainless eyes and say, 'and now, Mr. Big and Ugly, watch as I take all your figs from under your nose and run away!"

Thimblerig didn't hear the snort that came from just outside their hiding place because he was too busy making his point. Had he heard it, he would have thought that it sounded like the rush of a geyser under terrible pressure, erupting bursts of hot water and steam. Mullins heard it, and warily cocked his ears in that direction while Thimblerig continued talking.

"I'm so sorry that you're so brainless, Mr. Rhino, that you fall for the oldest con in the book, but it is the *shell game* after all..."

"Um, Thimblerig..." Mullins started.

"No, listen!" Thimblerig interrupted, fully enjoying painting the absurd scene. "I'd say, 'But Mr. Rhino, if you will please just stand there like the oversized chump that you are while I pick the figs out of your mouth, I would really appreciate it!' How's that for a cue, Mullins? Do you think you could remember all of that?"

Thimblerig sat back with a satisfied grin, picked up a particularly plump fig and fingered it, enjoying the way the shifting rays of light played off the dark purple and blue skin.

Mullins whimpered.

"Seriously, Mullins?" Thimblerig said. "If you're going to get all upset over a little criticism, you'll never make it in this business."

Mullins couldn't speak, but simply gestured behind Thimblerig. The groundhog turned and stared directly into the giant angry bent-horned face of the rhinoceros. The rhinoceros's eyes were slitted like a snake's, and he was shoving each breath

27

through his enormous nostrils with the force of a small hurricane. "You called me brainless," the rhinoceros rumbled. "That hurt my feelings."

"Ah, Mr. Rhinoceros! We weren't talking about you," Thimblerig started to say, slowly rising and turning around. As he turned, he bumped into his bag, spilling out the rhinoceros's bag, and several of the rhinoceros's figs rolled out onto the ground. All three animals looked down at the figs and the rhinoceros snorted again.

"You took my figs?" the rhinoceros asked in an even lower pitched voice, so low that the vibrations hurt Thimblerig's two big front teeth.

The forest closed down on Thimblerig, as if being shrunk around him, and it was hard to breathe. But Thimblerig was at his best in high-pressure situations, and so he forced a deep breath. It was time to use his golden tongue, which had saved him countless times before, and which would save him countless times to come.

"Mr. Rhinoceros, it's not what it looks like..."

Thimblerig's fur blew back as the rhinoceros snorted a wave of hot, angry air that smelled like the inside of an angry rhinoceros. Staring into the face as big as his body, Thimblerig's composure started to crack.

"You see, it's really that..." he stumbled. "...it all started when..."

A low rumble built inside the rhinoceros. It was a menacing sound, especially if you were the cause of that building rumble, and most especially if that menacing rumble was aimed right at you.

"It all started when I was a cub," Thimblerig sobbed, covering his face with his hands. "I had a really difficult childhood..."

Thimblerig peeked out at the rhinoceros through his claws to see if he was having any effect. The rhinoceros didn't look the least bit moved by the groundhog's performance. In fact, if anything, he looked even angrier. Apparently he wasn't as

28

gullible as Thimblerig had supposed. It was time to alternate strategies.

Catching his breath on a particularly heavy sob, Thimblerig looked up at the rhinoceros with the biggest, doe-iest eyes he could muster. Paws shaking, he pointed at Mullins.

"It was his idea…"

In the second it took for the beady eyes of the rhinoceros to shift towards the gazelle, Thimblerig grabbed the bag of figs and bolted. It was a move so quick that it surprised all three of them, Thimblerig included. He zipped under the tree-trunk legs of the rhinoceros, and shot out of the shelter like a bat out of a burning bush.

"Every mammal for himself!" he shouted as he disappeared.

But Mullins had already scrammed, not waiting for Thimblerig's shout, leaping through the underbrush in the opposite direction.

The rhinoceros yanked his head out of the thick wall of leaves and vines. Furious, he scanned the forest to the left and right, squinting as he tried to find the little groundhog in the middle of the festival crowd. He spotted him ducking behind a family of warthogs.

"Groundhog!" the rhinoceros thundered, the volume of his shout making every head turn, and then every animal attached to each turned head scattered as the rhinoceros charged.

Thimblerig's first rule of escape from large, angry, charging animals was get out of sight, and do so quickly. He was a good twenty minutes away from his burrow, so escaping underground wasn't an immediate option. Making a snap decision as he raced past the warthogs, he chose his next, best possibility – between the flabby brown legs of an overweight sloth.

The sloth had stopped slowly walking to slowly watch all the excitement. A large and surprisingly fast rhinoceros was charging after someone who had irritated it to the point of making

29

it want to charge. Someone, quite possibly the one the rhinoceros was after, had hidden between his legs.

He'd just been thinking that coming down from his tree for the festival was a big waste of time. After all, he moved too slowly to get any good figs, and nobody helped anybody these days. And then, just when he was about to go home, excitement had happened! The sloth couldn't remember having such an interesting time since the bananas fell.

Relieved to see the rhinoceros thunder past, and even more relieved to scurry out from underneath the sloth, who had apparently not bothered to dip himself into a bathing hole for quite a while, Thimblerig grabbed his bag of figs to head home. He was stopped in his tracks by a half dozen wild dogs standing in his path.

The wild dogs were not adorable floppy eared, warm-hearted, lick-you-in-the-face-and-play-fetch-with-sticks kind of dogs. They wouldn't curl up beside you and beg you to rub their tummies. These were the *wild dogs*, brutal authoritarian thugs, corrupt mafia, and anarchist hooligans, all rolled into one bloodthirsty pack. They would shake down animals of any shape and size for the last bite of a fig, or just for the sadistic pleasure of it. And now they were surrounding Thimblerig.

"What's that you have there, groundhog?"

A good half-dozen groundhoggian expletives flew through Thimblerig's brain as he stood before the wild dogs, but he quickly pushed them aside. Using any of those would be a good way to make sure his head ended up on a pointed stick in front of the wild dog's lair as a warning to other mouthy animals. Instead, he smiled broadly while subtly moving in front of the bag of stolen figs.

"Good afternoon gentledogs! It's a fine festival day, isn't it?"

"Lupo asked you a question," one of the other wild dogs growled, moving much closer to Thimblerig than the groundhog appreciated. "What's in the bag?"

30

"What, this bag?" Thimblerig answered, gesturing nonchalantly at the bag behind him. "Oh, it's nothing, just some knick-knacks for the burrow. You know, just sprucing up the place!"

The one called Lupo laughed a decidedly joyless laugh. "Knick-knacks? Do we look like fools?"

Yes you do! Thimblerig really had to bite down on his tongue to keep from saying this. But it didn't really matter, because Lupo wasn't waiting for an answer. He nodded at one of the other wild dogs who shoved Thimblerig out of the way, picked up the bag by the teeth, and dumped out the contents. The rhinoceros's figs rolled across the forest floor.

"I've really got to get a bag that cinches at the top," Thimblerig muttered as the wild dogs looked from the figs on the ground to him.

"Well, well, well. What have we here?" Lupo asked. "You wouldn't happen to be the groundhog that runs the shell game over on the east side, would you? The one that just took a rhino for a bagful?"

Any transaction, legal or not, was subject to a festival tax of fifty percent, payable to the wild dogs immediately. Of course the term 'festival tax' was just the wild dog's fancy way of saying they got half of whatever you made, whether you made it legally or not. Everyone paid it because the alternative involved ending up on a pointed stick. And Thimblerig hadn't paid the festival tax in quite a while.

Someone ratted me out, Thimblerig thought, and his options now were limited. Making a run for it was not a choice, as groundhogs were nowhere near as quick as wild dogs. If he denied being a con, they'd take all his figs and he'd probably end up on a pointed stick. If he confessed to being a con, they'd take all his figs and he'd probably also end up on a pointed stick. No matter what he did, a pointed stick was in his future.

Unless I can talk my way out of it...

31

"That's exactly who I am," he admitted with confidence. "You should have seen how I took that sucker! Had him right here in my paw from the start. I was just on my way to pay Kid Duffy when you stopped me. He and I have a private arrangement and he's expecting me."

At the mention of Kid Duffy's name, Lupo's eyes grew wide and the other wild dogs started whimpering. This was exactly the desired reaction. Kid Duffy was the wild dog known as "Blonger's Enforcer." Second in command of the wild dogs, and universally feared throughout the forest, Thimblerig was taking a huge risk. If Lupo called him on the bluff, he might be taken directly to Kid Duffy, and that would not go well. But one of the important rules of being a con is that you dare your mark to prove you wrong. So Thimblerig decided to up the ante.

"Actually, if you don't mind, maybe you could take me to Kid Duffy yourself? To help explain why I was late? That would really help me out. He doesn't like it when I'm late with his taxes."

Sweating profusely, the groundhog stood his ground fighting the urge to shift his feet. He stared at Lupo impassively, doing his best to project an air of confidence as he waited to see what Lupo would do. The wild dog stared back for a few moments, sizing him up, and he began to think that his con might just work.

Lupo walked up, and stood right over the groundhog, his muzzle just inches from Thimblerig's face. His breath smelled like rotten meat. "Kid Duffy wouldn't waste time or energy on a nobody like you." He turned to the other wild dogs. "Boys, get the figs."

The other wild dogs obediently collected his winnings and dropped them into the rhinoceros's bag. Thimblerig hardly noticed what the wild dogs were doing as the words "a nobody like you" echoed in his mind. Finally, when all the figs had been collected, Lupo turned to leave.

"Wait," Thimblerig said. "You're letting me go?"

The wild dog paused but didn't turn back. "Lupo don't waste his time on nobodies either. Enjoy the festival, groundhog."

Lupo and the six wild dogs sauntered off into the crowds in possession of Thimblerig's legitimately conned figs, nipping at any animal that came too close, leaving behind a groundhog with a devastated ego, only marginally relieved to still be alive.

CHAPTER 4
A CON IS BORN

"Nobody! He called me a nobody!"

Thimblerig sat on a rough wooden stump at Mulberry's Bar, in the middle of the crowd, nursing an old rotten fig and his wounded pride, speaking much too loudly to the koala sitting beside him. The koala was also sucking on a rotten fig, and spent quite a bit of time nodding. "I mean, didn't he know who I was?"

The koala nodded and took the last bite of his fig. He looked about sadly.

"You know who I am, don't you, Reginald? But did you know that I once took a fatcat giraffe for one hundred figs? One hundred! That's more than those wild dogs see in a lifetime, and I saw it after one game. And that wild dog has the nerve to tell me that I'm a nobody?"

The koala nodded, chewing the last bit of his fig.

"The thing is, I've run into some hard times recently. But times are tough for everyone, am I right?"

Nodding, the koala looked around for another fig, which Thimblerig handed him, and the koala immediately started to eat.

"And to be honest, I've been having some real strange dreams lately, and I'm not sure what to do with them. I mean, *strange* dreams. If I told you about them, you'd probably think I was nuts. Absolutely nuts. But it seemed so real!"

The koala was nodding, engrossed in his new fig, which was a bit more rotten than his last.

"I'm not crazy," Thimblerig said, shaking his head to clear out the cobwebs. "It seemed so real, but only a real sucker would believe it."

Then, as it hit him, the fig fell out of Thimblerig's paw. An idea of unparalleled brilliance broke through the confusion of the moment like a shaft of light breaking through the darkness. There *was* someone who would believe it.

"The believers..." he exclaimed.

There was a secretive group of animals in the forest, a small group of animals, who still held on to the old beliefs, claiming that the unicorns – like the one he'd just dreamed about - weren't gone forever. They were certifiable, holding onto old fantasy stories as if they were fact, wanting so badly for them to be true to the point of being blinded to everything else. They were called believers, and they were the perfect suckers.

If he could find some of those gullible fanatics, convince them that the flood was coming and that he knew where to go to be saved, then they would give him every last fig in their possession. Maybe even more.

It would be the ultimate con.

"Why didn't I think of this before?" Thimblerig muttered, grabbing his pack and pulling it over his shoulder and shoving his last three rotten figs into the surprised koala's paws. "It was great talking to you, Reginald!"

He pushed aside the vines that served as the entrance to Mulberry's, but paused before he exited. "This is going to be huge. Too big for me to pull alone."

He didn't like it, but if he could gather a small gang of cons he could trust at least a little, and if they succeeded, then they would all be set for life. Nothing else mattered, not having to work with others, not the wild dogs, not even the angry rhinoceros that was liable to still be skulking around somewhere, wanting Thimblerig mounted on the end of his horn.

"Gotta go find Mullins…" he said, and he ran off into the forest.

Mullins was where Thimblerig had least expected, hiding in some bushes on the outskirts of a small grassy meadow where the female gazelles liked to gather. Mullins was notoriously shy when it came to females, especially if he thought they were even somewhat attractive, which the five he watched now were, at least by male gazelle standards.

35

"Mullins! There you are!" Thimblerig announced loudly as he came upon him in the bushes. Several of the females glared at the groundhog, irritated by his intrusion. He just smiled and waved. "Sorry ladies, but I've just been looking for my pal. Turns out he's right here!" He grabbed the mortified Mullins by the scruff of the neck and pulled him out of the bushes. "See? Any of you girls want a piece of this?"

Mullins grinned uncomfortably, and with a definite air of superiority, the females turned their backs on the pair and disappeared into the forest.

"Thimblerig, what'd you go and do that for?" Mullins whined, yanking his head away from the groundhog, as he watched the last gazelle leave. "You scared them away!"

"Don't worry about them, Mullins," Thimblerig said with a wave of his paw. "I've got a new deal cooking, and I need you to go round up Soapy and Big Bunco to discuss it."

Mullins stared at Thimblerig, his mouth hanging wide open.

"Well, what are you waiting for?" the groundhog said, irritated.

"You actually want to bring someone else in on a deal? Are you serious?"

"As a heart attack, Mullins. But if you want in, you got to get your tail moving right now!"

Mullins didn't waste any more time and leapt off into the forest in the direction of the festival grounds. Thimblerig laughed watching him go, and hopped up and down clapping his paws together like he was a cub once again.

They met under Thimblerig's favorite eucalyptus tree, not far from the main square, tucked back in the shadows where only the shiftiest of animals went. The three animals sitting with Thimblerig all stared at him with mouths hanging wide open. Thimblerig just grinned as he surveyed the team he'd hastily assembled: Soapy the orangutan, a pickpocket with the sneakiest

36

fingers in the forest; Big Bunco, a floppy-eared pygmy elephant who had the reputation as an unflappable lookout. And then there was Mullins. Thimblerig still wasn't sure what the gazelle was good at besides keeping himself alive, but with such short notice he didn't have many options.

"A flood?" Mullins asked, breaking the confused silence. "I don't get it."

"Sounds wet," Soapy said.

"C'mon, guys!" Thimblerig exclaimed. "Where's your vision? This is the big-fig idea we've been waiting for!" He looked over at the elephant. "Please tell me you see the potential here, Bunco."

"I'm afraid not, 'Rig,'" she answered. "Maybe if you explain it again?"

Thimblerig sighed with frustration. Even Big Bunco didn't get it, and she was the sharpest one of the three. Thinking about his groundmother for the second time that day, Thimblerig could almost hear her saying, "If a student don't understand, then it's the teacher not explaining it right."

"Alright then, let me try a visual," Thimblerig said. He pushed aside the big eucalyptus leaf so they could see the forest beyond. All kinds of animals were walking back and forth, others sitting munching on figs, still others were standing around talking, all had their fig packs around their necks. "What do you see?"

"A bunch of suckers," replied Big Bunco.

"A bunch of suckers with a bunch of figs," Soapy said, a wicked gleam in his eyes.

"That rhinoceros from this morning," Mullins said.

Yep, there he was. The big galoot was stomping around asking questions of everyone. He might be a thickheaded, small-brained, one-animal wrecking machine, but Thimblerig admired his persistence. He lowered the leaf.

"Forget the rhinoceros," he whispered. "Think about what else you saw: a bunch of figs, belonging to a bunch of suckers, all ripe for the taking. Think about the way they fall for all the cons

37

at the festival! It's like they're begging us to take their figs! And why do they do it? Because they're a sorry, greedy, selfish, ignorant lot, and they just want more, more, more. They'll believe anything we tell them if they think they can get something out of it."

Big Bunco nodded, the light of understanding finally starting to gleam in her eyes. "So the flood story is just the bait."

"The long con is more Abernathy's speed," Soapy countered. "This isn't our kind of job."

"Why shouldn't it be?" Thimblerig replied forcefully. "We've been working at this for a long time, and what do we have to show for it? A few dried figs hidden away somewhere? Aren't you ready for the big payoff?"

"And you dreamed this?" Mullins asked.

"I did," Thimblerig boasted. "It was a gift from the unicorn, this dream. The ultimate con."

"But I still don't understand what the payoff would be," Soapy asked.

Thimblerig rubbed his paws together in excitement. "This is the best part, my friends, where we clean up. I'll use my skills of persuasion to convince them that I've had a vision, that the flood of prophecy is coming, and that only I know how to take them to safety."

"For a price," Big Bunco said, nodding her head.

"For a price," Thimblerig confirmed. "Two hundred dried figs per animal."

You could hear a mosquito pass gas in the silence that followed Thimblerig's suggested price. Two hundred figs? Most animals didn't have that kind of savings, especially these days. Any marks they could swindle would have to beg, borrow, or steal to pay up.

"They'd have to be crazy," Mullins said, stunned.

"The crazier the better," Thimblerig said, smiling. "Crazy figs are just as good as sane ones, aren't they?"

Soapy and Big Bunco exchanged glances. Thimblerig knew that they were each crunching the numbers in their heads, considering the potential just as he had. The possibilities were enormous, and made their typical cons seem like small potatoes in comparison.

"What's our cut?" Soapy asked, as serious as Thimblerig had seen him.

"That's the question, 'Rig," Big Bunco nodded.

"Fair enough," Thimblerig answered. "You each get fifteen percent."

Thimblerig was prepared to negotiate his way through this. If suckers were greedy, cons made them look like saints. He fully expected them to want twenty-five percent across the board after the wild dog's cut, so he dropped the big rock.

"And here's the kicker. We don't pay the wild dogs one purple fig."

If his colleagues had thought him a bit crazy before, now they figured he'd lost every bit of his mind. The wild dogs made a big show of chasing off the cons, but in reality, they just chased off the cons that didn't pay the festival tax. And those cons typically ended up on the end of pointy sticks.

"You heard right, friends," Thimblerig said. "We run this without the wild dogs."

"Without the wild dogs?" Mullins shouted. "Did you fall down your burrow and smack your skull?"

"The wild dogs don't like being out of the loop," Soapy added, shaking his head. "They don't like that at all."

"I should have known," Big Bunco said, leaning back and massaging her forehead with her trunk. "Thimblerig's gone Ponzi."

At the mention of the name "Ponzi", the others gasped, including Thimblerig. Ponzi had been a longhorn ram who had hatched a plan to borrow figs from anyone and everyone, promising that he'd pay them back with more figs later. What he didn't advertise was that he would borrow still more figs from other animals, promising them profits as well, and using their figs to pay off the other animals. He would always borrow more each time, keeping the profits for himself.

Ponzi had gotten away with it for quite a while, amassing a fortune in figs. But he'd gotten too greedy, and he'd taken his scheme to the wild dogs hoping for the big score. Blonger, the leader of the wild dogs, greedily took the bait and lost a substantial number of figs when Ponzi couldn't find anyone else to con. Ponzi's head ended up on a pointed stick, and his skull was there to this day as a warning to anyone who tried to pull the wool over the wild dog's eyes.

"This will not be a Ponzi." Thimblerig insisted. "Ponzi got stupid and greedy. We won't do either. This is why I say we keep the wild dogs out of the way. We do it quietly, get our marks, and get them out of the forest before Blonger has the chance to hear anything about it. Then we retire somewhere out beyond the Edge until it's all forgotten."

"I want twenty-five percent," Soapy said firmly.

"Yeah," Big Bunco agreed. "This is way too dangerous for fifteen."

"Listen, I'm the one taking the most risk here, because I'm the one who'll be the face of this operation. You guys will just be the shills helping to pull in the suckers, so the danger to you is substantially less. I'll give you eighteen. No more."

"Twenty-two," Soapy replied.

"Nineteen," the groundhog countered.

"Twenty," Soapy said. "Take it or leave it."

Thimblerig stared at Soapy for the requisite amount of time, then blinked. "Deal," he said. He'd hoped for less, but twenty was what he'd been expecting.

"Deal," Big Bunco agreed.

"Deal," Soapy matched.

"Poor Ponzi," Mullins said sadly.

The others turned to the gazelle, who had red, puffy eyes, and was blowing his nose on a nearby leaf.

"Well, Mullins?" Thimblerig asked. "You in or out?"

"What'd we say? Fifteen percent?" Mullins sniffed. "That sounds fair."

"Fifteen it is," Thimblerig said quickly, winking at the ape and the elephant, who shook their heads in amazement. "So, listen up. The wild dogs start their hunt in just a few days, and that will be the perfect cover for us to assemble our suckers and get out of the area. So here's what we got to do…"

CHAPTER 5
THE PROBLEM WITH BELIEVERS

Wild dogs appeared to be cobbled together with the leftover coats of other animals, with different shades of brown and orange fur haphazardly slapped on from nose to tail. They looked like a mess, and were smaller than many other predators, but their appearance ran in direct opposition to their skills. Working together, they were able to maintain control over all of the forest, and in the hunt, they would take down animals considerably larger than themselves.

Kid Duffy was an exceptional wild dog, bigger and more ferocious than any of the others, which had helped him to win the position of Blonger's enforcer; a pretty good gig if you played it smart, which Kid Duffy did. A good enforcer had to be cunning and merciless, and a healthy dose of deceitfulness mixed with an urge for self-preservation didn't hurt.

Right now, Kid Duffy's instincts for self-preservation were hard at work as he ran at top speed towards Blonger's Cave. He'd been shaking down the Silverback Gang for back payments on the festival tax when Blonger's messenger had arrived. "Blonger requests your company," had been the simple message, delivered just as Kid Duffy was about to sink his teeth into the shin of a particularly mouthy gorilla.

He'd not wasted any time.

The two wild dogs standing guard at the entrance to the big cave moved dutifully to block Kid Duffy's path. Without breaking stride, Kid Duffy uttered a single irritated growl that sent them scurrying.

Running past rows of decomposing heads that were mounted on sticks and displayed for everyone to see, Kid Duffy entered the gloomy entrance to the boss's cave. As he did, he slowed down to a trot, instincts hard at work, listening closely for anything out of the ordinary. Vigilant against any sort of threat or ambush, Kid Duffy proceeded with caution.

He entered the main passageway leading to Blonger's Great Hall. A pale green light was shining down on the corridor from the bio-luminous fungus growing between the stalactites above, it was a purposefully unsettling effect, and to keep from becoming disoriented, Kid Duffy focused on the shadows cast by the dim lighting until he reached the next passageway.

A series of murals lined the walls of the new passage, lit by holes in the cave ceiling; they were colorful and crude paintings that showed the history of the wild dogs, painted by the best ape artists, and Kid Duffy felt tremendous pride as he examined them. They represented the dark days when the wild dogs had lived under oppressive unicorn rule, the lost years when they were exiled from the forest, and their triumphant return. The final mural was a depiction of Aktamau, the greatest of the wild dog warriors, covered in blood, standing on the bodies of the unicorns he'd slain in the final battle.

"Kid Duffy!" an impatient voice snarled from the dark cave opening beyond. "The leader is waiting for you!"

With a final satisfied glance at the painting of the wild dog's triumph, Kid Duffy padded down the dark passage and finally into Blonger's Great Hall, which was decorated with orchids and lilies, violets and delphiniums, fragrant and colorful flowers brought in daily in homage to the leader. Even the wild dog guards, who always stood unmoving off to the side, wore garlands of wildflowers around their necks. The room was alive with the vivid colors of the blossoms – magenta, indigo, aquamarine, canary yellow; the mood created by the colorful flora stood in stark contrast to the terror that was typically experienced in the leader's presence.

"Answer me!" a gruff voice demanded.

Kid Duffy's attention was pulled to the activity in the center of the Great Hall. Six wild dogs stood at attention before the leader's empty throne of furs and on the ground in front of them, a female lynx was cowering, a bloody mess. Standing over her was the one who undoubtedly bloodied her, Kid Duffy's lieutenant Lupo.

"I want names, cat," Lupo growled. "Give me names."

"I don't have any names for you," the lynx coughed out, spitting up blood at the same time.

Standing back, waiting patiently for the interrogation to be over so he could have his meeting with the leader, Kid Duffy wondered what names Lupo was after. He also wondered where the leader was.

As if in answer to the enforcer's unspoken thoughts, a quiet voice spoke out from the shadows. "It's a pity. If you shared names, it would go so much easier."

Blonger, the leader of the wild dogs, stepped out from the darkness behind the throne. As soon as they saw him, all of the wild dogs threw themselves to the ground, prostrating themselves in submission. The leader was not impressive physically, and had no distinguishing features to mark him as the leader of the pack. Many of the wild dogs, including Kid Duffy, dwarfed him in size, others were faster, others had sharper teeth, but this supposedly average dog was the undisputed ruler of the wild dogs, and by extension, of the entire forest.

Stories whispered around the animal carcasses told of an ambitious but average dog that had been born into a family of rulers. He was not the oldest pup of the litter, but a series of accidents took the lives of his older siblings until he was the only wild dog left from Aktamau's line. Any opposition to Blonger's rule had disappeared years before and his word was now de facto forest law, supplanting the laws that came before.

Staring brazenly up at Blonger with open defiance, the lynx struggled against her pain and injuries to rise and stand on four legs.

"Kneel, horn lover!" Lupo growled while remaining down on the floor. "You're in the presence of your master, Blonger, leader of the forest!"

The lynx stubbornly stood her ground. "He is not my master," she spat out. And then, she unexpectedly raised one paw to her forehead and stuck out a single claw. "I serve the unicorn king."

In the back of the room, Kid Duffy was filled with rage. The lynx was one of the *believers*, and if he didn't have to stay in his submissive position, he would have torn out the cat's heart with pleasure.

Blonger stared dispassionately at the lynx. The room had gone deathly quiet; the only sounds were the cat struggling to breathe and the wild dogs struggling to keep from attacking her without permission.

"Lupo," the leader finally spoke. "Why don't you take our guest to the room we've reserved for her, and reason with her until she decides to share the names of her friends."

"Gladly, master," Lupo answered, rising with a wicked grin on his face. He barked an order at the other wild dogs who jumped up and began nipping at the legs and torso of the lynx, forcing her towards the shadowy doorway that led to the dungeons.

"He's returning, dog!" the lynx screamed back at Blonger as they pushed her through the doorway. "Do what you want with me, but you can't stop him!"

As she disappeared down the passage, her screams echoed across the Great Hall. Kid Duffy knew that his dogs would get the information Blonger desired, and that she would pay dearly for her foolish ideas. He just wished he could be a part of the interrogation.

"Enforcer!"

At Blonger's call, Kid Duffy resumed his submissive position and tucked his tail between his legs.

"Come forward," the voice commanded.

Kid Duffy began whining and dragged himself across the floor towards the leader, eyes averted. Finally he arrived at a blood-red circle painted onto the floor.

"I serve only Blonger," he said dutifully, eyes focused on the circle on the ground.

"Rise and face me, Enforcer." Blonger replied.

The enforcer fought the urge to swallow and shift on his paws. He had no idea why Blonger had sent for him, and he was thinking back, trying to imagine if he'd done anything worth punishment.

"I'm here at your command, leader," Kid Duffy chose his words carefully as he rose. "What is your desire?"

"Report this week's profit from the festival tax," Blonger said, sitting on his throne.

"At this point we are looking at seven to eight hundred figs."

"Why is it down from last week?" Blonger asked.

"We're still waiting for the patrols to report in from the outlying areas when they return for the hunt," Kid Duffy answered. "Once they do, we should be up to average levels for this time of year."

Blonger nodded. "Report on preparations for the hunt."

"Proceeding as planned, sir," Kid Duffy replied, relieved by the run-of-the-mill nature of the questions. "This year it will take place in the northern territory beyond the tree."

"Out towards the Edge," Blonger nodded.

"Yes, master," Kid Duffy replied. "The hunt will take us through the forest, across the steppe, and into the rock country."

"And the sacrifices?"

"The sacrifices will come from the prisoners, as you ordered, sir." Kid Duffy said, then added, "should the lynx be part of the sacrifice?"

"If she survives Lupo," Blonger said, rising and padding down the stone steps past the enforcer. "Rise and follow me."

Kid Duffy fell in behind the leader as he passed, trailing a head's length as custom dictated. Blonger led him into his private antechamber just off the Great Hall, away from the ears of his

46

private guards. The enforcer's heart pounded hard in his chest. The leader had something private to discuss, for his ears only.

As they entered the private quarters, Kid Duffy glanced at the paintings of Blonger on the walls, illuminated by sunlight shining down through holes in the ceiling. The most striking painting was the leader standing in front of a throng of wild dogs, highlighted with bright yellow, orange, and red paint. Green vines and fragrant lilies were placed around the room to add color, and the furs of zebras carpeted the floor, with the softest furs piled prominently in a corner of the cave room.

Three female wild dogs lounged on the furs, but one growl from Blonger sent them scurrying out a side doorway. The leader sniffed the furs and sat, turning his attention back to Kid Duffy.

"We're coming up on your one year anniversary, aren't we?" Blonger asked. "One year since you became my enforcer?"

"Yes sir," Kid Duffy answered, pleased that the leader chose to acknowledge his service.

"You took over from poor Monte," the leader continued. "He'd been my enforcer for many years, you know. It was a pity that he had to be let go, but that's what happens when a wild dog outlives his worth."

Kid Duffy wasn't sure where the leader was going with this talk, so he elected to stand at attention and wait until he was commanded to speak.

"Do you know why he was let go, Duffy?"

"I was never told, sir."

"A group of animals calling themselves "Children of the Unicorn" managed to get onto the field before the hunt and free several sacrifices. I caught them, and they were given the honor of being prey themselves during the hunt. Since that incident, our agents have reported a rise in the number of animals sympathetic to that cause. Have you wondered why you are kept so busy?"

"It's my pleasure, sir," Kid Duffy answered. "I serve you, and only you."

47

Blonger nodded, satisfied. "Monte accepted full responsibility for the breach, and suffered the consequences, freeing the job up for you. As to the believers, I can't stop them from believing what they will, but I can stop them from trying to weaken our hold on the forest. Do you understand what I'm saying?"

"I believe so, sir," Kid Duffy answered uncertainly.

"I don't know that you do, so let me make myself perfectly clear," Blonger said, standing up and strolling up to the enforcer. "If I see so much as a single hair of a believer, if any of these heretics try to disturb my hunt, if anything at all goes wrong, it'll be your neck in the teeth this time." The leader spoke in a whisper. "Now, I'll say it again. Do you understand?"

"I do, sir," Kid Duffy said, working hard to keep the timbre of his voice steady. "The believers will be nowhere near the hunt, except as prey."

CHAPTER 6
THE SEARCH FOR SUCKERS

The noontime sun streamed through the leaves and branches of Asarata onto the big, flat, high rock known appropriately, if not imaginatively, as "the Rock." This was one of the more popular spots during the festival, a place where animals would go to debate the issues or lecture about their philosophies of life. Crowds of animals came out each day after gorging themselves with figs, parked themselves in front of favored speakers, and listened.

On a good day, animals discussed their differing ideas and agreed to disagree, but often full-grown melees would erupt when animals refused to find common ground. The most famous disagreement in recent memory was known as the Poultry Riot, which started when an argument broke out about between two roosters over whether or not the egg had come first. Soon a couple of geese got involved, then a family of ducks, then a gang of turkeys, and things quickly spiraled out of control.

Many birds lost their lives that day.

Thimblerig usually steered clear of the Rock. He had no use for the things the animals said there, and their 'messages' made absolutely no difference to him. "They're just con artists trying to look more respectable," he'd told Mullins. "At least we're honest about our dishonesty."

But today Thimblerig stood in line, mingling with The Rock's usual con artists, waiting his turn to climb the little trail to the plateau where the speakers stood. Considering that the more superstitious, susceptible and foolish animals frequented the Rock, it was the perfect place to put his plan into motion. A pious-looking, white-bearded macaque stood at the front of the line, directing speakers to their places on the Rock, helped by a self-satisfied, long-legged, white crane, who Thimblerig took to be his shill.

Insanity comes in all shapes and sizes. Thimblerig turned his attention to the others standing in line. The crocodile standing in front of him kept glancing around as if paranoid that he was being followed, muttering something about "virtues of an unwilling soul", whatever that meant. The kangaroo who stood behind him appeared to have a tree's worth of leaves stuffed into the pouch where she was supposed to carry her offspring. Thimblerig started to ask why she was carrying all the leaves, but decided he was probably better off not knowing. The kangaroo noticed that he was looking, smiled pleasantly, and pointed ahead of him.

The line had moved forward, and so Thimblerig stepped up. The macaque was talking to the crocodile, and there was something about the infuriating look of certainty in the crocodile's eyes that really bothered the groundhog. They all had it, that same wide-eyed serious expression that said that the nonsense they espoused was right; that the gibberish they spoke was somehow special or divine.

It's a look I can easily imitate, Thimblerig thought.

"You there," the macaque called as the crocodile moved on up the path. "Marmot!"

"I'm a groundhog," Thimblerig corrected, stepping up.

"My apologies," the macaque said without a trace of regret in his voice. "I don't remember having a groundhog here before. Is this your first time?"

"I have answered the call," Thimblerig intoned, nodding and waving his hands in the air. "My message must be heard."

The macaque regarded him with suspicion. "I see. And I assume you can present your credentials?"

"Credentials?" Thimblerig hadn't expected this request. What sort of credentials was he expected to have? If he'd known, he could have had Inky the chimp make some good forgeries...

"Certainly," the macaque responded. He leaned closer to Thimblerig and reached out a paw. "Not just anyone is allowed on the sacred rock. As the guardian, it's my job to maintain the purity

50

of the messages that are spoken there. So you must present your credentials."

Some things were the same, no matter where you were in the forest. Thimblerig smiled, and discreetly pulled a fig out of his pouch. "Right. My credentials. How stupid of me to forget." He slipped the fig into the macaque's waiting paw.

"Everything seems to be in order, brother groundhog," the macaque smiled as the fig disappeared into his pack. It was as greasy a smile as Thimblerig had ever seen. He gestured up the path. "Please go to position seven. Your credentials get you fifteen minutes."

Fifteen minutes for a fig? It was a rip-off if there ever was one, but knowing you had to spend a fig to earn a fig Thimblerig smiled and walked away. As soon as he'd passed, he was forgotten, and he could hear the macaque shouting behind him, "You there! Kangaroo!" Being forgotten was just fine with the groundhog. The less remembered about him, the better.

The path twisted and turned as it inclined, following the contours of The Rock. As he reached the plateau, he saw that there were already a dozen or so animals spread out around the edges of the circular rock, each fervently preaching to groups of suckers. He counted animals until he came to the seventh position, between an ibex with impressively large curved horns, and a small hound dog with floppy ears and big black eyes.

It was midday, and so a respectable number of animals stood in the open area below the rock. He grinned, wondering which ones would take the bait when he started fishing.

"From the stars! We came from the stars!" the wild-eyed long-horned ibex to his left cried to the crowd looking up into the sky. "A long, long time ago, beings from another planet came and planted us in the forest, where we grew into the society you see before you today! I've seen these beings, and I can show you how to see them, too! You will feel such peace and tranquility…"

51

Only a few animals down below were paying any attention to the ibex, and Thimblerig couldn't blame them. He turned his attention to the hound dog on his other side.

"Right or wrong doesn't exist," the hound dog howled. "The only thing that matters is being true to yourself! Choose that which makes you happy! Only by doing this can you find true joy in life!"

A rotten fig sailed out from the crowd and slammed into the hound dog's face, stopping him in mid sentence. As it dripped down his long jowls and fell to the ground, a heckler called out, "that made me happy!" and the audience roared with laughter.

"Then it was right," the hound dog cried back over the crowd without missing a beat. "If that made you happy, then you were right to do it! That's the only truth!"

The audience nodded in approval, somehow agreeing with the hound dog, even though Thimblerig had no clue what he was talking about. But he smiled. The suckers were absolutely ripe for the picking, begging for something to believe in.

And he was going to give it to them.

Thimblerig stepped up to the edge of Rock and cleared his throat. He almost felt sorry for the uninformed masses down below because they had no idea what was about to hit them; how their lives were about to change because of the performance he was about to put on. He took a deep breath, held it for a moment for luck, and let loose his strongest and most persuasive argument.

"You're all going to die!" he cried. "Unless you listen to me, you will all die!"

Thimblerig waited for the cries of shock that he knew would come. But to his utter surprise, to his left the ibex continued his monotonous droning about star beings, and to his right the hound dog hadn't stopped his braying about truth. And the crowd hardly noticed him.

He wasn't used to being ignored when running a con, and so Thimblerig decided to put a little more fig on the fire. He scrunched up his face, took another deeper breath, and shouted,

"The flood from the old stories is coming! It's going to sweep through the forest! Nobody will survive unless you listen to me!"

Pausing, Thimblerig waited to see what sort of response his new enthusiasm would get. A wild boar on the front row belched so loudly that the rock under Thimblerig's feet actually vibrated, and someone farther back in the audience yelled out, "That's the most interesting thing anyone's said today!" Again, the audience roared with laughter.

Thimblerig's plan was unraveling before it had a chance to ravel. His was just another boring voice, giving another boring message, none of it original, none of it relevant, and all of it less interesting than a wild boar's expression of intestinal gases.

"You've got to do better than that, brother groundhog."

Thimblerig turned. The kangaroo was sitting behind him, removing the leaves from her pouch, and tying them onto her head with some vine forming a green and yellow headdress. "They hear that kind of thing a dozen times a day. If you really want to get their attention, you have to think outside the pouch. They're all sleepwalking down there, and they need to have their imaginations ignited to wake them up."

She winked and stepped up to her own spot on the other side of the hound. Then, she settled down on her haunches and sat, closing her eyes.

In spite of his allotted time ticking away, Thimblerig couldn't take his eyes off of the kangaroo and her strange display of nothingness. No speech, no movement, just sitting. Down below, some others also noticed and began moving closer for a better look.

And still, the kangaroo sat, unmoving.

A good two full minutes went by before things started to change. Finally, she raised her left paw over her head and gracefully rose. The leaves gave her the appearance of a tree sprouting out of the ground, and she stood still for a moment and then she began to dance.

53

Thimblerig couldn't believe his eyes! The tree was blowing in the wind as the kangaroo danced to music only she could hear. She was all smoothness and light, and it was hard to tell where the wind and the tree stopped and where she started, and it was all vaguely familiar.

The hound dog stopped his blathering to watch, and the animals down below abandoned the other speakers to get a better view of the kangaroo's flowing movements. She leapt in the air, twirling, eyes closed, and landed in a crouch. As she rose this time, her movements became more harsh and jarring. She moved back and forth, her arms crashing down, over and over and over again.

Then Thimblerig knew. Somehow the kangaroo was telling the story of the storm from his vision! Hadn't that been a tree in the beginning, tall and graceful? He could almost feel the wind and the water as he watched her push and pull, back and forth.

She twirled around a final time, finally collapsing in a heap on the Rock. The crowd erupted into a cacophony of appreciative cheers, which she acknowledged, breathing heavily, from her sitting position. She quieted the audience by raising her paw. "Now that I have your attention, please listen to what my brother groundhog has to say."

"Groundmother, are we there yet?"

"Not yet, cub! But we've got to hurry or we'll miss Aibek!"

Thimblerig found himself once more in a living memory. He was following behind his groundmother while she pulled a younger version of himself by the paw through the crowds.

Groundmother had always been quite capable of pushing her way through large groups of animals when she set her mind to it. She weaved around and about the larger animals, applied a well-aimed elbow when necessary, and finally got them to her favorite place at The Rock, right in front of Aibek the grizzly

54

bear, one of the most popular and controversial speakers of the last generation.

Looking up at the terrible grizzly, Thimblerig remembered how Aibek should have been every cub's worst nightmare, massive and brown, all claws and teeth and death. In reality, Aibek was the exact opposite. He was gentle and kind, and the children would fight over who would get to take a ride on his back after he had finished his lectures.

"You all don't seem to understand," the bear was saying, with a voice as golden and smooth as honey. "The problem isn't a few bad eggs, but the whole nest. The unicorns used to be here to hold our paws and help us make the right choices. But now they're gone, and it's up to us to hold things together until they return. And trust me, they are coming back, and when they do they're going to be putting together a whole new nest. Now, I don't know about you, but I want to be a part of the unicorn's new nest!"

Aibek brought a paw up to his forehead, and stuck out a single claw. All around them, Thimblerig watched as many of the other animals repeated the gesture. He glanced down at his younger self in time to see the cub looking up at his groundmother. Also showing the sign of the believer, she winked at him, and the young groundhog raised up his paw and stuck out a claw, with a big smile plastered on his furry face.

Clearing his throat, Thimblerig slowly raised his paw to his forehead and stuck out one claw. It was a risky move, because if the wild dogs had any spies in the crowd, he would quickly move to the top of their wanted list. But it also had the intended effect, with the gathered crowds immediately recognizing the gesture and quieting down.

Thimblerig lowered his paw and began to speak. "Thank you, sister kangaroo. Brothers and sisters of the forest, please listen carefully to my words, because they aren't just my words. They come directly from the unicorns themselves!"

55

The crowd shuffled nervously at this claim. It was one thing to speak an interesting message, but to declare it a message from the unicorns? It wasn't just outrageous, but it broke about a dozen of the wild dog's laws.

"Some will try to tell you that there were never any unicorns, that they are the stuff of myth and legend. But I can tell you first hand that the unicorns did exist. I can say this because I have seen one!"

Thimblerig could have directed a sizzling lightning bolt into the middle of the crowd and that would have been the only thing that would have shocked them more. And that shock was exactly what he wanted. It was time to hit them with the big rocks.

"He came to me just this morning in a vision, a vision that was as real to me as this moment is for you…"

Theatrically demonstrating hanging on Asarata's branch, flailing about on the ground as he recreated trying to swim through the water, swooping his arms in wide gestures to illustrate the waves crashing through the forest, the groundhog had the audience right in the pad of his paw. Finally, as Thimblerig neared the end of his story, he saw where Soapy stood out in the crowd. The ape gave him the thumbs up signal, and so the groundhog set the final part of the bait.

"The flood from the old stories is coming, friends," he concluded with as much seriousness as he could muster. "It's coming, and we can't stop it."

The animals were buzzing now, chattering to each other with a variety of responses. Thimblerig heard the words "crazy", "irresponsible", and "what if?" but he waited until he heard Soapy's voice call out over the noise.

"But what can we do?"

"Can anyone save us?" Big Bunco added, standing just off to the right. "Why tell us this if nobody can save us?"

"Those are all good questions," the groundhog answered. "I don't bring you this message without hope. The unicorn showed me the way to avoid perishing! He told me about a place of safety, and how to get there."

"Are you saying you can save us?" Mullins shouted from his place in the rear of the crowd. Thimblerig found him and locked eyes with the gazelle.

"I can save you, friend gazelle. With the unicorn's help, I can save all of you!"

Thimblerig was impressed by the conviction in his own voice. He let the words hang in the air and was immensely gratified to see so many doleful eyes gazing up at him. It was time to seal the deal.

"All you need to do is follow me..."

Suddenly, on the outskirts of the crowd, some animals started crying out in panic. Thimblerig glanced back and saw that near the spot where Mullins had been standing, animals were starting to scurry. What had that blasted gazelle done now?

"Wait! I can you to lead you to the place of safety!"

Now animals were flat out bolting, charging out of the area like the flood was coming now. The terror spread, and the animals in the front jostled, elbowed, and head butting each other in a panicked attempt to escape what was coming. He wasn't sure, but he thought he could hear Mullins' voice yelling 'Razzamataz!' over and over, but he didn't have time for that.

"You have to listen! You have to follow me!"

Then he saw that a squad of wild dogs was pushing and shoving their way through the crowd, their trajectory carrying them in his direction.

The game was up. The last place he wanted to be was in the clutches of the wild dogs, especially having just made the sign of the believers with the hunt just days away. He started to turn and make a hasty exit when a surprisingly strong paw stopped him by grabbing his shoulder.

It was the kangaroo.

"Don't run from it," she said with a spooky unwavering voice. "Don't run from what he's got for you."

Great, Thimblerig thought. *This loon's taking it seriously.* That would be great if the killer wild dog squad wasn't currently making a beeline for their exact location.

"Hey, listen, I really do appreciate your help back there, but I'm getting out of here before I end up as dog food. Look around! Your pals certainly weren't keen on hanging around. You should make yourself scarce, too."

She saw that he was right; the Rock had quickly emptied of all the prophets and messengers, leaving just the two of them. She nodded, and followed Thimblerig down the trail where they fell in with the dispersing crowd and disappeared into the forest.

CHAPTER 7
THE COMPANY OF ANIMALS

"Somebody must've ratted on us," Thimblerig said angrily, pacing back and forth. "The wild dogs never raid the Rock, and they chose to raid it today? While I'm in the middle of the job? And where are Soapy and Bunco? They knew where to go, didn't they?"

He and Mullins were sitting beside a bend in a stream. It was a shaded spot, concealed from prying eyes. Half his life was spent trying to be concealed from prying eyes. It was getting old.

"Sure they know," Mullins answered. "What's with your new pal?"

The kangaroo sat several feet off to the side, in some sort of catatonic state, not paying any attention to the gazelle or the groundhog. Her eyes were closed, her head bowed. It was like she'd fallen asleep sitting up, which is maybe what kangaroos did for all Thimblerig knew. Still, they spoke in hushed tones as a precaution.

"She's harmless," he answered, turning his mind back to the problem at hand. "What do we do next? I can't show my face back at the Rock again."

"They were into it, weren't they? And that dance was a brilliant touch, really whetted their appetite! You should have warned us about it."

"It was a spur of the moment decision," Thimblerig said, glancing back at the kangaroo. She was an odd one, that kangaroo. But the last thing he needed was some odd kangaroo hopping around after him. He'd ditch her as soon as he could.

"Well, it's a shame," Mullins responded, shaking his head. "If anyone could have pulled it off, it would have been you."

Thimblerig rested his head on his paws and resisted the urge to weep over his lost con. He'd seen it so clearly in his imagination: first, they demanded payment in dry figs, and stored them down in one of his deeper, colder burrows. Then, the suckers followed them willingly deep into the forest where they would be left high and dry; next, he and his partners would return to the burrow, where they would gather the figs and retire to someplace warm and sunny.

It was to have been the perfect con, the stuff of legend, and in an instant, it had been shot to ruin by a senseless squad of wild dogs.

Thimblerig hated when a con got shot to ruin. Come to think of it, he found that he hated the wild dogs, hated the suckers, hated his life.

"Mullins, do you know what I'm sick of?" Thimblerig asked, disgusted. "I'm sick of being at the bottom of the food chain. You and me, we're the ones everyone else thinks they can stomp on, chew on, and spit out. It's always been that way, and it will always be that way until we have something that makes us different. And you know what makes an animal different?"

"Figs," Mullins said, nodding his head.

"That's right. Figs." Thimblerig repeated. "Figs make the forest go around. Either you got sharp teeth, or you got figs. Right now, we got neither. This con was our ticket up."

"What's done is done," Mullins said, resigned, and he stood. "We should lay low and let things cool off."

"You might want to hang about," the kangaroo interrupted. She'd apparently woken up, or recovered from her trance, or whatever it was she was doing. Anyway, she'd decided to rejoin the world, and Thimblerig could care less.

"Listen, sister," Thimblerig mocked. "If you want to hang about, be my guest. But wild dogs don't just go out for afternoon strolls. They were there looking for someone, and I'm not going to take the chance that it was me."

"They weren't looking for you. They were looking for believers," she replied. "They will be looking for you soon, but they're not the only ones."

60

"I don't have time for this," Thimblerig replied, getting up. "C'mon, Mullins, lets get out of here. See you around the tree, sister."

"My name's Sheila," she said.

"Fine, Sheila," Thimblerig said. "We'll see you later."

Mullins got up and joined Thimblerig as he walked up the bank of the stream towards the clearing beyond. When they reached the top, Thimblerig stopped. Soapy and Big Bunco stood at the edge of the clearing surrounded by about a half dozen other animals.

"What's this?" Thimblerig asked, suspicious.

"There you are, brother groundhog! We want you to save us from the flood." Soapy replied, raising one hand up to his head and holding out a single finger. "We're believers!"

"He was as tall as ten of me," Thimblerig said, talking to the entranced suckers. "Jet black, with a brilliant horn as white as the whitest cloud on the brightest blue sky summer's day. It blazed out of the darkness like it was burning with some holy flame."

"Fire's orange," the duck said. "You said it was white. Which one is it?"

Thimblerig really wanted to scream, jump on the duck, and yank out all his white feathers by the pawful. The suckers had immediately started asking questions about his vision, and he'd been more than happy to provide them with the answers they wanted. But the whole time, the infuriating duck had been heckling him with nonsense and questions. It was starting to throw off his timing.

"I said 'like'. 'Like'. 'Like it was burning with holy flame'. It's called a simile." The groundhog's voice was dry like rough wood.

"Why don't you stop trying to be so literary," the duck countered, "and just tell us what you saw." The pair of llamas standing beside him nodded in agreement.

61

Thimblerig was too professional to let his exasperation show, although he really wanted it to. If it were possible to take snarkiness, embody it as a living, breathing creature, give it a modicum of intelligence and the ability to communicate, then snarkiness would have been this duck.

"Shi Lau – you did say your name was Shi Lau?" Thimblerig asked.

"I did," the duck answered. How was it possible to make two simple words sound so condescending?

"Fine then, Shi Lau," Thimblerig answered. "I'll just say this – the unicorn was bigger and wilder, more frightening, more amazing than I could have ever possibly imagined."

"That's the way Tannier Isa is described in the old stories," the large coffee-bean-colored camel said in awe. "What do they say? 'As black as the shadows he conquers, with horn of light he reigns...'"

"I just told him to stop being so literary," Shi Lau quacked impatiently, glaring up at the camel. "How are we supposed to figure out if this crackpot's for real if you keep egging him on?"

"Checking what he says against the stories is how we know if he's for real," the camel replied. "They won't contradict."

"I'm sure he's heard the stories too, Elbridge." The female gazelle next to the camel said, eyeing Thimblerig with suspicion. "They were widely known at one time."

This one was sharp, the gazelle. Her questions had been clever, and she was tougher than her little gazelle body would suggest. Thimblerig had an idea that if he could swing her to his side it would be a huge victory.

"Tabitha, is it?" Thimblerig asked, and she nodded. "Well, Tabitha, you're right. I have heard the stories. My groundmother used to tell them to me when I was a cub. But believe me, I'm telling you what I saw, not what I heard. It's what I experienced: from the unicorn to the flood. And it's coming."

As he spoke, the groundhog made a point to look each animal directly in the eye: the big camel, the annoying duck, that

62

earnest gazelle, the llama couple, and that enigmatic kangaroo. He summoned every ounce of the old bear that he could muster.

"The bottom line? Tannier Isa chose to give me the job of leading whatever animals would go to the place of safety, he said it's coming soon, and he said that everyone's welcome. I honestly don't know why he chose me, but he obviously had his reasons. If none of you want to go, you can bet your last fig that I'll be going, even if I have to go by myself." Thimblerig paused for dramatic effect. "Believe me, if the flood in reality is a tenth as bad as what I saw in my vision, I don't want to be anywhere near when it hits. And neither do you."

The animals nodded in agreement. Thimblerig suppressed the urge to smile. *As easy as falling off a log*, he thought, looking them over one by one.

Except the duck.

The duck wasn't nodding. In fact, he was looking at Thimblerig like he'd just rolled out of the toilet bush with used leaves stuck to his feet.

"I can't believe you're all falling for this," Shi Lau said with pessimism dripping from his bill like water. "Who is this groundhog? Has anyone here ever seen him at the Rock before? I know I haven't. He's just waiting to drop a big rotten fig on our heads. He wants something, I'll bet."

The duck, it turned out, was too smart for his own good, and a smart animal could potentially be a con's biggest problem. But if the con could figure out how to use their smarts against them, they could end up being the con's biggest score.

It was settled. He had to win over the duck.

"Shi Lau, you are careful and suspicious, and I appreciate that. That's how an animal stays alive in the forest, especially these days. And you're right that I've never had a message to proclaim on The Rock before. You're also right that I'm going to ask something of those who choose to follow me. But that's because I need to make certain that the animals that I lead are as committed to this as I am. If I don't, what's the use?"

63

"Here it comes," the duck snorted.

Trying his best to ignore the comment, Thimblerig pressed on.

"I have a chamber in my burrow, deep and cold enough to preserve dried figs for months. I'm going to require each animal who comes with me to make an investment in this trip by putting their figs where their mouths are. You'll need to make a good-faith deposit."

"A deposit?" the big cream-colored male llama asked. He and his brown-haired mate didn't look like that they had a fig to rub together, so it would stand to reason that he'd be nervous. The mate was looking at him with a concerned look on her face. "How much of a deposit?"

Here it goes, Thimblerig took a deep breath. *Make or break time.*

"Two hundred dried figs apiece."

Thimblerig had expected the sucker's responses: first shock and anger, and then when he'd explained that the deposit was fully refundable in case the flood never happened, safe and secure deep in the bowels of the earth in his paw-dug burrow, a final resignation.

"After all, who cares about losing some figs when the flood really does come?" he'd asked. They'd agreed, except for the duck, the lone holdout.

"This is ridiculous!" he quacked angrily. "Why should we trust this bum with our hard-earned figs? We don't know squat about him! And just where are we supposed to get that many figs anyway?"

"Beg, borrow, or steal, is what I plan to do," Soapy commented, trying to defuse the situation.

"Oh, and you're in tight with animals who have that kind of scratch?" the duck pressed. "What, hidden away up in bags in the treetops, are they?"

That's it, Thimblerig thought. *It's time to get this guy to put up or shut up.* He looked at Soapy and touched his nose. Soapy, who understood the gesture, winked.

"It's time to make a choice," Soapy announced, rising from the grass. "Nobody's forcing nobody to do anything, but we need to get going if we're going to be going."

"Good idea," Big Bunco agreed. "Let's do it."

A murmur of assent went up from the group, and Thimblerig smiled.

CHAPTER 8
MAKING PREPARATIONS

It couldn't have gone better if Thimblerig had written the scene himself. Not only had Soapy stopped the duck's argument before it could get started, but the duck had actually agreed to pony up the figs and join them.

"I still think you should have gotten rid of him," Mullins grumbled to the groundhog as they made their way to his burrow. "With that loose bill of his, that duck's going to be more trouble than he's worth."

"He represents thirty more figs than you had before," Thimblerig answered happily. "Each fig is a step up."

Mullins grunted, unable to argue the point. He was distracted momentarily by the brightly colored feathers of a trio of peacocks standing off to the side of the trail, talking to a couple of young hares.

"You gonna give us your figs, or does this gotta get ugly?" the largest of the peacocks had one of the hares grasped by the ears. The other two peacocks stood behind the two hares, preventing their escape.

"Oh, it's gonna get real ugly," the second hare replied, rising up to his full height and knocking the peacock back on his colorful plumage. "But not near as ugly as you, crow!" And he leapt on the peacock, while the other two rushed the other hare.

Ordinarily Mullins would enjoy watching a good fight, but today his mind was elsewhere, so he turned back to Thimblerig as they continued down the trail. "What did you think of Tabitha?" he asked.

"Who?"

"Tabitha," Mullins replied. "The gazelle."

"I guess she's okay," Thimblerig said. "A little too serious, maybe."

"I liked it," Mullins answered. "She's not like other gazelles." He looked down at the dusty ground as they walked the

66

well-worn path and was nearly trampled by a family of four yellow and black giraffes who came stomping down from Asarata. Thankfully, Thimblerig yanked him into the underbrush to avoid the long-necked animals who were not paying attention to smaller animals who shared their pathway.

"Mom! Bimba got more figs than I did!" one of the smaller giraffes was whining, knocking into the other small giraffe as they stomped past. "It's not fair!"

"Dad, tell Beryl to stop shoving me!" the other small giraffe whined as she shoved back.

"If you kids don't button your lips, I'll button 'em for you!" the big male shouted angrily, shoving both younger giraffes aside, pushing his way to the front of the quartet.

"Don't you threaten our children!" the adult female shouted from the rear.

The sound of the bickering giraffes faded as they rounded the bend, and Thimblerig and Mullins stepped back on the trail, and continued their conversation without missing a beat.

"You gonna talk to her?" Thimblerig teased.

"I might, if the mood strikes me," the gazelle said confidently. Thimblerig shook his head and laughed.

"What's so funny?" Mullins asked, offended.

"The idea of you talking to a pretty gazelle. That's really funny."

"I don't have a problem talking to the ladies," Mullins said defensively, stopping short. "I just have a problem when they try to talk back."

Thimblerig shook his head. Why was he bothering to get so buddy-buddy with the gazelle? This is how it always started. You relaxed your instincts, started to trust, and then they turned on you or turned you in. Thimblerig needed to rein himself in, and turn things back around to the scam.

As they crested a small hill they found the path blocked by a large dark green crocodile who was unconscious and collapsed on his back beside a black and white coated alpaca. The alpaca

67

was also out cold, his head resting on the crocodile's leathery belly. The remains of several old figs surrounded them, and both were snoring heavily. Thimblerig walked across the belly of the crocodile and leapt over the alpaca's head while Mullins hopped over to the side. They continued their discussion as they walked.

"Just don't get too attached. She might be pretty, but at the end of the day she's just a pretty sucker."

"You don't need to worry about me," Mullins said defensively. "She's nothing to me but thirty figs with really nice legs and a great personality."

Glad that they'd come to a natural break in the conversation, Thimblerig changed the subject.

"We got bigger things to think about, Mullins. The biggest one being how to get over a thousand figs into my burrow without attracting attention."

Mullins grunted, and they continued towards the burrow. Looking down at the love-struck gazelle, Thimblerig decided that a loudmouth duck wasn't the only thing he'd have to keep his eyes on.

"How many do we have?" Soapy asked as Thimblerig climbed out of his burrow, exhausted. It was close to morning, and they'd been moving bags of figs for the last two nights. Or, more exactly, *he'd* been moving figs since he was the only one small enough to fit down the burrow hole.

The marks had been given two days and two nights to come up with their deposits, and were instructed to deliver them overnight in small bags of twenty-five dried figs in an attempt to maintain secrecy about their plans. After all, Thimblerig had explained, the wild dogs would be on all of them in an instant if they got even a hint of what was going on.

"I count forty-six bags," he answered, standing, stretching out the kinks in his muscles, and then brushing the dirt off his fur. "The duck should be here any time now with his last two bags, then we should be able to set off in the morning."

68

"And you got our stacks counted off in there, too?" Big Bunco asked, peering down the dark hole. "We're taking a big risk, you know…"

"Of course I got your stacks, Bunco," Thimblerig answered, too tired to be insulted. He had no plans to cheat his partners. That would be bad business. "I promised you your cut, and you'll get it when the con is wrapped up. Now pipe down, here comes the duck.

In the small bit of light cast by the bright moon shining through the leaves overhead, they could see the dark silhouette of the camel, with the duck riding him like he was riding a steed.

"That duck's as much a con as we are," Soapy commented wryly. "How else could he convince someone to work for him the way that camel is?"

Thimblerig shushed him as the camel drew near. "Brother duck, do you have the last two bags?" he called up.

"First of all, I'm not your brother," the duck replied coldly. "Second, I said I was bringing them, didn't I?"

The bags dropped to the ground with a thud when Shi Lau pulled the cord holding them on either side of the camel's flank. Thimblerig went to the bags, opened one, and pulled out a dried fig to examine it in the moonlight. Then he did the same with the second bag.

"Twenty-five per bag?" he confirmed wearily, cinching up the tops of the bags.

Suddenly a white, feathery face accented by a large, flat orange bill filled his vision.

"Just so we're clear here, groundhog, I don't trust you," the duck said with a quiet, menacing voice. "And I'm going to be keeping a close eye on you. I better get all these figs back when you're proven a cheat."

Thimblerig didn't budge from the feathery face, but moved in even closer.

"If you doubt me so much, why don't you keep your precious figs, return to your pond, and see how long you can swim when the flood comes."

The two animals stood whiskers to bill, each waiting to see if the other would blink first. Thimblerig knew that if he lost face to the duck, it would squash his ability to pull off the con before it got started, and so he willed his eyelids to stay open by sheer force. The moments dragged on until the duck finally blinked.

"Fine," the duck squawked, flustered. "Take the figs. And if you *are* cheating us, then I hope you choke on the first one you eat." He turned and waddled away.

"Don't be late to the rendezvous spot in the morning!" Thimblerig called after them. "Your deposit is non-refundable!"

Without looking back, the duck threw up a wing in what could only have been a rude gesture in the world of ducks, then he flew up to the back of the camel, and rode off into the night.

"Two hundred is not nearly enough," Thimblerig grumbled to Soapy and Big Bunco as he hopped into the hole to store the last two bags of figs. "Not by a long shot."

It was late at night, and Thimblerig the teenager was sneaking into his groundmother's burrow. He'd been out again with Waldo the flying fox and the polecat brothers, but this time he'd been careful and he knew that she had no idea. He entered the family room and pulled off his pack, setting it triumphantly on the shelf by the door. He was about to tiptoe his way across the floor to his room when he heard the sound he'd been dreading.

"Having trouble sleeping?"

Thimblerig's head dropped. He'd have to think quickly to talk his way out of this one because considering where he'd been; he'd not just been breaking a family rule, but also wild dog law. He turned and saw that his groundmother was sitting on her favorite pile of green leaves in the darkness.

70

"I was just getting a snack," he said, grabbing a burberry root and starting off for his room.

"And that's all?" she asked, stopping him. He could sense his groundmother's eyes boring into him in the darkness.

"Yes ma'am," he lied, and turned to go to his room. "Good night!"

"You sure that's the story you want to tell?" she asked. "That's why you were out so late again? You weren't sneaking around with Waldo and the others?"

It was irritating, how she was so controlling, and how well she could read him. There wasn't any use lying more to her. "It's not like we were bothering anybody. We were just at Victory Field having a ghost hunt on the mound."

He'd been sure she'd already known where he'd been; she'd just wanted him to admit it, but the way she gasped made him realize he'd been wrong. She nearly lost her balance and he quickly went to help her. When she was standing steadily again, she grabbed him by the shoulders and pulled him close.

"Do you have any idea what you've done?" she said, her voice barely above a whisper.

"It's just a field, groundmother," he muttered with frustration, pulling away from her. "Nobody even saw us."

"Just a field?" she repeated, the sound of disbelief permeating her words. "Do you hear yourself? It's 'just a field' alright, 'just a field' where the wild dogs killed the unicorns. 'Just a field' where Tannier Isa struggled and killed Aktamau, before dying himself! The wild dogs claim that they tore up his body…"

"I know, I know," Thimblerig interrupted. "And others said that his body vanished in a flash of light. They also say that animals made of pure light battled on the side of the unicorns, and nightmarish creatures battled for the wild dogs. I know the stories, groundmother."

"And still you'd go trample that sacred ground?" The look of disappointment in her eyes made Thimblerig feel like a cub

71

again, and he didn't like it. "I may have told you the stories, but you obviously didn't listen."

And with that bit of scolding, Thimblerig felt something snap. A connection with his childhood, an irritation at the lack of respect he received, even if he was nearly an adult himself. Whatever it was, he was tired of it, and the words just came erupting from him like magma from a volcano.

"Of course I listened to your stories, but they're just stories! Nothing but stories!" Thimblerig knew he was shouting, but he couldn't stop himself. "Am I supposed to spend my whole life hoping that the unicorns will come back and fix all my problems? Well, I don't believe it. Maybe your generation did, but where did it get you? None of my friends' parents talk like this, and it's embarrassing! I'm sick of it all!"

Thimblerig expected his groundmother to get angry and toss him out of the burrow, but what she did was even worse. She stepped up, her eyes filled with tears, and she stroked his whiskers. "I'm sorry you feel that way, Thimblerig. But I believe that the unicorns have big plans for your life. I'm not giving up on you, and neither are they."

"Well, you should," Thimblerig muttered, pulling back from his groundmother. He had to get out. It felt like the walls of the little burrow were closing in on him, and so he grabbed his pack and started for the doorway.

"Where are you going?" his groundmother asked.

"Anywhere but here," he replied and he scurried up the tunnel without looking back.

CHAPTER 9
OFF TO A ROUGH START

Thimblerig stood on the edge of Victory field, the unpleasant memory of the argument he'd had with his groundmother still fresh in his mind. He forced it out of his mind as he looked over the wide untouched meadow and the mound that rose out of middle, said to be the place where all the unicorns' bodies had been piled after the wild dogs defeated them. Covered with tall inviting grasses that waved gently in the slight breeze, and dotted with multi-hued wildflowers, the field was lovely and unexceptional. Still, no animal ever went there to graze, to frolic, or lay out in the sun. In fact, it was the one place in the forest that most animals went out of their way to avoid.

It was fitting to Thimblerig that the small band of believers would meet here to start their journey. It would appeal to their mystic nature and their reliance on the old stories. It was a stroke of genius.

"The unicorn graveyard? Seriously? Whose bright idea was it meet *here*?"

The duck stood on the camel's head, staring out at the field in the morning light. The typical look of contempt was pasted on his face as turned back to the other suckers.

"I think it's perfect," Big Bunco replied, coming to Thimblerig's rescue before he gave into the temptation to strangle the duck. "I love the symbolism of it. Plus, we start here and nobody's the wiser because nobody ever comes here."

"And why do you think that is?" the duck replied. "The wild dogs consider this holy territory, and they execute anyone they find here."

The camel's hump deflated. The two llamas stopped mid-spit. Tabitha the gazelle turned and looked at Thimblerig. They all did.

"I've never heard of them executing anyone here," Thimblerig said, dismissing the duck with a wave of his paw.

"The wild dogs have plenty to do without worrying about a group of nobodies standing on the edge of a big, empty field. I used to come here all the time when I was younger, and never had a problem."

The forest had grown darker and more foreboding, especially the spot on which they stood. There was no way they'd get far if this dark mood persisted, so Thimblerig bent down and pulled out a tuft of grass, sniffed it, and then held it out for the others to see.

"Friends, you see these as simple blades of grass. But do you know what I see? I see hope." Thimblerig rose, still holding the grass. "I didn't choose this field as our starting point because it is a place of death. I chose it because I see it as a place of hope. This isn't where it all ended, it's where it all begins."

He stood and walked past each of the suckers, showing them each the grass. He had to get them all firmly in his corner, or they'd certainly peel off one by one when the going got tough, which it was probably going to do before they got far. They'd demand refunds, and maybe even threaten to turn him in to the wild dogs. That was a trail he wanted to avoid going down at all costs. He stopped in front of the camel and looked up at the duck.

"Tannier Isa has promised to help me guide you to the place of safety because the unicorns are starting everything up all over again! That's why we don't need to be afraid of being here. This place belongs to the unicorns, not the wild dogs! And now, it belongs to us."

The animals stood a little taller now, and even stopped glancing nervously over their shoulders. The duck had grown quiet, although he still didn't look like he was buying it. Thimblerig didn't care. As long as they could get things moving, Thimblerig could handle the duck.

"Well, then, how about we get a move on?" Soapy said, wiping his eyes. Thimblerig made a note to tell the ape later that he appreciated the touch.

Under the shadow of the unicorn's mound, their journey began.

Benny the wild dog was patrolling the outskirts of Victory Field, grumbling that he'd been given this job again. It was a thankless bum's job, away from all the interesting things going on in the festival. The worst part of it was the excruciating boredom; there was nothing to do, nobody to see, eat, or terrify. Just endless circles around the abandoned field, circling over and over and over again. Sure, every now and then some cub-pukes would venture into the "zone", and he'd have the pleasure of scaring the droppings out of them. It was actually the best part of the job, sneaking up on them as they traipsed through the sacred grass, and then letting loose with the most ferocious barks he could muster. Watching them jump all over each other trying to get away almost made the job worth it.

Almost, but not quite.

A more thoughtful wild dog would have felt awed by the historical significance of Victory Field, seeing walking this post as a sacred trust, the honor of guarding the birthplace of the wild dog's rise to power. But not Benny. To Benny, it was just a job, and a boring one at that, and he hated that he was given it so often.

He was so busy feeling sorry for himself that he nearly failed to spot the fresh tracks on the forest floor from at least half a dozen fully grown animals of different kinds! All the worthless animals in the forest knew that the zone was off limits, and that they'd pay with their lives if they were caught.

That meant it was hunting time.

Benny smiled, suddenly not minding the job so much, and lifted his head to howl the alarm.

The company of animals had been pushing their way through hanging leaves and underbrush for the better part of an hour when the howl shattered their peaceful hike.

75

"Did you hear that?" asked the male llama, Manuel.

The fact that everyone had stopped, and that all of the suckers wore fresh looks of alarm on their faces was a pretty good indication that, yes, they'd all heard it.

"Maybe it was just the wind?" Mullins suggested.

"If the wind has sharp teeth and strict rules against animals like us trespassing on Victory Field then it might have been the wind," the duck answered. "Otherwise, it sounded just like a wild dog."

"It probably doesn't have anything to do with us," Thimblerig answered, continuing to push on. "But anyway, we need to keep moving."

The suckers, led by Thimblerig and Mullins, with Soapy and Big Bunco bringing up the rear, started moving again. Ofelia, the female llama, pushed past a low-hanging branch, and it swept backwards, nearly knocking Shi Lau off his perch on the camel's back.

"Hey, watch it, longneck!" he squawked.

"Who you calling 'longneck'?" Manuel spat, stepping up to the duck and staring him down. "That's my wife, and you'd better apologize!"

Quickly, Soapy jumped up between the two. "Hey, easy, everyone. Calm down!"

"I'll be calm when the groundhog finds a trail we can use without getting knocked down every five minutes!" the duck said. "We paid two hundred figs for this, you know!"

"We're pressing on until we get to Passer's Trail," Thimblerig answered without turning around. "From there it's a straight shot north to the steppes, and then on to the Edge."

Thimblerig tried to ignore the bickering of the animals behind. He just wanted to get them to the Edge where he'd lose them in the caves or the maze of rocky outcroppings, and then he and his partners would disappear. They'd have plenty of time to move the figs to a different location before the suckers made it back to Asarata. *If they did make it back*, he thought. He wasn't so sure that this bickering lot would be able to actually make it back, based on what he'd seen so far. He doubted that anyone would miss them.

Thimblerig's wandering mind was snapped back to attention by another howl, and another only moments later, this time considerably closer.

Big Bunco moved up close to Thimblerig. "They're following us," she whispered.

"I know," Thimblerig answered. "They must have come across our tracks back at the field. Play it cool, though."

They stumbled out of the underbrush onto an actual trail, grass pressed and worn down by regular animal usage. As the others emerged behind him, Thimblerig looked for any familiar landmarks, but saw none. He stretched to relieve his cramped muscles.

"Do you know where we are?" he asked quietly as Soapy came up beside him.

"Hard to say, but it might be Passer's Trail," Soapy whispered back, looking for anything familiar in the tree line.

"I've only been out this way a couple of times," Thimblerig replied. He pointed at the twisted trunk of an ebony tree. "That tree looks familiar. Is this the trail to the Peekamoose watering hole?"

"Oh great!" the duck cried. "The groundhog's gotten us lost!"

While they'd been discussing things, the duck had left his perch on the camel's back and snuck up to eavesdrop. Now he was screeching for all the forest to hear, and if the wild dogs didn't know where they were before, they probably did now.

"Lost?" Manuel stammered, standing with the other suckers. "Did he say we're lost?"

All the suckers started looking up and down the trail as if expecting a snarling horde of wild dogs to descend upon them any moment. There was nothing but shafts of morning light shining through the overhanging branches, bringing out the rich tapestry of greens in the leaves all around them.

"Looks clear to me," Tabitha whispered, as if afraid that speaking too loudly would somehow break the spell and all the force of the wild dogs would descend upon them at once.

"Then what are we waiting for?" the duck exclaimed, flapping his wings madly in the groundhog's face. "They're probably right behind us! We've got to get moving!"

"Brother duck, you really need to calm down," Sheila hopped over and put a paw on the duck's back. "We don't know for sure that they're after us."

The duck jerked away from her touch. "Am I the only one in this group with any sense? We were only just in their no-no zone, poking around and talking about unicorns. Do you think they're just taking a morning stroll to help digest their breakfast?"

"Why don't you find out for us," Thimblerig asked.

"Excuse me?" the duck glared at the groundhog. "Why don't I what?"

"You're the only one of us with wings," Thimblerig said, struggling to keep his voice calm. "Why not put them to good use and go see just exactly where they are and what they're up to? Wild dogs can't fly, so you'd be safe."

Shi Lau sputtered and honked loudly at the suggestion. "You want me to do your work for you? You should have taken some of those figs and hired a flying lookout instead of relying on your clients. I can't believe you have the nerve to suggest that I…"

With that, Thimblerig had enough. With quick hands honed by years at the shell game, he grabbed the duck's bill, squeezed it shut, and held tight.

"You've already been trying to do my job by butting in every chance you get, and I'm sick of it." The menace in the groundhog's voice was tangible. "It's time for you to put your wings to use or pipe down and get out of the way."

The duck struggled, but the groundhog's hold was surprisingly strong. With panicked eyes, he looked at the other members of the company but found no allies, no one coming to his aid.

"Do we understand one another, Shi Lau?" Thimblerig asked, regaining the duck's attention. The duck nodded. "No more squawking?" The duck nodded again. "You're going to let me lead?" Reluctantly, the duck nodded a third time.

"Fine. Now everyone listen to the forest," Thimblerig said. "What do you hear?"

They all sat as still as statues. The sudden descent of silence, with no more duck shouting, had an immediate effect on them all. Insects buzzed, a slight breeze rustled the leaves, but there were no sounds of pursuit, no wild dogs with flashing teeth, no instant death; just the usual forest background noise. Apparently the forest was unconcerned about ducks throwing tantrums.

They all relaxed, and Thimblerig's anger started to ebb. He let go of the duck's bill. "Now if you are ready, we can start to head out..."

A single howl stopped Thimblerig in the middle of his sentence. It was one howl, just to the south, not far from where they'd just come. A second answered the first, just to the west. A third howl followed that one, to the east.

If the duck had not been petrified, he would have used this opportunity to deliver a resounding, "I told you so" to all the other animals. As it was, he dove behind the camel's hump and hid. The camel lowered his head between his knocking knees, while the female gazelle and the kangaroo stepped closer together and the kangaroo rested a comforting hand on the gazelle's back. The two llamas stood with their heads high, eyes open wide, and looked like they might bolt at a moment's notice.

"They're boxing us in," Soapy said quietly.

"Folks, we've got a new plan," Thimblerig said, turning to the animals. "We got one way out of this, and not much time to get there." He pointed his paw up the trail to the north – in the direction of the Edge. "I suggest we double time it."

Thimblerig started out thinking that he'd have to push the company to move quicker, but as it turned out it was all Thimblerig could do to keep in front of the long-legged camel. And it was all the long-legged camel could do to not panic and stomp everyone in his pursuit of escape.

The trail led up a steep tree-lined incline at first, and then suddenly descended and wound about a small hill that rose to their right. The forest was thick, limiting visibility and creating a claustrophobic atmosphere for the company of animals, which increased their instinctual sense of panic.

Things had gone wrong so fast, and with so little warning! When things went wrong in a shell game, it was every con for himself, and you blended in with the suckers as you made your escape. But being out in the middle of the forest, far from the familiar ground around Asarata, running for his life with a bunch of suckers? Thimblerig reluctantly admitted to himself that he had no clue what he was doing.

And so it was, the groundhog was just as caught off guard as any of the rest of the group as they rushed up the trail and into a clearing filled with waiting wild dogs.

CHAPTER 10
DEALING WITH KID DUFFY

A dozen wild dogs closed the trail behind them, cutting off any hope of escape. They were growling, teeth bared, saliva dripping, but they weren't moving in for the kill.

Thimblerig glanced at the suckers, and it was clear that they all expected slow and painful deaths. The llamas had their eyes closed, heads bowed close together, and they were whispering to each other. The camel stood tall, but his knees were visibly and audibly knocking together. On the camel's back, the duck was only visible as a few white feathers poking out from behind the camel's hump. To his left, Sheila was standing next to Tabitha, her paw resting on the gazelle's back, like a mother comforting a child. Thimblerig was impressed that the gazelle looked defiant, not afraid. His partners, the consummate professionals, had unreadable faces, even Mullins.

Thimblerig sighed. It was going to be up to him to get them out of this. He took a deep breath and turned back to face the wild dogs with a big grin plastered on his face. "Hey, look who we got here! Wild dogs! Glad to see you all out here, keeping the forest safe!"

"You violated sacred ground," one of the wild dogs snarled. "And now you got to pay the fine." Benny the wild dog, eyes on fire with blood lust, stepped out in front of the others. He moved between the animals, sniffing each prisoner in turn. "What have we here?" He stopped at Tabitha, grinned, and licked his chops. "Boys, looks like we're having venison for lunch."

"No!" Thimblerig heard Mullins cry out, and from nowhere, a brown blur slammed into the side of the wild dog. Thimblerig's eyes were wide as he saw the gazelle knock the wild dog onto his side, and then collapse on top of him, flailing about. The other wild dogs were too stunned to move at first, not expecting such an act of aggression by their prey, especially not expecting it from a gazelle, which gave Thimblerig only seconds to act before they recovered and tore his partner to shreds. He rushed over and pulled Mullins up, shoved him aside, and turned his attention back to the wild dog on the ground.

"Hey, sorry about that. He tripped! Listen, can we make a deal here?"

The wild dog was up in a flash, and with a snarl Thimblerig would remember for the rest of his life, rammed his head into the groundhog's gut. Thimblerig crumpled to the ground in a heap beside the camel's feet, and Soapy was quickly at his side.

Benny turned to face Mullins. "I'm gonna enjoy this, gazelle." Two wild dogs moved behind the gazelle to prevent his escape, so he had no choice but to stand and watch his death approach. Before anyone could react, Tabitha leapt up beside him; eyes still defiant, facing Benny by his side.

"Two for the price of one," the wild dog said, grinning wickedly. The wild dog settled back on his haunches, preparing to strike, when an order was barked out that changed everything.

"Hold!"

As one, the wild dogs dropped to the ground, their tails between their legs, and started whining. Even Benny dropped at the sound of the commanding voice. The only wild dog still standing, the one who had just entered the clearing, looked to be twice the size of the next largest.

"Kid Duffy," Soapy whispered in awe.

"Blonger's enforcer," Thimblerig said. Soapy nodded, a slight but barely perceptible motion. The ape wasn't taking any chances of getting the enforcer's attention.

But Thimblerig just smiled. *We might just get out of this after all*, he thought. *If I can shift my shells the right way.*

--

"Report," Kid Duffy ordered.

"I found these animals trespassing on Victory Field," Benny replied. "We were about to make them lunch."

Kid Duffy considered the pathetic animals shaking in fear before him, surrounded by his wild dogs. There was a lanky camel, a fat duck, a gamy-looking kangaroo, two llamas with nice coats but not much meat, a familiar looking ape, a baby elephant, a couple of four-legged snacks, and what appeared to be a large rat.

"Not much of a lunch," Kid Duffy replied distastefully.

"You got that right," Benny chuckled, relaxing. "But still, you're welcome to join us."

In a flash, Kid Duffy had Benny's neck in his jaws, pressing down, drawing blood. Benny went limp and whined louder than ever, but the enforcer kept biting down harder and harder until the other wild dog was blubbering and begging to be let go. Finally, he dropped Benny to the ground, a sobbing, bloody mess.

The enforcer leaned in and said, loudly enough for the other wild dogs cowering nearby to hear, "I'll join you when I want, not when I'm invited."

Benny nodded miserably.

"Now get outta here!" Kid Duffy barked at the humiliated wild dog. Benny crawled past the other wild dogs and out of the picture.

"Anybody else want to invite me to lunch?" The enforcer asked the rest of the pack. They all shook their heads wildly, except the big rat, who stepped forward and raised a paw.

"I have an invitation for you, Mr. Duffy, sir."

Kid Duffy cursed silently. He really wasn't in the mood to eat a rat.

As it turned out, the big rat was actually a groundhog, and Kid Duffy stood with him away from the pack and the prisoners. He'd been ready to separate the animal's head from his shoulders when the groundhog had mentioned making a deal. Kid Duffy knew that meat bled from all sides, and a good deal could come from the most unlikely of places, so he gave the groundhog two minutes.

"Here's my deal," the groundhog said, speaking quickly. "I know you guys have your hunt coming up, and I want to offer you the best prey in the forest. Us."

"You want to what?" Kid Duffy was used to animals begging for their lives. They didn't usually beg to be hunted.

"We'll be your prey. You need someone to hunt, and we're sitting ducks. Especially the duck. Give us a head start, and then hunt us!"

The enforcer glanced back at the rest of the animals. Pathetic. It was a pitiful group, no matter how you bit them.

"No deal," he replied. "There's no challenge here."

"You're exactly right!" Thimblerig nodded. He was improvising, completely making it up as he went along. He wasn't sure what he was doing; he just knew every minute not being eaten was a good minute. "But you're Blonger's enforcer! You're not the kind of wild dog who stops with surface observations..."

Kid Duffy's unimpressed face told Thimblerig that he'd get nowhere with flattery, and turning the curve sharply, he changed tactics. In this case, it might just work if he told the truth, embellished a bit, but the truth nonetheless.

"See, they may look ordinary, but they're far from it," he said. "They're *believers*."

"Believers?" Kid Duffy had been on the hunt for believers ever since the meeting with Blonger, but he had been beginning to believe that there weren't any left, since he hadn't been able to track any down. And now he'd stumbled on a gang of them out here in the middle of nowhere?

"Yeah, they believe in the unicorns!" Thimblerig said, noting the look in the wild dog's eye. It was the same look every mark got when they imagined they knew where the pea was hidden. But the enforcer was still not taking the bait. He needed to make the figs look sweeter. "They claim the unicorns are coming back to overthrow you guys! And they've been talking to others about it, trying to get others to join them in their mission."

"Mission?" the enforcer asked, his curiosity piqued.

"Oh, sure. That's all they talk about, this mission of theirs. They say that before the wild dogs are overthrown, the unicorns are sending a flood! So all the believers are going to gather together in the Edge to escape the destruction!"

"*All* the believers? There are others?" Kid Duffy asked.

"Oh, sure!" The groundhog winged. "Herds and herds! And they're all meeting up at the Edge."

Kid Duffy grimaced at the unfortunate timing of this news. If word got back to Blonger that believers were gathering *en masse* during the hunt, his career – and maybe his life - would be over. On the other hand, his position would be cemented if he were the one to help catch that many believers in one spot. But one look at the groundhog was all he needed for his cynical instincts to kick in, as he was reminded of the questionable source of this valuable information.

"Why are you telling me this?" he growled. "You're one of them, aren't you?"

"Of course not!" Thimblerig answered quickly, waving his paws back and forth. "I'm just their guide! They hired me to get them to the Edge, that's all! I don't buy into their wacky beliefs. I'm just trying to walk away from this in one piece!"

Having heard enough, the enforcer stood and walked away. He had to think. Most likely, the groundhog was full of scat, and was attempting to fast-talk his way out of being executed. The idea that herds of believers would be gathered in one place was too good to be true. If he decided well, he'd receive Blonger's pleasure. But if he made the wrong decision...

Kid Duffy wasn't superstitious, but he found himself wishing for a sign, something that would tell him what he should do. *But leaders don't wait for signs*, he thought. *Leaders make decisions.*

And so he decided.

"They're doing what?"

The duck, uncharacteristically quiet since the wild dogs showed up, suddenly found his voice.

"They're letting us go," Thimblerig answered quietly.

The animals couldn't believe what they were hearing, and yet it was true. The big, ugly wild dog that had arrived last was barking orders at the others, and one by one the others were peeling off from the circle and returning to the forest. Finally, big and ugly was the only one left, and he padded up to them.

"You've got one day, groundhog," he snarled. Then he also turned and trotted up the trail out of sight.

The clearing was quiet, but not in a comforting way. It was an eerie quiet, as if a giant predator was about to attack from behind a tree.

"What did that mean?" Tabitha asked. "'One day'?"

"It means that in one day, we're not just going to have a handful of wild dogs after us, but the whole pack." Thimblerig said, matter-of-factly. "So we should be heading out."

"Wait a minute," the duck interrupted. "Are you telling us that you traded a few for the entire pack? That's the best you could do?"

"I negotiated," Thimblerig replied. "Like it or not, it's the hunt, and we're headliners. Seems like Duffy was particularly fond of the idea of hunting down a group of unicorn lovers, and so he gave us a day. Now we could sit here discussing this, but I bought us a day, and time is passing. We need to get this show on the road."

CHAPTER 11
A SURPRISING REVELATION

The journey, which had started out with such promise, had taken a dark turn. No one was feeling particularly inspired, the big exception being Mullins. The gazelle was hopping ahead on the trail as if on the way to the feast rather than running away from becoming one. Thimblerig caught up with him.

"You seem excited," he said.

"Did you see the way she stood there with me?" he gushed. "She was standing there right beside me! That wild dog was going to kill me, and she jumped up and faced him with me!"

Thimblerig couldn't help but smile, even given their dangerous situation. The gazelle had gone and done something foolhardy and heroic, and now the girl was paying attention.

"So, what's your next move?" he asked as they trudged up along the trail.

"My next what?"

"Something usually happens next. You know, you save her life, she risks her life for you, you have a conversation or something…"

"A conversation?"

The gazelle stopped skipping, and in a moment his newfound courage dissolved. He looked as if a stray leaf landing on his shoulder might send him barreling down the trail away from the danger.

It was probably for the best, Thimblerig thought, considering what they would have to do when they reached the Edge. It would be easier for Mullins to leave the girl behind if he wasn't emotionally attached.

"C'mon, Mullins," he said. "We're blocking the trail."

The forest had been growing steadily darker and more ominous with each passing moment, and so it was with enormous relief to the company of animals that they finally arrived at trail's end, and the end of the forest. Beyond the forest lay the wide-open expanse of the steppe, an immense flat plain blanketed with high rustling grasses, which gave way to hills dotted with scrubs of dry vegetation. Above it all, the setting sun ignited the sky with flaming purple, orange and red clouds as it continued its daily journey to brighten far away lands. In the distance, a dark range of mountains lined the horizon.

"That's our destination, folks," Thimblerig said, gesturing toward the mountains. "The Edge."

"How long will that take to cross?" the camel asked.

"It looks a lot farther than it is," Thimblerig said. "We'll go tonight for a couple of more hours and then rest. If we get started before sunrise, it shouldn't take more than a day."

"More than a day?" Shi Lau said. "We already have less than a day until the wild dogs come after us, and then we're going to be out there in the middle of nowhere, sticking out like sore wings? This is a fantastic plan."

"Would you rather return to the forest?" Tabitha asked.

They all turned and stared back into the imposing darkness of the forest, which seemed even gloomier in the dimming light of dusk. The place that had been their home and sanctuary for most of their lives had lost its welcoming appeal. Even the duck shuddered looking back.

"Death waits behind us," Sheila said simply, and then as she turned to look out over the grassland, her face was bathed in crimson from the setting sun. "Life waits ahead."

On that note, Thimblerig moved forward into the tall grass. One by one, the others followed, leaving their forest home behind forever.

"I always felt different then the other camels in the herd," Elbridge said to the others as they pushed their way through the grass. "While they were mostly interested in filling their bellies, I was interested in asking questions."

Nighttime had fallen on the steppe, but Thimblerig had elected to keep moving as long as they were able. The stars would peek out from behind the clouds from time to time to help them keep their bearing, and they walked closely together to avoid getting separated in the darkness.

"Questions?" Sheila asked as she hopped along beside him to his right. "What sorts of questions?"

"The big picture kinds. Why was I born? Do I have a purpose in life? What happens after we die? Most of the other camels weren't concerned."

"It's not just camels," Ophelia said from the camel's other side. "Most llamas could care less."

"Gazelles, too," Tabitha agreed as she walked along beside the llama. "But it's hard to fault them. When you're just trying to survive, you don't have much time for big picture questions."

"I disagree," Elbridge replied kindly. It was such a relief to have found others with whom he could discuss these issues without being put down; it gave him a new confidence to express himself that he hadn't felt in a long time. "We're all trying to survive, but we make the choice about what things are important. For me, it's important to understand my purpose."

"For me, it's important to get some sleep!" Shi Lau said crossly from the camel's back. "Why don't you all shut your grass holes!"

"You are such a freeloader," Manuel the llama said, and then he spat.

"Manny…" Ophelia started.

"No, Ophelia, I need to say it. Hold up, Elbridge," Manuel interrupted, trotting over to the camel to look the duck in the eye. "Duck, I want to know why you don't do something besides sit up there talking down to everyone. You've been doing it all day, and I'm tired of it! In my opinion, you should hop down and carry the camel for a change."

The feathers on Shi Lau's back stood visibly, their whiteness standing out against the blackness of the night, and he stuck his bill in Manuel's face.

"Let me tell you what you can do with your opinion, llama…" Shi Lau growled.

"Shi Lau, Manuel, that's enough," Sheila interrupted, pushing her way in between the two animals. "We're all following the unicorn together."

The duck turned on the kangaroo. "Are you seriously talking to me, nut case?" Looking back at the llamas he asked, "Am I the only one getting sick of this whole 'one with the unicorn' act she's putting on?"

"Be careful, duck," Tabitha replied, hopping in front of Elbridge, and speaking with such venom in her voice that the duck felt instantly grateful that he was not on the ground. "You need to be more careful with your words."

"What's the hold up?" Soapy called out forcefully from the rear of the group. "We need to get moving if we're going to put enough space between us and the wild dogs."

The mention of the wild dogs was the motivation that the animals needed to declare a temporary cease-fire. Grumbling, they started moving forward once again. Soapy sprang ahead of the others to Thimblerig, who walked alone.

"Never mind the wild dogs," he said quietly to the groundhog as he leapt up alongside him. "That duck will be lucky to survive the other animals."

Thimblerig responded with a grunt. He was keeping his eyes on the dark sky, doing his best to find a single star that they could follow in the right direction to get to the Edge. It had been growing progressively cloudier as the darkness set in, and what few stars he'd been able to follow before were now safely tucked away behind the clouds. If they got off course just a tiny bit and kept moving forward, they'd find in the morning that they'd gone a considerable distance out of the way. That was something they

90

couldn't afford to do if they were going to make it to the Edge before the wild dogs tracked them down.

"What's the grunt for?" Soapy asked. "Worried about something?"

"What am I *not* worried about?" Thimblerig answered, laughing humorlessly. He glanced back to make certain the duck wasn't eavesdropping again, and spoke quietly. "I can't see any stars, Soapy. I'm not sure we're going in the right direction."

A spot of light in the dark clouds above gave him a quick burst of hope, which quickly faded away as he recognized that it was only a firefly flying in curious circles directly overhead. This just reinforced the sinking feeling he'd been having that he had gotten them all in over their heads. Still, he was too proud to admit that much, even to his partners. He glanced at Soapy, managing a cocky smile. "But hey, we've gotten this far, so no worries, right?"

This time it was Soapy's turn to grunt, and then for the next several minutes they trudged along in silence. Finally, Soapy spoke up once more.

"You know 'Rig, Bunco and I were talking back there, and we were both just saying that we've never seen anyone talk their way out of anything with any of the wild dogs, let alone Kid Duffy. You actually got us away from the wild dogs! Not only that, but you've gotten us out of the forest, and even with that loudmouthed duck, we haven't lost any of our suckers. All in all, I'd say it's going pretty well, thanks to you."

The groundhog was touched by the encouragement, and walked along silently, unsure how to respond. He was so used to working alone that he wasn't comfortable with others offering compliments. Suddenly a distressing thought occurred to him; was Soapy trying to play him? Had he and Big Bunco cooked up a side con walking together in the back of the group? Was this all part of a new scheme to con him and somehow worm more figs out of him?

91

Thimblerig was usually pretty good at reading other animals. You had to be in his line of work, or else you didn't last very long. Soapy seemed sincere, but then again, it was his job to make animals glad to shake his right hand while he was stealing their figs with his left. And Thimblerig had been burned before.

Soapy couldn't have really meant it.

Could he?

Another bit of glowing green light circled Thimblerig's head and flew past them before disappearing into the darkness.

"Did you see that?" Soapy asked.

"You mean the firefly?" Thimblerig asked. "What about it?"

"I didn't know that fireflies lived out here," the ape answered, eyes on the sky. "I thought they stuck to the forest, close to the trees. Look! There's another one!"

Sure enough, another firefly flew past, following the same basic path as the others Thimblerig had seen; they flittered silently around his head and then faded away into the night sky. Thimblerig was about to say that fireflies weren't the most unusual creatures in nature when another four fireflies chased each other around his head, then another three, then at least six or seven more.

"What's happening?" Tabitha called from behind. The other animals were starting to chatter among themselves again, and the frustrated groundhog turned to tell them to quiet down when he saw what was heading their direction from the forest behind, and his mouth just hung open.

The sky to the south was lit up with thousands of tiny bits of green, blue and yellow lights flowing like a river up and over their heads, as if the stars themselves had come down into the atmosphere and joined together as an endless flock flying overhead. Weaving and bobbing as they went, some winging down to fly circles among the other open-mouthed animals before rejoining their brothers in the sky, thousands of fireflies were all heading in the same general direction straight ahead.

"What does it mean?" Ophelia said as a firefly momentarily landed on her nose, ran tiny black arms across its antennae, and then sailed off again into the now-glowing sky.

"I'd say it means that someone wants our groundhog to know that he's taking us in the right direction," Sheila answered, a wide grin on her face. All the other animals turned and looked at Thimblerig, who stood, still open-mouthed, washed in the neon light of the endless stream of fireflies.

"Thimblerig?" Soapy said, awed as he watched the thousands of tiny lights sail over their heads. "You gonna say anything?"

The groundhog felt as if he were surfacing from another vision as the tail end of the flock of fireflies flew past, high aboveground. In the wake of the fireflies passing, the clouds parted above them like water in the wake of a swimming crocodile, and a row of stars shone out clearly.

"Yeah, sure," he said, finally finding his voice. "Time to get moving."

"Can you hear it?" Sheila said. "The unicorn is talking to us through the wind, telling us to keep moving forward."

Thimblerig glanced over at the kangaroo who lay on her side, serenely gazing at the row of stars that continued to twinkle above, apparently listening to the unicorn speak as the wind rustled the grasses. Of all the crazy animals he'd come across in the forest, she was definitely in the top five. She knew he was looking, and she smiled. "You think I'm crazy."

"I never said you were crazy," Thimblerig said. Thinking and saying things are different, so technically, it wasn't a lie. He looked past her at the other animals, sacked out on the grass. The duck's snores were particularly loud, apparently amplified by the shape of his bill. Having volunteered to take the first watch, the groundhog thought everyone else would be sound asleep.

"It's alright," she continued. "Lots of animals think I'm crazy, even some of the other believers. They call me "Hopping Mad Sheila." Ever get called names like that?"

Thimblerig considered this question for a moment. As a con, he had been called every name in the book. He deserved it most of the time, but that didn't make it enjoyable.

"I've been called worse. You get used to it," Thimblerig said. Then remembering the role he was supposed to be playing, he added, "You know how it is, being a believer and all. Following the unicorn is definitely not easy."

The kangaroo didn't respond to this, but went back to her stargazing. Thimblerig had no desire for small talk, so he breathed a quiet sigh of relief. Besides, he really did think she was crazy, and he wanted to steer clear in case it was catching.

"He does things in interesting ways, doesn't he?"

Apparently, the conversation wasn't over. Thimblerig was glad that the darkness made the grimace on his face difficult to see.

"Who's that?" he asked.

"The unicorn," she replied. "Tannier Isa."

"Yeah, interesting," he responded politely. "Listen, Sheila, you really should get some rest. We've got a long day tomorrow..."

"You have no idea," she said cryptically. Thimblerig decided to play her game to get her to pipe down.

"Yeah, but the fireflies prove that the unicorn's with us, right? So I'm not too worried." She was quiet again, and Thimblerig made a satisfied mental note that speaking wacko talk was a good way to keep a wacko from talking too much. He would have thought the opposite would be true.

He settled back down and started plotting where they'd be heading in the morning, and how to put the wild dogs off their trail as long as possible. If he could, he would try to put them off the trail completely, but he couldn't begin to fool himself into thinking that he would really be able to accomplish that. He

94

regretted that he hadn't brought along someone more familiar with the steppes to help them find their way through, but he hadn't imagined that the wild dogs would pay them any mind...

Working the streets for so long had helped Thimblerig develop a sixth sense for when he was being watched. His instincts were tickling him right now, and out of the corner of his eye he noticed that the kangaroo had shifted her attention from the stars to him. She wasn't saying anything, just staring, propped up on her left arm.

"Can I help you?" he asked, irritated.

"You are really something, Thimblerig," she answered.

"Thanks," he mumbled uncertainly, relieved that she was finally not just staring, but wishing that she'd go back to staring at the stars instead of him.

"It wasn't necessarily a compliment," she said. "I've seen you before, you know."

"Excuse me?"

"At the festival. I've seen you there. You run a street game. With shells and peas?"

"I don't think so," Thimblerig stammered, alarmed at this turn of conversation. "All us groundhogs look alike to other animals."

"No, I'm sure it was you," she replied. "You were obviously palming the pea, but the other animals saw what they wanted to see, didn't they?"

What was happening here? Thimblerig felt as if were being shoved down into the floodwaters again, but this time he was being shoved under at the paws of an insane kangaroo. Or was she insane? Pitilessly, Sheila continued.

"The other day you were playing a game for figs with a rhinoceros and you took him for a bagful. I can't imagine he was very happy about it when he finally figured it out. Oh! And the gazelle was there, too."

I got sloppy, Thimblerig thought. He should have been smarter with Sheila. He'd let down his guard with her, and she'd been playing him the whole time. He had to recover this somehow.

"I just met the gazelle..." he started to say defensively.

"I may be crazy, Thimblerig, but I never forget a face," she answered, looking back up at the stars. "I've seen Soapy and Big Bunco working the crowds too, although I didn't see them at your rhinoceros game. And now here you all are, together, with a monstrously big pile of figs sitting in the middle of you. Isn't that a coincidence?"

Thimblerig was sitting up straight now, looking back at the kangaroo. She was barely illuminated by the ambient light of the stars at which she was gazing, and she was impossible to read. She held all the figs, and with one word could spin the con down into the dirt. Professionally, he admired her skill. He decided that it was time to speak normally to her, con to con.

"You're good," he said. "I'm just trying to figure out why I don't know you. Are you working for someone? The fox sisters, maybe?

"No, I don't work for the fox sisters," she replied, laughing. "I'm not that crazy."

"So you're an independent contractor. All right then, how much do you want? That's what this whole 'believer' act has been about, right? You want a cut of the action?"

"Oh no, I really am a believer," she answered, laughing more now. "I'm just amazed, that's all."

"Amazed?"

"Sure! Think about it!" Sheila sat back up again and faced Thimblerig. Even in the darkness, her eyes were shining as if by some inner light. "Tannier Isa came to you, and you don't even believe it. You've taken this incredible honor that animals better than you have waited for their entire lives, and you turned it into a big shell game with bigger stakes. I'm amazed at the ego you must have to even make such an attempt. But the really crazy part is that he's using you anyway, even though you don't believe a word that you say."

What's this? Thimblerig thought, stunned. *She's not a con?*

"Let me get this straight. You've known what was really going on this whole time and you still wanted to be a part of it? You still scrounged up two hundred figs and came out into the wilderness with us? Why would you do that?"

Even in the darkness, Thimblerig could sense Sheila's smile. She laid her head back down, and resumed her examination of the stars prickling the sky above.

"Because I'm a believer, Thimblerig. I believe it all. I believe you're really leading us to the place of safety, because the unicorn is leading you. It doesn't matter to me what you think you're doing, because what the unicorn is doing is much more important. I just hope you figure that out before it's too late."

They sat silently in the darkness for several minutes, Thimblerig not sure what to say, Sheila apparently at peace that she didn't need to say any more.

"For the record," Thimblerig said, finally breaking the silence. "I really do think you're crazy."

"I've been called worse," she replied, closing her eyes to go to sleep. "You get used to it."

The animals were up and moving well before dawn, and Thimblerig was impressed in spite of himself. Even though the previous day's march had gone well into the night, they hadn't needed any prompting to get going. They were up quickly, continuing to discuss the events of the night before, and each offering his or her interpretation of the meaning of the "river of fireflies".

Thimblerig found that he wasn't terribly bothered by either the fireflies or the boulder Sheila had dropped on him. The firefly incident had just been a freak of nature, like the time when he'd seen a massive flock of starlings that appeared to be flying as one before an approaching storm. As to the kangaroo, she was a die-hard believer, and she wanted this trip to succeed, so she wouldn't squeal on them. He and his partners would leave her behind just as quickly as the rest of them, so in the end she was only going to be able to tell the others that she'd known, for all the good it would do them, or her.

No, Thimblerig was concerned for other reasons. The wind had been blowing lightly across the plains from the west when they'd first started across the steppes. Overnight it had shifted to become a distinct headwind, blowing cooler air in from the north. Also, he'd seen some flashes of lighting over the mountain range in the distance in the purple darkness of the early morning, which reminded him too much of the lightning in his dream. What were the odds that a storm would hit now?

He stopped himself from going down that trail. The flood had been a dream, and nothing more, no matter what the kangaroo said. It was a dream inspired by his extremely creative subconscious, and it had helped come up with this brilliant scam, and that was all. There were no floods coming, and no magical unicorns. He had enough to worry about that was very real: wild dogs, obnoxious ducks, love-struck partners, insane kangaroos, and seeing this highly profitable con to the end...

I'm getting too distracted, he thought. *Got to get my eyes back on the prize.* He forced himself to stop worrying about the dark clouds up ahead, and made himself stop thinking about the bothersome animals he was leading behind, and instead focus on the grass in front of him, one step at a time.

A gleam of light off in the distance caught his eye. He'd nearly missed it, but there it was again – something reflecting in the distance ahead. What was a gleam of light doing on the steppe during the day? There wasn't any water out here, so what else could reflect light?

"Did you see that?" he asked Mullins, who was walking close by.

"See what? Where?"

"Out there, ahead of us," Thimblerig said, keeping his eyes on the spot where the light had been. "I thought I saw..."

The steppes were as barren as usual, nothing but an empty, endless hilly vista as far as the eye could see.

"Thought you saw what?" Mullins asked.

"Nothing," Thimblerig answered finally, shaking his head. "Just the sun playing tricks on me."

"You okay?" Mullins asked, concerned.

"I'm fine. Just didn't get enough shut-eye last night. Why don't you take point for a little while?"

Nodding, the gazelle bounced up ahead, leaving the groundhog gratefully alone. He was wondering about the light, pondering what he had seen, when he saw it again. Only this time he also saw the source of the light.

The black unicorn from his dream was running freely through the grass about fifty yards ahead, the light from the sun gleaming off the brilliant horn that jutted out from his forehead. The unicorn was galloping away from them, on a course directly in line with their own – directly towards the dark clouds and the Edge.

The unicorn stopped, turned and looked back at him. It stamped the ground, turned, and then was gone. Vanished – like a mist burning away in the morning sun.

Thimblerig hadn't even noticed that he'd stopped walking, but stood as if carved from a rock, staring hard at the spot where the unicorn had been standing. He rubbed the palms of his paws in his eyes, grinding hard, not daring to believe what he'd just seen. He looked again and saw empty steppe.

"What's wrong?" Shi Lau shouted. "Why'd we stop?"

"Did anyone just see…" Thimblerig stammered.

"What?" Elbridge interrupted, alarmed. "Is it the wild dogs?"

"No, not the wild dogs," Thimblerig said. "I thought I just saw…" he trailed off, refusing to say what he thought he'd just seen.

"You saw *him*, didn't you?" Sheila asked, hopping up beside the groundhog.

"I couldn't have," Thimblerig protested. "It was the sun playing tricks. And I didn't get much sleep. And..." the groundhog was suddenly aware that everyone was staring at him. "...we really need to get moving."

"It's a good sign," Sheila persisted, blocking his path, with a quiet voice that only Thimblerig could hear. "You should tell the others. It'll lift their spirits."

And then it hit him like a big heavy bag of figs. Of course he hadn't seen a unicorn, of course it was the sun and his lack of sleep and all of that, but why *couldn't* he have seen him? It was perfect. His instincts and abilities buried deep in his subconscious were hard at work, even when his conscious self was distracted.

"You're right, Sheila," he said, rustling up his old confidence. "This is a very good sign for all of us."

He turned and faced the group.

"Fellow animals, I have just had another vision, even as we were walking along." Thimblerig lowered his voice dramatically. "Just ahead of us, on the top of the next ridge, I saw Tannier Isa."

"He was here?"

"You saw him again?"

"I didn't see anything..."

The questions and comments came quickly from each of the suckers with Soapy and Big Bunco throwing out a few to play along. The duck hopped up on the camel's hump and scanned the grasslands ahead of them and Thimblerig threw up his paws to quiet everyone down.

"I don't have any answers except to say that he was there. Sheila thinks it's a sign and I can't help but agree."

"A sign of what?" Ophelia asked.

"That we're heading in the right direction," Sheila answered. "That the unicorn continues to lead us."

"Don't you get tired always being so upbeat?" Shi Lau asked Sheila, exasperated. "I didn't see anything, and I think it's pretty convenient for the groundhog that once again, he's the only one who did."

"Did any of you see the vision of the flood? Any of you?" Thimblerig asked. The animals shook their heads. "Could it be, Shi Lau, that Tannier Isa has chosen only to appear to me?"

The duck flapped his wings in disgust. "Isn't that handy? It works out great for you that you're the only one who gets to see him. I'm beginning to think that it's time we…"

"Thimblerig's not the only one who saw him."

Everyone turned to look at Mullins, shocked. He was staring out over the steppes, a face so somber and serious that nobody could challenge him.

Brilliant! Thimblerig thought. *I should have thought of that myself!* In an instant, Mullins had doubled his credibility.

The gazelle turned and faced the animals. "He was galloping just over the rise of the next hill. He was as big as a boulder, black as night. He was just like Thimblerig described him…"

They all looked at the gazelle, and finally Tabitha broke the silence.

"If both Thimblerig and Mullins say they saw him, then that's good enough for me. I say we keep moving forward." She was radiant in the sunlight, and her vote of confidence was just what the others needed.

"So let's keep moving," Ophelia said.

"To the Edge!" Manuel agreed with enthusiasm.

Thimblerig smiled and glanced proudly at Mullins. He winked, but Mullins shook his head, turned, and started back in the direction of the Edge. Wondering about the cold response, Thimblerig scurried forward to catch the gazelle.

"Hey Mullins, that was brilliant improvisation!" he said cheerfully. When Mullins didn't respond, Thimblerig continued. "What's wrong? That was great!"

"Nothing," Mullins answered crossly.

"I think I'm getting to know you, Mullins," Thimblerig said. "And something's eating at you."

Mullins glanced back to make sure they were far enough from the others so as not to be overheard.

"I wasn't improvising, Thimblerig," Mullins whispered. "I really saw him."

Thimblerig couldn't believe what he was hearing. It wasn't possible for Mullins to see the unicorn, because there wasn't any such thing. It was all Thimblerig's fertile imagination at work.

"He was galloping in the direction of the Edge, just like you said. He looked back at us, and then disappeared. It was insane."

The wide-eyed look on Mullins' face made Thimblerig's whiskers twitch. It was the same look that the kangaroo hopped around wearing - the look of the believer. Thimblerig knew that he had to handle this situation carefully. "That's great, Mull! What do you think it means?"

"I don't know, 'Rig," Mullins said. "But if it's true, then that means that the con is on us!"

"On us?"

"Yeah! Think about it! We started out trying to scam these others, but if he's real, then we were being scammed ourselves the whole time!" Mullins said, the serious look on his face melting away as he started laughing. "It's the unicorn's grift! He's been conning us all along!"

"By 'he', you mean Tannier Isa," Thimblerig said, laughing, too. *Great,* Thimblerig thought, still smiling with as much genuineness as he could muster. *It's worse than I imagined.*

"That's fantastic, pal," he said. "Hey, you stay up here on point, okay? Maybe you'll see him again. I'm going to go back and check how the others are doing."

"No problem," the gazelle added, a smile on his face. Thimblerig started to turn. "And 'Rig?"

"Yeah, pal?"

102

"It's like one of those old stories, isn't it? Like the ones we heard when we were kids! Only this time, we get to be a part of it!"

If he'd had thumbs like Soapy, Thimblerig would have given the gazelle two of them straight up. Instead, he just nodded, smiled, and turned back to conference with the two members of his team who were still sane.

CHAPTER 12
THE HUNT BEGINS

The mid-morning sunlight flooding Victory Field was deceptive, clothing the field with a bright cheerfulness that ran in direct opposition to the occasion for most animals.

The wild dog's hunt was about to begin.

Victory Field was overrun with hundreds of growling, snarling, snapping wild dogs, from all over the forest, all impatient for the hunt and thirsty for the blood of the prey. The hunt was always held during Asarata's festival, marking the occasion of Aktamau slaying the last of the unicorns many years before, and it was the biggest day of the year for any wild dog.

Other animals surrounded the field, chosen at random by the wild dogs and pulled away from their families in male and female pairs, so that all kinds would be represented. The animals being forced to watch the opening of the hunt were terrified, but also relieved to be observers and not participants, an unfortunate honor that was reserved for a select few. The audience stood quietly; meat and plant eaters alike, setting aside their differences for the moment. All animals knew that an argument in the spectator circle would likely result in the offenders being pulled out and forced into the hunt without warning. There would be plenty of time later to settle scores for stepped-on toes and the cross looks, but for now, compliance was the rule of the day.

Kid Duffy paced back and forth in front of the animals who were prey for this year's hunt. The leader had accepted his reasoning for releasing the believers, but Kid Duffy was distracted by second thoughts. Of course they would catch the ones he'd let go, but what if the groundhog had been lying, and there were no "herds of other believers" when they got there? It had been an enormous gamble, and Kid Duffy had foolishly gone all in.

The rustling of the prey brought his attention back to the business at hand. They were the fastest, strongest, angriest, or most vicious of all the animals kept in the wild dog dungeons, and this year, there was at least one believer; the lynx who was being interrogated in Blonger's cave earlier was there, showing a surprising lack of emotion. In contrast, the male ram beside her was busy foaming at the mouth and beating his curved horns into the dirt in a vain and obvious attempt to fool the wild dogs into thinking he was rabid. Even if he were, it wouldn't make any difference. Prey is prey.

The tenth in line, restrained by dozens of vines tightly crisscrossing his back and head, was the hunt's star attraction: a cliff-sized great bull elephant. He was perfect prey material, certain to get the wild dogs excited, with his vile temper and willingness to stomp on just about anyone who got in his way. But that wasn't why he was taking part in the hunt. In fact, under different circumstances, Kid Duffy would have enlisted the elephant to work for him as hired muscle. This particular elephant had earned his position as the biggest attraction in the hunt by trying to run down Blonger a few weeks earlier, an act that would usually warrant immediate execution. Fortunately for the elephant, the hunt had been coming up, and so his execution had been delayed. Or perhaps it was unfortunate. It was all a matter of perspective.

Kid Duffy noticed with irritation that the elephant, like the lynx, was also standing still and quiet. How could they start the hunt when the star attraction was being so docile?

A disturbance near the entrance to Victory Field pulled Kid Duffy's attention away from the elephant. The wild dogs were snapping and snarling at the animals in that area, forcing them to create an opening in the circle around the field. Six wild dogs entered, each wearing the fur or feathers of a strong hunter of the forest – a grey wolf, a hyena, an eagle, a wild boar, and a lion. It was the capital guard, Blonger's elite, and their arrival heralded the entrance of the leader, and the start of the hunt.

Kid Duffy felt a strong mixture of pride and gratitude. A ripple of tangible fear raced along the crowd like a wave, causing them to whimper and whine. Even the elephant had finally started acting like himself, yanking on the vines in desperation. At the same time, joy spread through the ranks of the wild dogs, and they raised their heads, yelping and barking as one. Joining them, Kid Duffy felt immense gratitude that he had been born a wild dog, and so extremely proud to serve the leader!

When the chaos had reached a crescendo, Blonger made his entrance.

Blonger felt immense satisfaction as he entered the circle onto the field. It was as if darkness and terror trailed behind him, causing all the animals to fall deeper into madness. It was all a feast to Blonger's spirit: an intoxicating, maddening, chaotic feast, and he fed off the anarchy and confusion in much the same way that common wild dogs fed off flesh. He was the undisputed center of the forest, and could feel the pleasure of it radiating from the tips of his ears to the nails on his paws.

As he reached the base of the mound in the center of the field, he turned to face the prey being held across the field, and was further pleased by the despair he saw there. His attention was quickly drawn to the bull elephant struggling mightily against the vines that bound him. He was very satisfied to see this, because it meant that the hunt would be a challenge. It was always better when the ones about to be sacrificed refused to go easily. Gratified, the leader was about to turn and begin his speech that would begin the hunt when two things happened at once. First, some of the vines holding the elephant snapped. Second, the beast was straining against vines that led back to a large tree at the edge of the field. They were triple and quadruple wrapped, and yet the force of the elephant's heaving and jerking was causing the upper part of the tree to bend over.

The wild dogs guarding the prisoner were so caught up in adoration of their leader that they failed to notice what was going on behind them. "Get up!" Blonger hissed at his capital guard who lay in submission at his feet, but they couldn't hear him.

The crack of the tree shattering was so powerful that it broke through the chaos and immediately grabbed everyone's attention as it came crashing down in pieces, scattering the animals who had been standing nearby. Free at last, the bull elephant shook off the remaining vines, raised his trunk, blasted a trumpeting rage, and charged directly at Blonger.

The capital guard jumped up to form a protective shield around the leader while the rest of the pack turned to face the threat barreling down on them. Many slower wild dogs were trampled instantly, while others bit at his tree-trunk-sized legs and feet, attempting to leverage their numbers to bring him down before he could reach the leader.

Kid Duffy appeared between the elephant and Blonger, gripping a vine in his teeth that was tied around the necks of several young animals; a hippopotamus, a zebra, and a lion. The enforcer yanked the vine, violently dragging the group of young ones to the ground. He barked, and in an instant, three of the capital guards surrounded them, teeth bared, growling. Kid Duffy stood in the path of the oncoming elephant and growled a challenge. This had the intended effect. Throwing both front feet to the ground, the elephant slid to a grinding halt. He was breathing so heavily that Blonger could feel the hot breath washing over him in waves. The oversized beast radiated anguish as he stared down at Kid Duffy's captives.

The elephant turned his attention back to Blonger, and the despair transformed into hatred. "You'll pay for all of this one day, dog," the elephant rumbled. And then, too fast for most of the dazed wild dogs to react, the elephant turned and charged for the edge of the field. In moments he crashed into the forest, and the sound of trees falling echoed as he raged his way deep into the dark woods.

Blonger's own rage threatened to overwhelm him. His moment of triumph had been stolen from him, his pack lay in ruins, and the idiot masses were undoubtedly questioning his authority. He needed to recover the moment.

107

"And so it begins, animals of the forest," he called out, voice shaking beyond his control, and everyone was immediately silent. "The hunt! The triumph of the wild dogs! Any animal that dares stand against us will die as the prey in our hunt. It doesn't matter the strength or the size, no one who sets themselves against us will survive."

He glowered at the animals standing around the field, hating them more than ever before. He barked an order to the wild dogs guarding the remaining prey, and they preserved their lives by responding immediately. The wild dog guards lunged at their captives, biting and nipping, and herding them to the edge of the field, where one by one they finally scattered into the forest, with the exception of the lynx.

She stood in the middle of the animals, ignoring the wild dogs who continued to growl and bark threateningly at her, and turned to look back at Blonger. With a triumphant gleam in her eye, she raised one paw to her forehead, stuck out her claw, and smiled. Then she turned back to the forest and disappeared into the darkness.

Howling and barking, cheering the departure of the prey and the start of the hunt, the wild dogs waited for the cue from their leader. Blonger stood still for a moment longer, soaking in the anger and the hatred and the vitriol, and then howled once more for all to hear. The pack joined him, and then with a rush of pounding feet and snarling voices, they tore into the forest after their prey.

The hunt was on.

CHAPTER 13
THE UNICORN'S SPRING

The day before, when the company of animals had stood at the threshold of the forest, the steppes had seemed easy to cross. While not liking the idea of being so out in the open, the passage itself had appeared to be a simple enough obstacle. What they hadn't counted on, from Thimblerig down, was the fact that the steppes were a great deal vaster than they had appeared. The Edge wasn't getting any closer several hours into their second day yet most of the company of animals continued forward stoically.

Most of them.

"I'm dying up here!" Shi Lau cried from his perch atop the camel. "I need water!"

"It's not so bad," Elbridge replied.

"Not bad to you, because you're a camel!" the duck spat.

"You'll just get thirstier if you keep talking about it," Tabitha replied from up ahead. "Just don't think about it."

"Don't think about it, she says," Shi Lau muttered. "How can I not think about water? I'm a duck!"

"I'm with Shi Lau," Manuel said from behind. "My tongue feels like it's made up of lizard skin. I can't even work up a decent spit."

"There's some good news," Shi Lau replied. "You and Ophelia have been spitting all over the place this whole trip. It's disgusting!"

"It's a part of our culture," the irritated llama said. "Is it duck culture to be annoying?"

Shi Lau slumped back down on the camel's hump trying not to think about his thirst. Of course, this meant that it was the only thing he could think about.

Meanwhile, in the front of the line, Thimblerig was plodding forward as thirsty as the rest of them, but not about to complain. He wasn't exactly sure what he was going to do about this problem, either. Why hadn't they thought to bring some water skins with them? The more he thought about it, the more aggravated he was with how ill prepared he'd been to make this journey.

"It's ironic, don't you think?"

"What's that?" Thimblerig said, wondering when Big Bunco had come up beside him. He hadn't noticed.

"Here we are, all complaining because we don't have any water, while on our way to escape a flood."

"I'm not a big fan of irony, Bunco." Thimblerig said.

They walked along in silence. If not for the thirst, which was getting more and more desperate, Thimblerig might have actually enjoyed being out on the steppe. It lacked the lush living greenness of the forest, but there was beauty here. The open skies that appeared to go on forever, the shadows of the billowy clouds playing tag on the rolling green hills, there was a ruggedness to the steppe that Thimblerig would have found inviting in other circumstances.

"What are we going to do?" Big Bunco asked finally, breaking the silence.

"The unicorn will provide," Thimblerig said with a smirk.

"Amen!" Sheila called from behind. Thimblerig groaned, and kept walking.

Hours later, the sun continued to beat down on the little company of animals and their thirst was growing more desperate. Thimblerig had taken the point, and just behind him Tabitha was now walking beside Mullins, although the gazelle still couldn't talk to her. Shi Lau was taking the worst of the heat from on top of the camel, but he stubbornly refused to come down. The llamas were walking quietly behind the camel, bearing it up a little better than the others. Sheila no longer hopped, but shuffled her feet to continue forward. Soapy, wearing a hat he'd woven out of tall grasses brought up the rear alongside Big Bunco.

The flatness of the steppe was giving way to more hills, and over the mountains beyond the hills the sky was growing more and more dark and ominous, with more than a passing resemblance to the sky in Thimblerig's dream. But it was just coincidence, pure and simple, and didn't deserve to be pondered.

Then Thimblerig saw movement up ahead. *Not again*, he thought. He paused and squinted, trying to blink out the dust from his eyes. Yes, there it was again. Something dark popped over the top of one of the hills and then vanished again.

"Did you see that?" Mullins asked from behind.

"I did," Thimblerig answered, holding up a paw to let the others behind know they should stop as well. "What was it?"

"The unicorn?" Tabitha asked with a weak but enthusiastic voice.

"No," Mullins answered. "Whatever this thing was, it was trying not to be seen."

"Wild dogs?" Elbridge asked. "A scout, maybe?"

"Can't say," Thimblerig answered. Turning to face the company, he was greeted with the view of a group of disheartened, fearful animals.

"Listen, I know you're all thirsty and tired, but we can't let ourselves be spooked by shadows. I promise you that we'll get there if we keep pushing ourselves. There will be water up ahead, but we just have to get to it."

"It's a little late for inspirational speeches," Shi Lau grumbled. "We're out here because we trusted you. We don't have any water because you didn't think to bring any. The wild dogs are after us because of you. If we die, it's your fault, because you led us here."

"Thimblerig didn't force any of us to come. We're all here by choice." Sheila said.

"And the unicorn will provide," the llamas said in unison, and most of the others nodded in weary agreement as they muttered "amen" with dry and dusty throats.

The only exceptions were the duck, and Thimblerig, who for different reasons, were not so sure that he would.

111

The company of animals started moving again, unaware that they were being closely observed by not one, but two pairs of eyes. To be more exact, two different pairs of eyes had just been observing them, but the owner of one pair had ducked down and was now scolding himself for being seen.

"Careless!" the cinnamon-colored saiga antelope muttered irritably as he lay on the ground. His head was angled at an extremely uncomfortable position in an attempt to avoid having his two spiral horns pop up over the hill. "They weren't supposed to see me."

"They look to be in bad shape," the tiny golden-furred gerbil standing nearby replied. He was brazenly standing on the hill, not at all concerned about being seen. Being invisible was just one of the many benefits of being tiny in a big animal world.

The saiga antelope grunted, twisting his head, trying to keep his bulbous nose out of sight while he peeked over the lip of the hill. It was the antelope's enormous nose that typically gave him away, making his head look like it was mostly nose. But this didn't bother him, because all saiga antelopes prided themselves on the size of their noses, and his was respectably huge.

"I don't care what kind of shape they're in as long as they keep moving."

"What are they doing here, Kuandyk?" the gerbil asked, rubbing the tuft of fur under his chin, a habitual action that helped him think. "Those look like forest dwellers to me. You don't suppose it could be *them*..."

"Oh, I know exactly what they're doing here," Kuandyk responded coldly. "They're thieves! Here to steal the treasure."

"They don't look much like thieves to me."

"Nurlan! Of course they don't look like thieves!" Kuandyk hissed conspiratorially. "Thieves would never want to look like thieves, because if they did everyone would know they were thieves!"

"I suppose that makes sense," Nurlan answered, still unsure.

112

"Of course it does! We need to scare them off before they can steal it."

The tiny gerbil looked at the big-nosed saiga skeptically, unable to believe what he was hearing. "Scare them off? Have you seen us? We couldn't scare ourselves off, let alone a group like that."

"Exactly," Kuandyk grinned. "That's what we want them to think, too. We have the element of surprise and we need to use it to our advantage!"

Nurlan nodded. His partner's argument actually made pretty good sense. Nurlan leapt on Kuandyk's neck like a rider mounting his steed, and grabbed hold of his antlers. With a shout of "Death or glory!" the pair charged over the hill to confront the dishonorable forest treasure thieves.

The company had come to the bottom of yet another hill, and with the noonday sun beating down from above, they were just working up the energy to ascend when Big Bunco stopped Soapy.

"Do you hear something?"

Soapy cocked his ear to the wind, and after listening for a moment, nodded. "I do," he answered. "Sounds like it's coming from back there."

They turned and were surprised to see an animal off in the distance galloping towards them, and it appeared to be shouting. The creature was too far away for them to make out what had it so upset.

"Thimblerig?" Soapy called.

The groundhog glanced back and was just as surprised to see the animal. As it drew nearer, he thought that it looked awfully front-heavy, like its nose was going to pull it down face-first to the ground.

"Is that a gazelle? Mullins? Tabitha? A cousin of yours?"

Mullins and Tabitha looked at each other and shrugged. "Maybe some sort of antelope?" Mullins replied.

Thimblerig's first thought was that they should prepare themselves somehow, after all, they were being stormed by an unknown entity in the middle of the steppe, but he just couldn't bring himself to be concerned. First, he was exhausted and incredibly thirsty. Second, the animal didn't look like much of a threat.

Calmly, they all stood and watched the big-nosed antelope come screaming down the hill. It took a couple of minutes, but eventually he was close enough that they could make out that he was screaming "Death and glory!" over and over and over as he ran. Thimblerig started tapping one foot on the ground, impatient to find out whose death was upsetting him so much.

Finally, the animal stopped about ten feet away, gasping for breath. When finally able to speak, he shouted, "That's far enough, thieves! You'll steal no treasure today!"

A smaller animal that had previously gone unseen jumped on the larger animal's neck and waved a tiny little furry fist, screaming, "We'll rip out your fur and poke you in the eyes! Then we'll pluck out the duck's feathers and force feed them to the camel!"

"You'll do what?" Elbridge and Shi Lau both looked up at the same time.

"Easy now," Thimblerig said, putting his paws up in a sign of submission. "We come in peace. We're not here to steal anything."

"Likely story," the big-nosed antelope spat. "That's just what a thief would say!"

"Yeah, nice try! You'd have been more convincing if you'd said you *were* here to steal the treasure!" the smaller animal, a gerbil, said.

"Who would believe that?" Big Nose said, nodding in agreement.

Thimblerig had a firm suspicion that these two had been in the sun for too long. He'd seen prolonged sun exposure do some strange things to animals. Perhaps he could use their madness to his favor?

"So if we told you we were thieves, you'd believe that we weren't?"

"Of course!" the gerbil shouted. "Anyone honest enough to admit that they're thieves can't be anything of the sort!"

Thimblerig glanced back at Mullins, who shrugged in response. *What the heck*, he decided. *You have to eat the figs you find.* "Alright then," he called out. "You've convinced me to come clean. We *are* thieves, and we have travelled for days to steal your treasure. Every last little bit of it."

Both the antelope and the gerbil grew wide-eyed at this revelation. The antelope huffed loudly and stomped the ground, and he looked as if he might explode. Hopping up onto the antelope's head, the gerbil whispered into his ear, and they both looked at Thimblerig again.

"I don't know…" the antelope said. The gerbil whispered again, which caused the antelope to stamp his feet again, and turn around in circles. He appeared to be in pronounced distress, as if suffering from a severe headache.

Finally, without warning, he turned back to face them. Both he and the gerbil smiled. "Well met, weary travellers!" the antelope chirped brightly. "What brings you to our little corner of creation?"

Thimblerig gaped at the pair, unable to move or speak, amazed that his gambit had paid off. Fortunately, Sheila stepped up. "We're so glad to meet you," she said with as much cheerfulness as she could muster. "But in the name of the unicorn, can you tell us if there is any water nearby?"

The transformation on the antelope's odd but friendly face was immediate. It was the look a sucker got when they figured out they were being conned; a mixture of anger, surprise, and gassiness that would have been amusing if they weren't all so thirsty.

"You! What? Water? That's..." the antelope stammered incoherently, slowly backing away from the kangaroo as if she were a hungry leopard about to pounce. Then he found his coherence. "You *are* thieves! The lot of you! Here to steal the treasure! Curse you! Curse you and the camel that you rode in on! Let's get out of here, Nurlan!"

The antelope turned and galloped as hard as he could towards the hill behind which they had originally seen him, the gerbil hanging on for dear life. Thimblerig couldn't help but wonder what sort of treasure these two could have out here in the middle of nowhere that would have them so worked up.

And then it hit him. What else could be considered treasure in the middle of the dry and arid steppe? If he was right, they had only moments to act before the opportunity would be lost. He glanced back at the company of animals and made an on-the-spot decision.

"Elbridge! Follow them! We'll be right behind you!"

Without questioning the order, and with the squawking duck hanging on for dear life, the camel took off after the retreating antelope.

"Everyone follow them!" Thimblerig ordered, scurrying as fast as he could behind Elbridge. "We can't let those two out of our sight!"

"Why, Thimblerig?" Mullins called after him. "They're steppe-crazies!"

"Yeah, but I think they're steppe-crazies with water!" Thimblerig cried back, pushing his own stubby legs to keep up with the long-legged camel.

Kuandyk hadn't run this hard since he'd been caught in the middle of a yak stampede. Putting every ounce of energy into putting as much distance as possible between himself and the lying thieves whom they had come dangerously close to trusting, his heart felt like it would explode, but he forced himself to continue pounding dirt to escape.

"Kuan... Kuan... Kuan..." the gerbil muttered from his place on the antelope's head, and while Kuandyk was sorry that Nurlan was having such a rough ride, this mad dash across the steppe was all that was saving both of their miserable hides. Reaching a ravine below a particularly large steep hill, he immediately ducked behind a large rock to hide and collapsed on the ground; breathing heavily, dust billowing with each breath that rushed through his disproportionately huge nostrils.

"Kuandyk!" the gerbil yelled, finally able to speak. "What are you doing?"

"Protecting the treasure from those thieves," he panted impatiently.

"Didn't you hear what the kangaroo said?" Nurlan asked.

This was certainly irritating to the antelope. He'd heard exactly what the kangaroo had said. "Why do you think I took off? She wanted water."

"Before that!"

"I don't know. What does it matter?"

"It matters! She said 'in the name of the unicorn'!" The gerbil hopped excitedly off the saiga's head. "That's exactly what she said."

The saiga blinked at the gerbil as this information processed.

"I did not hear that," he replied simply.

"That's what the boss said they'd say! And you ran them off!"

"Technically, that's not true. Technically, I ran myself off." Sulking, he raised his nose in the air. "Whose fault is that?"

The gerbil reached up and grabbed the jowls of the saiga with his two tiny paws, forcing his face back down. "You've stopped making sense! We need to go back and get them!"

"We do, don't we?" Kuandyk replied sheepishly.

"No need," an out-of-breath voice said from behind. "We're already here."

Shocked, Nurlan and Kuandyk looked up to see the groundhog standing over them on top the rock, panting, thirstier than ever.

The treasure had indeed been water, and it was the coolest, sweetest, most refreshing water that Thimblerig had ever tasted. It came from a small pool fed by an underground spring, bubbled down the ravine, and disappeared around a bend.

The company of animals drank until they couldn't drink any more, and they ate their fill of olives from an olive tree growing on the banks of the little stream. Sitting in the shade of the tree, they felt more refreshed than they'd felt in ages. The gerbil and the saiga waited on the little company like exceptionally gracious hosts at a fancy fig party, sharing some grain that they'd culled from the grasslands as the company rested.

"What's up with you two?" Soapy asked, interrupting the constant stream of talk from the saiga. "A few minutes ago, you couldn't wait to get rid of us."

"Yeah," Big Bunco agreed. "Why the change of heart?"

Nurlan and Kuandyk exchanged nervous, excited glances, then Nurlan spoke.

"Just a few hours ago, Kuandyk and I were minding our own business, doing some gardening," he pointed to a little plot of land a few feet away where some vegetation was trying hard to keep from dying in the heat of the steppes. "When something really strange happened…"

"You're going to bore them to death!" the antelope interrupted, stepping forward. "Let me tell it. It was a sunny day just like this…"

"It was just a few hours ago," said the gerbil.

"My partner and I were doing our best to survive in this arid and desolate land we call home," the antelope continued dramatically. "Where every day is a struggle for life over the

118

elements, where you don't know when you wake in the morning if you will still breathe when night falls…"

"Oh, for heaven's sake," the gerbil cried, scurrying up onto the antelope's nose. "The unicorn showed up!"

"Here?" Sheila asked, a bit of the old passion creeping back into her voice. "He was here?"

"Right here!" the gerbil replied, puffing out his chest. "He stood right on this very spot!"

"I was getting to that…" Kuandyk brooded.

"He told us that you were coming, and he told us that we were supposed to help you!" The gerbil's squeaks were incomprehensible, as he grew more and more excited. "Then he struck the rock with his horn and water gushed like we've never seen before, and this olive tree sprouted and grew in a matter of moments! He said that we were to guard these treasures, and bring you here."

"And don't forget the most important part," the antelope added. "Right before he left, he said that you'd take us with you."

Thimblerig had been enjoying the fairy tale up to that point. In his experience, there was nothing more entertaining than finding a good crazy animal and parking yourself in front of them. It had been a welcome distraction from the stress of the past twenty-four hours. But this grabbed his attention.

"Hold on a minute," he interrupted. "Take you where?"

"With you!" the gerbil answered. "He said you'd be heading to safety, and that we were to go with you to escape the flood. He said that there'd be others."

Thimblerig couldn't believe what he was hearing. It was one thing to let a crazy animal entertain you, but you didn't bring him home and give him a place on the floor of your burrow. He was having enough trouble with his own little group of suckers without adding a couple more to the mix. Especially two more that probably couldn't pay.

"No, no, no," he said. "These animals have each paid a substantial sum to be taken to the place where I'm taking them. It

119

wouldn't be fair to them if we just picked up stragglers along the way."

Thimblerig was certain the others would agree with his assessment of the situation. But when he turned to look, to his shock, they were glaring. At him.

"Thimblerig," Tabitha started coldly, "how could we leave these poor animals here? They'll never survive."

"Agreed," Elbridge said. "I begged and pleaded for the camels in my herd to join us, and they laughed at me. If these two want to come, I say we let them."

"Everyone's welcome," Sheila added.

She would throw my words back at me, Thimblerig thought. Certain that at least the duck would object, Thimblerig glanced his way, but the duck just grinned. "Everyone's welcome," Shi Lau repeated spitefully. Thimblerig had not wanted to strangle the duck more than he wanted to at that moment.

"Just hold on now," Thimblerig responded. "This isn't a democracy. I'm the one who had the vision, I'm the one who sees the unicorn, and I say they don't make the trip unless they can pay up."

Thimblerig crossed his arms defiantly, and waited for the suckers to fall in line behind him.

It would be a long wait.

CHAPTER 14
A RATHER LARGE ADDITION

Kid Duffy ran alongside Blonger, leaping over fallen trees and dodging ditches. The leader was once again proving his position with this hunt, having already personally taken down five of the prey. Reports were coming in that other members of the pack had eliminated three others, and only two were left, including the elephant. The elephant was either incapable or uninterested in hiding his tracks, and all they had to do was follow the trail of flattened trees. Once they'd gotten rid of these last two, they'd go after the believers, saving the best for last.

Blonger brought the wild dogs to a sudden halt, and sniffed the ground around a particularly large fallen tree. The other dogs assumed defensive positions around the area, creating a perimeter.

"Enforcer!" Blonger barked. Without wasting a moment, Kid Duffy jumped up beside the leader. "What do you see here?"

Kid Duffy approached Blonger's question very carefully, first taking in the area as a whole, and then focused on the area where Blonger was standing. The obvious signs were the downed trees and enormous tracks. These were a clear indication that the bull elephant had crashed through this part of the forest. But that was too simple and too obvious. There had to be something else...

Then he saw it. Behind an outcrop of dark green ferns something white lay on the ground. A feather. He nudged his muzzle closer still, sniffing the ground around the feather, and his mind flooded with images as the scents activated his memory.

Duck, camel, gazelle, llama, ape, elephant, kangaroo, groundhog...

"The believers..." he said. "They came this way."

Thimblerig was angrier than he'd been in a long time. Not only had the suckers in the company stood together to demand that the antelope and the gerbil accompany them, but Mullins,

121

Soapy, and Big Bunco had agreed! *It's mutiny*, he thought. But that wasn't exactly right. They weren't overthrowing him; they still believed he was the one that was supposed to lead them. They'd just insisted that the company take on the two crazies, for free.

And so it was, after each took a final long drink from the unicorn's spring, they set off once more for The Edge, and whatever destiny awaited them.

Finding her way to the front of the line beside Thimblerig, Sheila spoke quietly, so only he could hear. "You shouldn't be upset," she said. "Would you really leave those two behind?"

"Yes I would," he answered bitterly. "And it would have been better for them. At least they would have had a stream and an olive tree. That's more than we have here."

"So you're only looking out for their best interests," she said. "I didn't realize that you'd become so considerate. Have you had a change of heart since our last conversation?"

"Of course I have," Thimblerig replied sarcastically. "I now care more about two strange animals I met out on the steppe than I do my share of figs back in my burrow."

Sheila hopped along silently with the groundhog for a few moments. As much as he appreciated the lack of conversation, he knew that it didn't mean she was finished talking. She just was working on the next thing she wanted to say. It was a fairly irritating personality trait.

He glanced back at the company of animals. Their march across the steppe had led them to a rocky trail on the side of a steep hill overlooking a surprising thick grove of trees. It wasn't difficult for the smaller animals, but Eldridge and the llamas didn't find the going easy, and had to watch their footing carefully. More than once, a rock would come dislodged and tumble down the side of the hill into the tree-filled ravine below. The duck was even finally forced to abandon his usual place on the camel's back, waddling in front in an attempt to help his larger big-hooved companion find sturdier footing.

122

"You know that they wouldn't have survived," Sheila said, finally breaking the silence. "The wild dogs would have found them and killed them."

"Maybe, maybe not," he answered coldly. "Who knows? The unicorn could have been watching out for them."

"What's that?" Sheila asked.

"I was being facetious, Sheila," he answered, growing tired of always being taken seriously when discussing fantasy. "It'll take a lot more than a couple of bad dreams to convince me…"

"No, I mean what's that, down there?" she interrupted. "Look at the treetops."

Following her line of sight, Thimblerig didn't see anything at first. The trees below grew so thick that it was impossible to see anything but a sea of yellow and green leaves which stretched from one end of the ravine to the other. Then he saw it. Something was walking through the grove, carelessly knocking into the trunks hard enough to shake the treetops. He motioned for the animals behind him to stop.

"Everyone quiet," he whispered. "There's something moving down there."

"What is it now?" the duck said, exasperated.

"The wild dogs?" Tabitha asked.

"That's no wild dog," Soapy said, concern written on his face. "That's something big."

"Kuandyk, what kinds of big animals live out here?" Thimblerig asked, continuing to watch the progression of the – whatever it was. It was moving their way.

"Oh, I'm one of the biggest," he answered proudly. "My father and my grandfather were not quite as large as I am, but my family has always been among the hugest of animals on the steppe. In fact, if you include the size of our noses…"

"Whatever it is down there, it's where we need to be," Thimblerig said, cutting him off. "We have to cross through that ravine and there's no other way around."

The groundhog's first inclination was to try and wait the mystery creature out, hoping it would continue on its way if they just held their position. But one look back at the camel was all it took to tell Thimblerig that waiting wasn't an option. Elbridge had pushed himself up against the hill on the far side of the trail, trying not to look down. His knees were knocking together again, and he was muttering and whimpering incoherently.

We've got to get off this trail before he slips and brings the whole trail down with him, Thimblerig thought. The fall probably wouldn't kill them, but it would injure enough of them that they'd be stuck, easy pickings for any predators who happened by, and certainly easier prey for the wild dogs.

They had to continue, and they had nowhere to go but down, to whatever awaited below. He motioned to the others to continue as quietly as they could, and he began back down the trail.

Thimblerig didn't see the loose rock on the edge of the trail, and neither he nor any of the others had time to react when the rock slid out from underneath him, and took him tumbling down the hillside. He threw out his arms in an attempt to slow his fall, but there was nothing to grab onto, and so he fell, arms reaching to the sky. Time slowed, and he could clearly see the wide eyes of the company of animals growing smaller as he plummeted down.

The limbs of the trees whipped painfully against his back, but he wasn't able to use them to slow his fall. When the end came, it was not at all what he expected. Instead of crashing down into hard rocks and sharp edges, instead of breaking bones and puncturing lungs, he simply stopped falling.

So this is death, he thought. *It hurt, but it wasn't nearly as painful as I expected it would be.*

"It's painful, isn't it?"

Thimblerig stared at the black-circled eyes of the lemur who was glaring down at the shells sitting on the stone table in

124

front of him. The groundhog was trying to get a read on him, but was having a difficult time of it, and he couldn't afford to lose any more figs.

Thimblerig had been trying to horn his way into the festival scene for a while now, trying to get better at his shell game, and had not been doing as well as he'd hoped. His growling stomach kept reminding him that he also hadn't eaten a decent meal in three days. His mentor, a red-haired orangutan named Frankie Four Fingers, sat silently behind them on a stump chewing on some long sweet grass and pretending to be uninterested.

"It's on the left," the lemur finally said.

"Are you sure about that?" Thimblerig asked.

The lemur looked up angrily. "Why would I have said it if I wasn't sure?" He glanced over the groundhog's shoulder at the orangutan. "What kind of bonehead operation you runnin' here, Frankie?"

"Lay off, Tsito," Frankie grumbled. "Give the kid a chance,"

The lemur scowled from Frankie back to Thimblerig. "All right, big shot. I'm sure it's on the left. Happy?"

Fighting the urge to leap across the stone table and show Tsito just how happy he was, Thimblerig lifted up the shell on the left to show that the pea wasn't there. He grinned his snarkiest grin, picked up the middle shell, and accidentally dropped the pea he was palming before he could place it. He and the lemur watched the pea roll across the stone table and drop to the forest floor.

"Chump," Tsito said as he picked up the two figs and walked away, laughing. "That's a real pro you got there, Frankie! A real pro!"

Thimblerig grabbed the edge of the stone table and heaved it over with a grunt, scattering shells and a couple of extra peas across the forest floor. Then he collapsed on the ground at Frankie's feet. "I stink at this, Frankie," he said. "I'm hopeless."

"You are pretty bad, kid," Frankie agreed. "But you're not hopeless. Frankie don't waste his time with hopeless cases. You just need practice, that's all."

"Thanks, Frankie," Thimblerig replied. Then, swallowing his pride, the groundhog muttered, "Listen, about the figs I owe you..."

"Hey, don't worry about that right now, kid. You got enough on your back." Frankie leaned over and put his four-fingered hand on Thimblerig's back. "Mooch just told me about your groundma."

"Yeah," Thimblerig answered quietly. Truth be told, he'd just heard about his groundmother dying himself. "I was out in the scrubs when it happened. She was old."

And senile, he didn't add. *Always babbling about unicorns.* He'd been embarrassed by her for years. If he were honest, he'd have to admit that he was glad that he wouldn't have to be embarrassed any more. If he were even more honest, he'd have to admit that he felt lousy for being glad.

"Still, it's rough when someone goes to the other fields," Frankie answered. Thimblerig nodded, and then they sat in an uncomfortable silence for a few minutes, listening to the lemur arguing with a ferret down the way over a dropped fig.

Finally, Thimblerig got up and picked up the stone table. He gathered his shells and peas, and started to practice again. He was determined to get this game down if it killed him.

Mullins was caught unprepared. One moment his partner was walking in front of him, the next he was gone. The only sign that the groundhog had been there at all was a small cloud of dust that rose from the edge of the trail where he fell.

"Thimblerig!" The gazelle leapt to the edge, careful not to suffer the same fate. But he was too late, getting there just in time to see Thimblerig disappearing into the green treetops below.

Not waiting to see what the others would do, Mullins tore down the trail. He quickly reached the level area where the trail stopped descending, and turned back to the left in order to head back to the spot where Thimblerig would have fallen. The gazelle wasn't thinking about danger, or whatever animal might have been in the trees waiting for them. He just cared that his partner – his friend - was lying, broken, possibly dying, needing his help.

He leapt over underbrush and ducked under tree branches, not able to see more than a few feet at a time, but moving quickly knowing instinctively that Thimblerig wasn't far.

A tall bush blocked his path, and just beyond he could see the dark outline of something big. He couldn't tell what it was, but it was huge, and it was right where Thimblerig had fallen. He paused for just a moment before taking a deep breath, leapt the bush easily, and landed in a clearing under the shelter of a stand of trees. The largest elephant he'd ever seen stood before him, grasping Thimblerig firmly with his trunk. The other members of the company came bursting into the clearing behind him just in time to see the elephant lower Thimblerig to the ground and back away.

Sheila, Tabitha, Mullins, and Big Bunco rushed up to the groundhog, patting him on the back and nuzzling him affectionately, relieved that he was unharmed. The others voiced their relief while eying the elephant suspiciously.

For the first time in his adult life, the groundhog was speechless. He wanted to say thank you, to assure them that he was unharmed, but the words lodged in his throat. When was the last time anyone cared about what happened to him? And here was a group of suckers visibly relieved that he was alive?

"Groundhogs falling from trees, just like he said…" the bull elephant was muttering, his cavernous voice filled with awe.

Thimblerig turned to the mountain of animal standing back from the others. "What's that?" he asked.

"He told me where to be, and when to be there," the elephant answered. "I didn't think I'd make it, but here I was, and here you came. Guess I shouldn't be surprised, anything can happen when the unicorn's involved…"

Oh no, Thimblerig groaned.

The saiga antelope stepped forward. "You've seen him, too? Impressive, isn't he?"

Quickly forgetting Thimblerig's brush with death, the company surrounded the elephant, begging for details.

"Three festivals ago Anastasiya and I were married, and soon afterwards had Sasha, our first calf," Pavel said. The animals were all gathered around the big elephant, listening intently as they made their way through the tree-filled ravine.

Once again, Thimblerig had been outvoted, and they had yet another freeloader along for the ride. They'd taken a bit of time to make sure he didn't have any hidden injuries, and then resumed their journey. Thimblerig sulked, walking ahead of the others, looking for the right moment to lay into his supposed "partners" for the betrayal. Things hadn't been necessarily going his way, but at least he'd had a modicum of control. Now, he was being swept along, flaying and thrashing his arms to keep from going under, and he had nothing better to do than keep moving the increasingly large group forward.

"We'd always talked about making the trip to Asarata when we started have children, but others in the herd warned me that the festival was too dangerous with thieves and outlaws running the show. I really wanted my daughter to see where the unicorns had walked and the great tree, so I insisted, thinking I could handle anything. Eventually my daughter's begging forced Anastasiya to agree, and we joined a caravan making our way across the southern grasslands to the tree."

"What a trip it was! I was sure I'd made the right choice. As we journeyed, Sasha would jump for joy and squeal with delight over every new kind animal we'd come across. When we arrived at the festival, it was everything I'd thought it would be. My wife was like a child again, Sasha ate so many figs that she got a stomachache, and I let my guard down."

128

A dark shadow fell over Pavel's face, and Thimblerig was drawn into the story in spite of himself.

"What happened?" Mullins prompted quietly. Pavel looked down with tears in his eyes.

"She was only a child, hardly understanding the difference between right and wrong. She didn't know that the fig she picked up belonged to a wild dog who stood nearby. She just loved figs, and they were everywhere. He attacked her. The wild dog attacked my beautiful, precious child over a fig."

"By the unicorn..." Tabitha muttered.

"When Anastasiya realized what happened, it was too late. She went mad with rage and trampled three wild dogs before they..."

As the elephant paused, Thimblerig glanced back at the company of animals and saw the despair on the elephant's face mirrored on the faces of the others. Even Shi Lau looked devastated. Sheila was looking at him with an unreadable expression, and he turned away.

"The others wouldn't let me go back to the tree. They told me that it wouldn't change anything, that nobody there would help me, that I should forget it. I struggled against them, but over time I came to understand that they were right. There would be no justice for my family if I depended on the laws of the forest."

"The wild dog's laws," Soapy corrected.

"That's right. But I didn't forget it," the elephant continued. "I convinced the others that I wasn't going to do anything, and started quietly asking questions. Finally, I found a leopard who'd seen what happened. He didn't want to talk, but I convinced him to tell me the whole story. He told me who the wild dog was that killed my family. It was Blonger."

The mention of the leader of the wild dog's name turned Thimblerig's blood to ice. It was no surprise that the little elephant had been murdered, if she had taken one of the leader's figs. Thimblerig had heard this story too many times, or stories similar, from other animals.

"When I had the chance, I went after him. It wasn't easy, but I was patient, and I nearly got him under my feet."

"Nearly?" Mullins asked. "What happened?"

"I missed," Pavel said. "I had two shots at him, but I missed both times. I thought I was clever, planning it all out, waiting and playing the part of the loyal wild dog subject until I had the chance. I decided that the best chance was the hunt."

"Blonger always kicks off the hunt in person," Thimblerig said.

"I would run him down at the hunt and tear him to bits. I didn't care what happened to me. It was all I could think about, day and night. But the unicorn's ways aren't our ways, and one night before the hunt, Blonger was out walking the festival grounds with his guard. The sight of him sent me over the edge, and I attacked. I was so angry that it was like I was watching from above, watching some other elephant attack. But I was too rash, and his guards stopped me before I could even get close."

"They let you live?" Manuel asked.

"It was just a few days before the hunt, and they decided I would make good prey. They dragged me in their darkest cave and had their apes tie me down."

The elephant stopped walking as he came to this part of the story. They all stopped, surrounded by the gloomy trees, which were growing gloomier as dusk approached.

"I struggled, but the more I struggled, the tighter the vines became. I wanted to die, but they hadn't even given me that relief. I'd failed my wife, my daughter, everyone that mattered to me. What use was there in going on? A gust of wind blew through the cave, coming from the shadows. It was like a breeze out in the grasslands, warm and fresh, and I smelled grass and dust like back home. Then light poured into the cave like the sun was riding on the wind."

"And then he was there. Tannier Isa was there. How an animal can be so dark and so light at the same time, I can't explain. And I was afraid; I'm not ashamed to admit. I knew he

130

didn't want to hurt me, but I was still afraid. He walked over to me and touched the tip of his horn to my forehead. Then he pulled back and said my name, 'Pavel'."

The company of animals, Thimblerig included, were entranced, listening to Pavel's story. The wood itself had grown quiet, as if the trees and the insects had also stopped to listen.

"He told me not to be afraid. He told me that Anastasiya and Sasha were safe in his fields, but it wasn't my time to join them. And he told me I needed to find you, groundhog."

"I'm sorry," the groundhog interrupted. "He told you to do what?"

"Find you," the elephant repeated. "He told me that when the hunt started, I needed to make my way out here, and be here when you fell through branches. He told me it was my job to save the one who would save many."

CHAPTER 15
CONNING THE CONS

Thimblerig should have been pleased with Pavel's statement. After all, it effectively removed any lingering doubt in the minds of the company of animals. Even Shi Lau was treating Thimblerig with a new respect that bordered on awe, but it was just as irritating to the groundhog as his constant cynicism. But he didn't feel pleased at all. He felt uncomfortable. It had to be coincidence.

The suckers were still suckers, and the way they were looking at him, with such reverence, didn't change that. He was scamming them, and he was going to have more figs than any groundhog had a right to have when it was through. This was all that mattered, and the unicorn business that kept coming up was just nonsense. Nonsense and coincidence.

He forced his thoughts back to the fact that the elephant represented another two hundred figs not going into storage in the burrow back at Asarata. And his partners were buying into it all, too, just like the suckers. How was he supposed to finish the job without them? When it came time to turn back, would they be willing to do it, or would they blow the whole deal? The whole system was breaking down, and he didn't know how to stop it.

As they came to the end of the ravine they were all pleased to see that the Edge was closer, within striking distance. The bad news was that the skies above the mountains had grown even darker with threatening clouds, and the wind had picked up, blowing harder from that direction.

A storm was definitely on the way.

After having experienced the terror of the rain and flood in his dream, the last thing Thimblerig wanted was to get caught out in the open in a rainstorm. He continued pushing the company towards the ridges ahead, away from ravines and low-lying wooded areas.

The terrain continued to transform as they walked, with rocky outcrops becoming more frequent, and the rolling grassy hills fading into the background. Night was falling, and Thimblerig decided that even with the storm ahead and the wild dogs behind that they would have to stop to rest.

"Have you thought about the wild dogs lately?"

Mullins had been walking with Tabitha since they left the woods, and this was the first time he'd spoken to Thimblerig in that time.

"Of course," the groundhog answered. "They're back there, and they're coming. That's why we've got to make it to the Edge."

"What do you think we'll find there?"

Thimblerig wasn't able to answer this question. Mullins had been spending too much time with the female gazelle, and he'd seen the way that they looked at each other, the growing affection between them. The worst part was that Mullins had bought into the scam just like a sucker, but he was supposed to be one of the cons! Could he be trusted with the truth? Thimblerig didn't think so. But he had to say something.

"I don't know," he answered.

"Have you changed your mind?" Mullins asked.

Here it comes, Thimblerig thought. "About what?"

"About the plan. About the con."

And there it was. Thimblerig should have known better, bringing Mullins into this. "Don't trust anyone," Frankie Four Fingers had taught him, over and over again. His instincts were always to work alone, and in the excitement to get the con off the ground, he'd gone against his instincts. Now it was coming back to bite him in the tail and he had to see how bad the damage was.

"If not, you planning on ratting me out?"

"Of course not," Mullins said. "But if you're still planning on leaving them behind, I…"

133

"You'll what?" Thimblerig would have been willing to bet one hundred figs on what Mullins was about to say, and he started to get angry.

"I won't be going back with you," Mullins said.

"Uh huh," Thimblerig said. "She got to you, did she?"

"Who? Tabitha? No, that's not it at all," Mullins answered defensively. "It's not just me, Thimblerig. Soapy and Big Bunco feel the same and have just been trying to figure out how to tell you."

Feel the same? If Mullins told Thimblerig that Soapy and Big Bunco were actually brother and sister he may have been more shocked. He turned to look back at his partners, and saw it on their faces. Shame. Embarrassment. Betrayal.

"But we want you to stay, too," Mullins continued, his voice rising with excitement. "Can't you see that the con is busted? I know you really saw the unicorn, because I saw him, too. Kuandyk and Nurlan saw him, Pavel saw him. Why can't you admit that you saw him? Your dream wasn't just your imagination! Look at the sky ahead! It's real, and it's coming, just like you said!"

Thimblerig had to find a way out of the mess. It was a disaster, and it was becoming more and more of a disaster with each passing moment. He wasn't so surprised by Mullins' change, although the timing aggravated him. It was a given that the gazelle was eventually going to fall for a pretty face. But Soapy and Big Bunco? They were old pros, and as cynical as an animal could come. How could they have been duped so quickly?

And then it hit him. They were playing him! They'd cut a deal behind his back and now they were planning their own con. This was exactly why the groundhog preferred to work alone, where you didn't have to worry about someone filling in your burrow when you'd gone below for a nap. But what could he do?

The answer came to him clearly; although it wasn't the solution he would have chosen. In his mind, he was on his own now, and he had to figure out the best way to finish the con and make it back to the burrow alone.

He was going to have to con the cons.

"We're stopping!" Thimblerig shouted, bringing the caravan to a halt.

"Don't tell me. You see Tannier Isa," the duck called out. "Maybe we can all see him this time?"

"No, I don't see Tannier Isa," Thimblerig answered. "I just need some time to be alone and meditate." He gestured towards the mountain range looming ahead, visible even in the disappearing light of day. "See that pass directly ahead? That's where I've been heading, but I'm not convinced it's the right way. I need guidance. And you could use some rest, I think."

The company of animals nodded while looking at him with complete awe. He knew what they were thinking, and he was exhausted by their reverence. Still, he'd use it to his advantage if it meant finishing the job.

"Mullins, Soapy, Big Bunco, why don't you join me? Manuel, you keep first watch."

Leaving the company settling down in the little clearing, the groundhog shuffled ahead, just behind a rock outcropping, and plopped down, weary and achy to the bone. The partners joined him, and sat in silence waiting for the groundhog to speak. He chose his words carefully.

"I've been thinking," he finally said. "Listening to Mullins, and you know this is just all becoming really strange. What if my dream wasn't just in my head? What if it really was a message?"

"We've been thinking the same thing," Soapy agreed.

"Really? Well, here's what I say we do: we continue to the Edge and see what's waiting for us there. If it is real, and the unicorn is guiding us, then we don't have any worries. We'll get there, and everything will be right."

"What if it isn't real?" Big Bunco asked. "Are we leaving them to fend for themselves?"

"That's a fair question," Thimblerig said. "If we get there and find a big goose egg waiting for us, then we help the others get past the wild dogs and back to the forest, where we return all the figs. It's what Tannier Isa would want, I think."

The three looked at each other and – was it exhaustion or was an unspoken signal given? It really rubbed Thimblerig's fur the wrong way that he didn't know. Since when do partners come up with secret signals against each other?

"Agreed, Thimblerig," Mullins said, relieved.

Soapy got up and wrapped his long arms around Thimblerig's neck in a crushing hug. "Glad you're with us, bud."

So that was it then. No argument, no attempts to make Thimblerig stick with the plan. It would have been nice to have at least a bit of sanity left in the team. But as his groundmother used to say, the burrow needs digging, and so he nodded and smiled. "Me too," Thimblerig answered, patting Big Bunco's trunk for good measure. "So listen, I'm not sure how this meditation thing is supposed to work, but I'm going to give it a go. Why don't you go back to the others and I'll see if I can make contact, or whatever it is I'm supposed to do."

Soapy and Big Bunco left with much more spring in their step, but Mullins hung back.

"You're making the right call, pal," he said sincerely. "I believe in you, Thimblerig. May the unicorn help us, but I really do." He was both embarrassed and proud as he walked around the outcrop of rocks, leaving Thimblerig alone to 'meditate'.

Thimblerig lay down and rested against the coolness of the rock; proud of how he'd handled his partners. He'd figure out a way to lose them all when they got to the Edge, and then he'd just have to go solo back to the forest. He'd have no trouble finding some other animals to help him move the figs, which was fine with him. As far as he was concerned, his partners had forfeited their cut.

"From now on, I work alone," Thimblerig said, yawning. It felt good to be sitting for a change. He knew that he needed to keep alert, that the wild dogs were certainly on their trail by now, but fatigue from the trip had caught up with him, and the groundhog could barely keep his eyes open. He noticed some flashes of lightning in the distance, and then he stopped fighting and fell sound asleep.

CHAPTER 16
THIMBLERIG'S DREAM, PART TWO

The storm raged all around him. Again.

Thimblerig was seriously ticked off about being back in the storm. When he'd lain down by the rock, it was because he'd wanted to rest, not have another unexpected dream or vision. But here he was again, being pummeled from all sides by raindrops as big as stones. There was no shelter; nowhere he could run to escape it. The rain fell harder, the sky was darker, and he was stuck out in it.

If there was a silver lining, it was that at least he wasn't trapped up at the top of Asarata, in danger of plummeting through fig branches to his doom. This time he was standing on a rock on the side of a mountain. Above him, the mountain rose high, the top lost in the haze of the storm. It occurred to him that if the flood came again, he'd want to get to higher ground. So he turned and started trying to climb the rock face. But the rocks were especially slippery, thanks to the pouring rain. Every time he would get a paw hold and start pulling himself up, the howling wind would blow harder and the rain would fall harder, and he'd lose his grip and slide back down.

"Give me a break!" he shouted to the storm. "Give me a freakin' break!"

The storm didn't answer back, and so Thimblerig mulled his options. He could continue trying to climb up, but considering his lack of rock climbing skill, this didn't seem to be the best choice. He could stay where he was, huddle down under an overhang somewhere, and wait it out. But not knowing how long this dream would last; it could be a long wait. Again, not the best choice. The last idea was to go against his instincts and head for lower ground; at least until he found a more easily navigated trail that would take him back up.

With the driving rain and flashing lightning making it difficult to see where to step, Thimblerig took a deep breath and slid down the side of the mountain onto the flat ground below.

Thimblerig walked towards the left, and saw that the mountainside in this direction was sheer rather than rocky. There were no trails he could climb, no way to get higher.

"Stupid dream," he muttered. "Stupid rain-soaked, never-ending, pointless dream…"

Thimblerig stopped his muttering as the ground rumbled and shook beneath. Then through the horrific clashes and rumblings and rain, he thought he heard someone calling out. The voice was faint, and he couldn't make out what it said. Had he imagined it? Who else would be out in a storm like this if they didn't have to be? Then he heard it again, this time it louder and clearer.

"Someone help us, please!"

There were others out here somewhere? Whoever they were, they sounded like they were in big trouble.

"Hello!" he called out. "Where are you?"

"Please, can anyone hear me?"

The voice was coming from above, up the mountain. Thimblerig shielded his eyes from the falling rain, and tried to see if he could tell where exactly it was coming from.

"Who's there?" he shouted, but there was no answer.

Then a flash of lightning illuminated a silhouette on a precipice on the side of the mountain wall, shaped like a kangaroo. There was only one kangaroo that would dare hop into one of these insane dreams.

"Sheila?" he cried. The wailing wind carried his voice in the wrong direction, and he was sure she couldn't hear him. But even if she had, what could he do to reach her? She was standing on a precipice that was dozens of feet up the side of the mountain wall. What was she doing all alone up there? It was maddening to see someone he cared about in danger and not being able to do anything about it, even if it was only a dream.

Wait a minute. Someone he cared about? Did he really just think that?

"Thimblerig!"

Elbridge? Had he just heard Elbridge call his name?

"Help us!"

There it was again. Elbridge did not do well on high, small spaces. In fact, he was surprised the ledge was holding even now. Dream or not, Thimblerig had to do something. He ran back and forth, from left to right, hopping up and down in a vain attempt to see if there was anything on which he could climb to reach them.

"I can't get up!" he shouted. "Can you climb down?"

His yelling didn't stand a chance of getting through with the storm blowing as hard as it was. Thimblerig's heart began racing as he thought that they would think he wasn't doing anything to help them, that he'd abandoned them.

The next burst of lightning revealed that the situation was worse than he'd imagined. He could see their faces clearly; each sucker that he'd conned into making this trip on the precipice huddling together against the force of the storm, waiting for him to lead them to safety.

Feeling a renewed sense of urgency to get up the side of the cliff, Thimblerig stepped to the right, into a puddle of freezing cold water. The earth shook with more violence than before, followed by an explosive concussion that knocked the groundhog off his feet. He fell into the frigid water, ears ringing, thinking that the world was coming to an end.

"Can you hear me?" he called, scrambling to his feet, his attention swinging back to the suckers on the ledge. "I'm trying to figure out how to help you!"

"Too late," a voice snarled from behind. "They belong to me."

As if appearing from nothing, the wild dogs stood all around him, eyes burning like emerald flames in the darkness. The largest, most ferocious wild dog he'd ever seen stood right

140

beside Thimblerig, growling furiously. He could feel the hot breath of the beast through the pouring rain.

Ignoring him, the wild dog leapt to the side of the cliff and scurried up as effortlessly as a spider climbing the side of a tree, heading in the direction of Sheila and the others. He howled and the pack followed him up, barking and yelping as they went, dozens of pairs of glowing green eyes disappearing into the mists above.

Crying out in horror, Thimblerig ran to the side of the mountain and tried to scramble his way up after the pack. It was useless, because his feet and claws slid off the rain-soaked walls, and he slid back to the ground, sitting in bone-chilling water now up to his stomach.

The gale force winds and constant rain prevented Thimblerig from hearing anything from the precipice above, but he could perfectly imagine the horrifying scene - his friends being torn limb from limb as the pack reached their precipice. They'd been counting on him, and he'd let them down! He was supposed to lead them, and he'd led them to slaughter.

Being so focused on what was going on with the wild dogs, Thimblerig failed to notice that the water pooling around him was receding rapidly, pulling out into the deep. Moments later, a mammoth wave crashed down, picking him up and tossing him around until he somehow managed to break through to the surface. He was shoved up against the wall of the cliff, and could feel the wall speeding past as the swiftly rising water level pushed him up, up, up.

He swirled and sputtered in the raging water along with tree trunks, branches, and other animals. These, he realized by their flaming green eyes, were mostly wild dogs, being washed away by the wave. He looked for any member of his company of animals among the debris, but couldn't find them.

Thimblerig was splashing around, trying to keep from going under, when the trunk of a tree rushed by. The groundhog grabbed hold, and held dearly. He was swallowing lungfuls of

141

water and trying to grasp what was happening. Thankfully the waves were calming, and the rains lessening, but still the floodwaters rose. There was no end to the water, no end of the wall rising beside him, no end of the nightmare.

Hopeless and out of ideas for self-preservation, the groundhog remembered that the last dream ended when he'd been pulled under the water. He was about to let go and allow the undercurrent to take him when he saw a golden light in the distance shining out like hundreds of fireflies flying in tight formation. It was moving, heading his way, growing larger as it came, and leaving a glowing trail that reflected on the surface of the dark water.

Thimblerig knew exactly what it was.

How foolish he had been to not recognize the light when he first saw it! His heart leapt in his chest as the light came near enough for him to see that it was the glowing spiral horn of the black unicorn, Tannier Isa, who was running effortlessly across the surging waves. The unicorn came galloping up, and stood a few feet away. For long moments, they stared at each other in silence. Thimblerig had so many questions, but they were stuck in his throat. Was any of this real? Why was it happening to him? What did the unicorn expect him to do? All he could do was hold onto his log and stare.

A sudden wave splashed over the groundhog's head, and he gasped and spit out the water, desperately wiping his eyes out of fear that he'd find he was alone once more.

"Tannier Isa," he sputtered.

"Thimblerig," the unicorn replied.

"I need help," Thimblerig said, his desperation welling up and threatening to choke the words before they could come. "I don't know what to do."

"It's not complicated," Tannier Isa replied. "You just need to follow me."

"But I don't even believe in you!" Thimblerig answered honestly, painfully. Why was he even having this conversation?

142

What did he expect to happen? He was talking to a unicorn in a dream about a flood, and was obviously losing his mind. But was it a dream? The unicorn's eyes were so penetrating, as if he knew the groundhog better than he knew himself. Could that happen in a dream, so clearly, so gut-wrenchingly?

"Belief will come," the unicorn replied. "For now, I just need you to do as I say."

That was the answer, wasn't it? Doing what the unicorn said. He'd screwed up the whole con by trusting his own instincts. When he'd gone the way the unicorn wanted him to, when he'd done what he knew the unicorn wanted him to do, things had gone better, hadn't they?

"I will," the groundhog said. "Just tell me what to do."

"You need to continue leading the others to the Edge, and there you'll find the place of safety."

"The Edge is enormous," Thimblerig said. "How will I know where to go?"

"You know the answer to that question, Thimblerig."

"Follow you," the groundhog said, nodding.

"And you'll know the place of safety, because it will be unlike anything else you'll find in the Edge. It's been made for you all."

Thimblerig was confused. What could be made that would possibly help them survive a flood like this? Tannier Isa knew what the groundhog was thinking. He smiled and said, "Look up, Thimblerig."

Following the unicorn's instructions, Thimblerig looked up to see that the glow from the unicorn's horn extended out and up the side of the cliff wall. He gasped at what he saw and nearly lost hold of the tree. The wall was not stone at all, but wood. Enormous logs, cut and shaped to fit together much like a wall rising up into the sky as far as he could see. It also extended out to the left and the right beyond his range of vision, across the water. Did it ever end?

The wall of wood moved, riding up a swell in the waves. It was floating just like an unimaginably large tree. It didn't make sense, that such a huge object could float, and also that it appeared to be as the unicorn had said – made, not created – put together with purpose. In the forest, only the apes had the skill to build, but Thimblerig knew that they would never be able to construct a thing of such magnitude.

"What is it?" he asked, dumbfounded.

"It's called an ark," Tannier Isa replied. "And it was made for you and the others, so that you can survive."

"Who could make that?"

"It was made by a kind you haven't encountered yet, but you will. But now you have to hurry, Thimblerig. The storm is coming. Judgment has been withheld long enough."

"Judgment?"

Thimblerig didn't like the way the word tasted on his lips. And the way the unicorn had said it; he could tell it was a difficult word for him as well. What would happen to the forest? His home? Everything and everyone he knew? Could it really happen? "But why?" he pleaded.

"The forest has become flooded with darkness, Thimblerig. Eventually, the darkness will annihilate everything, including all the animals of the forest. I won't permit that to happen."

Thimblerig could hear his groundmother's voice clearly, repeating the stories over and over again in his mind, begging and pleading with him to remember. And what had he done? He'd turned his back on it all, embracing the darkness as resolutely as the worst of them. He'd become the living embodiment of all that was wrong with the forest.

"Clean start," Thimblerig whispered.

Tannier Isa snorted in response. "Clean start, with the animals who haven't forgotten, who have the best opportunity to bring back the light. It's the forest's only hope."

But this wasn't right, the groundhog thought. If the flood was going to wipe out those that didn't listen and refused to change, he deserved to be the first one in the water. What business did he have surviving, let alone trying to lead others to survive?

"You've made a big mistake," the groundhog said. "I should be at the bottom of your list, not leading anyone to safety. The choices I've made…"

"Such as?"

The way the unicorn was looking at him, Thimblerig felt shame. He hadn't felt that emotion since the last time he'd seen his groundmother, and he didn't like it. Not one bit. Maybe confessing his bad choices would help alleviate the emotion somehow. He took a deep breath, and then spoke.

"I've cheated and lied. I've taken advantage of animals who had nothing, stealing their last fig right out of their mouth and congratulating myself for my cleverness. I've spent my life looking out for nobody but myself, not giving a rip what happens to others. And you think I should be the one to lead these other animals? Well, you're wrong. It's as plain and simple as that. You're wrong!"

Tannier Isa stepped up close to the groundhog so that their faces were inches apart. Thimblerig could see his worthless face reflected in the onyx pool of the unicorn's eye.

"Let's get something straight, Thimblerig," Tannier Isa said forcefully. "When I say I chose you for the job it's not because I see some redeeming quality in you that makes you worth choosing. Not at all. I say it's you because you are the one that I choose." The unicorn's voice softened a bit as he pulled his head back. "Yes, you've made bad choices, Thimblerig, but don't be defined by those choices. Be defined by my choice. And I choose you to lead."

Thimblerig felt like he was standing furless in front of the unicorn. The golden flame from the spiral horn burned brighter and brighter until Thimblerig was forced to close his eyes. The light grew so bright that it hurt his eyes, even closed. He covered his eyes with his paw, but it didn't help matters at all. It was like the light was going to overwhelm him and burn him to ash.

"Please!" he cried. "It's too much! I can't take it anymore!"

A gigantic wave lifted the groundhog's log and tossed it, Thimblerig holding on for dear life, into a direct collision course with the solid wood wall of the ark. Thimblerig braced for impact, and when he was just about to crash into the side of the ark he woke to the sound of someone screaming his name.

CHAPTER 17
THE AMBUSH

Thimblerig rubbed his eyes, groggy as one is when waking suddenly from a dream. But had it been a dream? He still felt waterlogged, and surely – and strangely – enough, he was actually soaking wet.

Hadn't he heard a scream? Or was it an echo from the dream?

"Thimblerig!"

It was Sheila's voice, but it wasn't an echo of the voice from the dream. It was clear, loud, and desperate, and it was coming from the other side of the rock he'd been sleeping behind. "Sheila, I'm coming!" Thimblerig cried, jumping up and scurrying around the rock and into his worst nightmare.

Huddled together in the gloom of the moonless night, his company of animals was surrounded by a pack of at least three dozen snarling wild dogs. Even Pavel was trapped, encircled by the lion's share of the pack. Thimblerig was stunned, wondering how they'd been found. *You'd been sleeping, you idiot,* he thought. *If you had just kept everyone moving...*

"Well, if it isn't our little con," a familiar rough voice said out of the darkness. The pack parted to reveal Kid Duffy, grinning triumphantly. "I'd have bet you would at least make it to the Edge, give us that much of a challenge. But imagine our surprise when we came upon the lot of you, napping out here in the open like figs ripe for the taking."

Helplessly, Thimblerig looked at his friends, and their terrified faces didn't make him feel confident about the situation. He was still trying to shake off the effects of the dream, and having the enforcer standing right over him just made the situation that much more hopeless.

"Where are the others?" the enforcer asked.

The groundhog blinked, having a difficult time forcing the wild dog's words to make sense.

"Others?"

Kid Duffy's eyes narrowed suspiciously as he began to growl, and it all came rushing back to Thimblerig – the agreement when they'd been let go and the story he'd made up about a large number of believers.

"The others! Right!" Thimblerig said loudly enough for his partners to hear, and he hoped that they would pick up on what he was trying to do. "The other believers, of course. Sorry, I was a bit thrown off… didn't expect you to be here so soon. You're wondering where the other believers are!"

"Listen con, I stuck my neck out because there was supposed to be a whole herd of believers out here. My boss won't be happy when I bring back only half a dozen. And I'm not happy with the one who causes my boss to be unhappy with me." Kid Duffy sneered. "The leader's gone after the last of the prey, and he sent me to track you down. Turns out that wasn't much of a challenge. I'm supposed to go back to him with this sorry lot?"

Thimblerig's nimble mind sprang into action, and he knew immediately what he had to do. He just didn't know if it would work.

"Hey, look Mr. Duffy, I know when I've been beat. But if you'd found us just a few hours from now, you'd have had the whole lot of believers. They're all just up there in the Edge, like I told you before! Let me take you there!"

The mountains of the Edge rose above them, illuminated in the darkness by occasional flashes of lightning that lit up the outline of the jagged peaks. The groundhog also felt a flash of urgency as he considered what the lightning meant, what was coming, how little time was left. He had to shove that feeling down. Kid Duffy was clever and Thimblerig needed all his wits about him.

"I'm not buying it this time," the wild dog answered coldly. Thimblerig's heart dropped as he realized his bluff was being called. "I don't trust you, groundhog, and I never should have."

He turned and faced the company of animals, surrounded by his pack of wild dogs. The enforcer was gratified to see the fear in the eyes of some of the prey, but he was irritated that it wasn't in the eyes of all. The kangaroo and the pair of gazelles looked especially defiant. That wouldn't do. If he couldn't make them fear, perhaps he could crush their spirits.

"Under the authority granted to me by Blonger, leader of the wild dogs, I find you guilty of breaking wild dog law. You will pay with your lives at the discretion of our leader. But you should know who you have to thank for your fate." He gestured back at Thimblerig.

"Thimblerig tried," Sheila replied. "He was doing the will of Tannier Isa."

Kid Duffy's ears perked up at the mention of the name. It was strictly forbidden by Blonger himself for any animal to say the name of the long-dead unicorn, and if the kangaroo weren't already under a death sentence, she certainly would be now. But knowing that also helped Kid Duffy figure out what he needed to do to crush them all.

"Is that so? And did your unicorn king tell him to sell you out to me?"

The animals now looked confused as well as fearful. The kangaroo and the female gazelle exchanged confused glances. "It's not true," the gazelle said. "He was helping us get away from you."

"I suppose I could have misunderstood the terms of our agreement," Kid Duffy replied, gratified. He turned back to Thimblerig, grinning. "What was it you said, little squirrel? 'I don't buy into their wacky beliefs. I just want to walk away from this in one piece.' Do I remember your words correctly?"

Thimblerig wanted to deny it. He desperately wanted to claim that Kid Duffy was making it all up, that he was purposefully trying to drive a wedge between them. But he couldn't, because it was true. He had fully intended to abandon the company of animals as soon as it was convenient. He had fully intended to betray them if it meant saving his own hide.

"It's true. I said those things," he murmured. "But it's not how I feel now!"

"I knew it!" Shi Lau exclaimed triumphantly. "I tried telling you all this the entire time. He's been looking out for himself from the start!"

"They weren't supposed to catch us," Thimblerig started to say, but Kid Duffy cut him off.

"You were pretty serious about it when we made our bargain," Kid Duffy interrupted, regaining control of the conversation. "If fact, as we agreed, you are free to go."

The members of the company gasped. Thimblerig felt shame rising up again as he imagined what they were feeling. As far as they knew, they'd put their trust in him, let him guide them all the way out to the borders of the Edge believing that he was leading them to a place of safety, when all the while he'd been setting them up for destruction at the sharp teeth of the wild dogs.

But he'd changed, hadn't he? After everything they'd been through, after all the visions, after seeing the light of the unicorn's horn, he believed it now, didn't he? The reality of his confession came crashing down on him like the storm from his vision. The unicorn *was* real, the flood *was* coming, and it was *his* responsibility to save the animals. He believed it all!

"I believe…" he said quietly, amazed.

And he knew what he had to do. "Wait," he cried, leaping in front of Kid Duffy. "Take me too! If you're taking them, take me with you!"

Everything stopped as Thimblerig made his insane request. The wild dogs looked particularly perplexed, not having seen an animal ask to be taken prisoner before. Kid Duffy saw the reaction of his pack and lunged at Thimblerig, knocking him to the ground and ending the discussion. He pressed Thimblerig close to the earth and held him there.

"It's over, groundhog," he whispered. "You lied to me about what I'd find here, and I will have to face Blonger because of it. This is my payment to you: you will go free, but you will live the rest of your pathetic, meaningless life with the knowledge that these others animals died slowly and painfully because of you, and I will make certain that they do."

Kid Duffy was pleased by the look of utter hopelessness on the groundhog's face. If he didn't have to face his own humiliation when he returned to Blonger, then the groundhog's reaction might have made the whole enterprise worthwhile.

"Yes, little squirrel, you will go free," he shouted for all to hear. "You are free to live your life, find a mate, and have little squirrel babies, while the believers go back with me to face Blonger's justice, *as we agreed.*"

All Thimblerig could do was lay there, under the pressure of the huge wild dog who was holding him down, speechless for the first time in his life. He couldn't deny what the wild dog said, even though he felt like he'd changed in the short time since they'd made their agreement. The wild dogs weren't interested in his changed thinking; they were only interested in victory. And the enforcer had his victory.

Kid Duffy stepped off the groundhog and growled an order to his subordinates to move out. It was time to bring this charade to an end, and to salvage what he could. Maybe he wasn't going to bring an entire herd of fanatical believers to Blonger, but at least he'd bring this group. It wasn't much, but he did have the elephant, and it might just be enough to keep him from being shafted to the bottom of the pack, or worse.

Helpless, Thimblerig watched as his friends were led away by the wild dogs, past the trail that led to the threshold of the Edge, until they were out of sight.

Finally only Kid Duffy remained. He turned to face the groundhog, a final remark posed on his lips. But he decided against it, turned, and padded away, leaving Thimblerig alone with his misery.

151

Thimblerig had heard about the idea of depression, but hadn't realized what it was until this moment. He wanted to get up, run and hide, find a dark hole where he could bury himself and sleep until the floods came. But he couldn't do it. He was rooted to the spot where he'd been left, and all he could do was stare at the spot in the distance where he'd seen the last of them go.

They were gone.

They were all gone, and there was nothing he could do about it.

He'd failed them, even as he'd just realized that he didn't want to fail them. Even worse, he'd failed Tannier Isa.

But he'd told him, hadn't he? In no uncertain terms he'd begged the unicorn to find someone else, he'd told him that he was the worst animal for the job, but the unicorn had persisted. The unicorn had gone all in, and lost the bet.

"I told you I was the wrong choice," he muttered.

And as the groundhog sat with heavy heart, paralyzed with fear and indecision about what to do, a single drop of rain landed on his nose.

Nurlan the gerbil lay on a tall mound of seed freshly plucked from the lushest wild wheat that grew on the steppes. The sky above was more brilliantly blue than he could remember, but to be honest it was hard to recall anything with his mouth packed so full with the meaty grain, which was more salty and flavorful than any he'd ever eaten.

It would be an understatement to say he was enjoying the experience, but he still had a nagging itch in the back of his mind that something was a bit off. In all his life, Nurlan hadn't even seen more than twenty or thirty pieces of grain at one time, and now he was reclining on a bed of it?

And what about his friend? The one with the big nose? What was his name? Kuan-something or other. He struggled to remember. Kuanbar? No, but it did start with Kuan... Kuanbano?

152

Kuanden? Kuandyk? Kuandyk! That was it. Where was Kuandyk? He'd love to share a bite of this delicious seed.

Nurlan lifted his head to see if he could find the big-nosed one that was usually nearby, but things started to turn fuzzy, and the mound of grain beneath started to dissolve, like a mound of salt in the rain.

"No! That's okay! I don't need Kuandyk!" he muttered, lowering his head and clenching his eyes tight. He needed to get the grain to come back. But as he concentrated, the world turned upside down, and the gerbil vomited out the grain he'd been enjoying.

Through squinted eyes, he saw that he'd been dreaming, and in reality he was lying on his back on a patch of ground, with a dark and foreboding sky above. His mind began to connect the events of the past few hours, and as it did so, he remembered that he wasn't only with his friend Kuandyk, but the group of new friends that the unicorn had given them. Then he remembered the wild dogs attacking, and he sat up as suddenly as his lean gerbil body would allow.

"Kuandyk!" he shouted, concerned. Then it all came rushing back to him – how they'd been ambushed by the wild dogs, how he'd tumbled off the antelope's back as they were herded into a group, and then darkness. Had he hit his head and blacked out? The painful lump he felt on the back of his head confirmed that this had been exactly what happened.

Had they noticed he was gone? Had Kuandyk tried to find him? He certainly wouldn't have left him on his own, although it could be that the antelope thought he would go unnoticed by the wild dogs, and could affect a rescue attempt, which of course he would do if he were able.

But he was alone. The realization crashed down on him in an instant, and at the same time, a drop of rain plopped on his head. He looked up just in time to see a bright flash of light spider web across the sky.

"It's here?" he muttered quietly. The storm was here? And his friends weren't? Where exactly had the wild dogs taken them? How could he find them? How could he rescue them? Nurlan had no answers to these questions, but he knew that he had to try. And he knew he didn't have much time to figure it out.

He hopped up with the intention of scurrying back in the direction in which they'd come, hoping it was the right way, but stopped and had to steady himself. Waves of nausea made him feel like the ground was rocking. He sat still for a moment, breathing deeply, listening to the soft pitter patter of raindrops falling around, and as he did he noticed a strange rock just a few feet away that was shaped like a groundhog.

Thinking it odd and strangely coincidental that a rock would look like the very same groundhog that he'd been following just a short time before, he decided to waste a moment investigating. The nausea having subsided, he crawled quietly across the ground until he was quite close to the rock.

The darkness made it hard to see anything, even standing up close. Fortunately, another bolt of lightning lit up the sky, and showed him clearly that the rock was not actually a rock, but the very groundhog he'd been thinking about.

"Thimblerig!" he shouted, hopping up to the rock-shaped groundhog. "Thank the unicorn! You're still here!"

He was a bit surprised and offended that the groundhog paid him no mind. It was like he wasn't there at all! He just sat in the middle of the path, rocking back and forth, muttering something about wrong choices.

The gerbil sighed. Nothing on the steppes was ever as easy as you hoped it might be.

CHAPTER 18
OUT OF THE DARKNESS

"Groundhog!" Nurlan shouted as loud as he could. "Wake up! Thimblerig, you need to snap out of it!"

Every second the groundhog wasted locked away in his little world was a second that the wild dogs were getting away. He had to get the groundhog's attention, but he wasn't sure what to do.

He stared up at the mountain of groundhog sitting before him, and decided he had to climb.

Maybe the unicorn hadn't chosen him at all. Maybe it was because he'd led such a detestable life, taking advantage of the gullibility of the other animals just to get a fig here or there, and now he was being punished. Could the unicorn really be so crafty that he'd set someone up like this? But if it was judgment, then it was what he deserved until the floodwaters would come and put him out of his misery. After all, he was responsible for the deaths of the company of animals that he'd been tasked to save.

"I deserve this," Thimblerig said.

He was surprised to feel the earth shaking and shuddering. Could it be the flood, already here? Already slamming into the earth hard enough to cause an earthquake?

His eyes started to focus as he shook, and a little face came slowly into sight, and it was babbling some sort of little face madness. Then it hit the groundhog that the earthquake was actually the owner of this little face, grasping his whiskers and shaking his head back and forth.

Then he felt the pain.

"Argh!" he cried, grabbing the pint-sized animal and jerking him away from his face, taking a few of his precious whiskers with him. "Are you insane?!?" He was about to throw the mass of squiggling arms and legs as far away as he could when he heard a voice he thought he knew.

"Thimblerig! Snap out of it! We've got to get going!"

Drawing the animal closer, the little thing looked familiar, but Thimblerig wasn't sure.

"Who are you?" he asked. "How do you know my name?"

Frustrated, waving Thimblerig's whiskers in his face, the gerbil screamed, "It's Nurlan! From the unicorn's spring! What's wrong with you?"

"Nurlan?" Thimblerig asked, recognition dawning. "You got away?"

"There's no time for that," the gerbil said, pulling himself away from the groundhog's paws and dropping to the ground and then gesturing upwards. "Don't you see what's going on?"

The sky was now completely dark. A splatter of cold, wet rain fell on his face, mirroring the coldness he felt inside.

"It's starting," he mumbled.

"You're right it's starting," Nurlan responded. "Who knows how much time we have to find the others, get them away from the wild dogs, and make it to safety? We need to get going!"

The gerbil started up the trail but stopped when he saw that the groundhog hadn't moved. He was still sitting in that same position, looking up at the sky with a vacant look in his eyes.

"What are you waiting for? Come on!"

"I can't do it."

Nurlan couldn't believe what he was hearing. This was the chosen one – the one Tannier Isa had told about – the one who was supposed to lead them all – and he couldn't do it?

"Is this some sort of groundhog joke?" he asked, running back to the groundhog. "Because if it is, I've got to tell you that I don't get it."

"It's no joke. I can't do it. I'm done."

The gerbil's disbelief held for a moment longer, and then washed away, leaving behind bedrock of righteous indignation and anger.

156

"You have got to be kidding me!" he cried. "The unicorn gave you the job of protecting and guiding a handful of animals, and you're giving up?"

"He was wrong!" Thimblerig snapped. "I was the wrong choice!"

Nurlan felt white-hot rage now. "You are the only wrong one, and you're wrong about this," he said coldly. "He doesn't make mistakes. Like it or not, you're the one he chose, and it's time you started acting like it."

A sudden flash of lightning served to underscore what the gerbil was saying. Looking up at the rocks of the Edge above them, Thimblerig fully expected to see the silhouette of the unicorn against the night sky. Instead, all he saw was the rolling black clouds, and the steadily falling rain.

"But what if I'm not?" he asked, the desperation palpable in his voice. He saw the gerbil now as if for the first time. "What if I screw things up?"

The gerbil's anger faded. Satisfied that he'd finally gotten through, he patted the groundhog's paw gently. "Well bud, you already lost the ones you were supposed to be saving. I don't reckon you could screw things up worse than that, could you?"

"This is the worst idea I've ever heard," Thimblerig whispered. "And I've heard plenty."

Thimblerig sat with Nurlan behind a small outcropping of rocks, sheltered for the moment from the drizzling rain. The pack of wild dogs was just on the other side of the rocks. Thankfully, they hadn't been moving quickly or working hard to cover their tracks, and the duo had managed to catch up with them.

"It'll work like a charm!" Nurlan whispered back. "I've done it myself. You should have seen how I scared Kuandyk one time when I popped out of the hole shrieking like a stomped rabbit!"

Thimblerig was covered from head to toe in a variety of grasses, tied in bunches to give him the appearance of some sort

157

of hideous grassland monster, and he was apparently supposed to shriek like a stomped rabbit. This was a very, very bad idea.

"There's a big difference between a pack of wild dogs and a saiga antelope," Thimblerig replied. "He probably didn't try to bite your face off."

"Hey, I'm the one actually entering the enemy camp. You just distract them and I'll do the rest," Nurlan answered.

Without waiting to hear any more criticisms, the gerbil skittered around the edge of the rock and started making his way towards the closely guarded company of animals. He crawled towards a clump of grass as near to the wet ground as he could, counting on the rain and the darkness to help make him invisible to any attentive wild dogs. Wild dogs were notoriously good at smelling out animals, and he didn't want to take any chances.

Successfully arriving at the clump, he pulled the tall grass back slightly, and was rewarded with an unobstructed view of the company of animals huddled together around Pavel. Nurlan counted twenty wild dogs surrounding them in two circles, with the inner ring keeping a watchful eye on the elephant and the outer ring facing the darkness, in case of attack. The rest of the pack was scattered about, and appeared to be waiting for something.

Where's the enforcer? Nurlan wondered. That was the clever one, the one he'd really have to watch out for. Finally, he saw Kid Duffy at the far perimeter of the encampment, talking with three other wild dogs, who nodded their heads and disappeared into the darkness. Nurlan wondered briefly where the enforcer might be sending them, but decided not to dwell on this question. He had enough to worry about.

Speaking of worrying, it was now up to the groundhog to provide the proper distraction. Would he do it? This was really their only chance, and it wasn't much of a chance. After all, it was a couple of insignificant rodents going up against the wild dog pack. And it all came back to the groundhog, who had lost his moxie. Together, their chances were small, but the chances would be slim to none if he had to go at it on his own.

Any minute now, groundhog, any minute. After several minutes of waiting, he muttered a few discouraged words in his native gerbilese. Apparently the groundhog had chickened out and he was going to have to do this on his own. He took a few deep breaths to try and get his adrenaline going and prepared to make the dash to the closest sleeping wild dog, thinking that he would use the brute for cover.

Suddenly, a brilliant light flashed out over the rainy landscape, followed by a crack of thunder that shook the ground. Nurlan was dazed and couldn't see anything except dancing flashes of light. He rubbed his eyes and to clear away the stars and looking back at the rock. There he was! The groundhog was standing on the top of the rock, hopping up and down and screeching like an angry owl who'd had his lunch swiped from his beak. It wasn't a stomped rabbit, but it would do. The wild dogs reacted immediately, jumping up and moving towards the rock where the strange creature was making so much noise.

Quickly, Nurlan slid out from behind the grass, rolled to avoid the oncoming wild dogs, and scurried forward until he stood unobserved in the middle of the company of animals.

It was time to let them in on the plan.

A few moments earlier, Thimblerig watched Nurlan crawl away to put his insane plan into motion. His fear and concern were replaced by an unpleasant feeling that he had trouble identifying. The feeling had started with the realization that a tiny gerbil was exhibiting courage and bravery while he sat uselessly, paralyzed with fear.

"It's shame," a quiet voice said; a voice that rode the raindrops and blew in with the wind. "That's what you're feeling."

159

Ordinarily, Thimblerig would have been concerned about hearing ethereal voices. But after the events of the past week, it was perfectly reasonable.

"I don't like it. I don't like it one bit. How do I get rid of it?" He answered, not even attempting to figure out from where the voice was coming.

"You know the answer."

The groundhog closed his eyes and sighed. He didn't want to admit it, but he did know the answer. It went against every survival instinct that screamed for attention in his subconscious. He had to do the right thing and stand up to the wild dogs.

"I didn't choose you so you could live in fear and shame, Thimblerig," the voice continued.

"But I can't," Thimblerig whispered. "I'm not even sure who I am anymore."

"It doesn't matter who you are," the voice said. "Open your eyes and see who I am."

The groundhog wanted to obey the quiet and reassuring voice, but he couldn't. If he obeyed and he saw what he thought he would see, those piercing eyes, and that magnificent horn, then he would know for certain just how lost he was. How could he stand being in the same place as the unicorn? How could he do it and not be reduced to ashes, his life burned away by the understanding of how small and insignificant he was?

"Thimblerig," the voice persisted. "Look at me."

Slowly, painfully, Thimblerig looked up and gasped. Even though he'd seen the unicorn three times already, twice in visions, once from a distance, those encounters hadn't prepared him for the reality standing before him in the falling rain now.

The unicorn appeared to be carved from ancient ebony, as dark as the night. His coat rippled with energy from within, as if his fur was made of lightning, and the rain sizzled as it struck him. And then there was the horn; if the unicorn's coat was alive with dancing energy, then the horn must have been the source, burning with a brightness that made the sun seem dim in

160

comparison, and yet paradoxically, Thimblerig could look directly at it with completely open eyes.

"You've made the first step," the unicorn said.

"The first step?" Thimblerig whispered. "I haven't done anything."

"I told you to look at me, and you did," Tannier Isa responded, stepping closer. "Are you willing to take the second step?"

"Is it as easy as the first?" he answered.

"That depends on you."

"On me?"

"You have to give me your shame."

Thimblerig couldn't believe what he heard. Give the unicorn his shame? First, he didn't know how he was supposed to give away a feeling. If he'd asked for something physical like a foot or an arm, he would understand. But shame? How was he supposed to give away part of who he was, inside?

Something else bothered the groundhog about this request. The unicorn was *good*, and Thimblerig felt it the way that you know the sun is shining by feeling its warmth. Just like he didn't doubt the warmth of the sun, Thimblerig didn't doubt the goodness of the unicorn. His shame would ruin that goodness.

"I can't do it," he said.

"It's the only way," the unicorn answered. "Right now your shame is paralyzing you, and rightly so. You've made some terrible choices, Thimblerig, from the moment I called you. You are responsible for what happened to the animals you were supposed to protect. If you didn't feel shame, we wouldn't be having this conversation, because you'd be beyond my help. Your shame is what will save you, but only if you give it to me."

The unicorn was asking too much, and Thimblerig curled down into a ball in the sloppy mud as he realized it. Sure, he didn't want to keep his shame; he detested it and was eager to forget the feeling altogether. But it was *his*. He'd earned it, and he had no right to allow someone else to just take it from him.

161

"It's the only way," the unicorn persisted. "Otherwise your friends will be dead before morning."

This was probably intended to spur Thimblerig to action, but instead it drove him further into despair. Suddenly an idea came to him, and so he bolted up, water splashing around him, and looked at the unicorn with hope.

"You can do it!" he exclaimed. "Just show yourself to those wild dogs for a moment! They'd go insane and take off!"

"It would be useless," the unicorn said. For the first time, Thimblerig sensed sadness in his voice. "They wouldn't even see me."

"How could they miss you?" Thimblerig said. "You're huge! Not to mention that you have this whole glowing thing going on."

"It doesn't matter. They still wouldn't see me, because they choose not to. Believe me, I've tried speaking with them, and to all the animals of the forest. You're very unusual, Thimblerig. Very few animals listen to me these days, and I won't force anyone."

"Seems like you forced me..." Thimblerig muttered.

"Thimblerig, you need to trust me," Tannier Isa said. "What is your decision?"

Of course Thimblerig knew what he needed to do. His friends were just on the other side of that rock, at the mercy of the wild dogs, and he and the little gerbil were their only hope.

The gerbil? How long had it been since the gerbil had crawled into enemy territory? Had he been captured already? Was he just sitting there, waiting for Thimblerig to do what he was supposed to do? It was time to act.

"Let's do it," Thimblerig said resolutely.

Without wasting a moment, the unicorn stepped forward through the rainfall, leaned down his head, and drove his horn directly into Thimblerig's chest.

162

CHAPTER 19
COSTLY FREEDOM

Thimblerig sat in the pouring rain, just a stone's throw away from the pack, sitting in conversation with the king of the unicorns, who just a day earlier had been nothing but myth, and who now had his horn embedded in his chest.

And he felt warmth.

That was the shocking part. Had you asked him just a moment before what it would feel like to be impaled by a unicorn horn during a rainstorm, he would have listed 'excruciating', 'mind-numbingly painful', 'ridiculously and freakishly agonizing', as possibilities. But warmth? That sensation wouldn't have made it in his top one hundred list of options.

He looked down at the base of the horn, which was the only part he could still see, and which only seconds before had been burning so brightly. The light was now pulsing, and with each throb of light from the horn, a wave of warmth passed through his body.

Tannier Isa pulled his head back slowly, carefully withdrawing the horn from Thimblerig's chest. Thimblerig dropped to the ground, breathing heavily, but amazed to be alive. He grasped his chest, expecting blood, but there was nothing but fur that was wet with water.

"I'm alive," he gasped, amazed, holding his chest. He looked up at the unicorn with amazement. Tannier Isa was standing unsteadily, like he could fall if the breeze blew a bit harder. "Are you alright?"

"I'll be fine," the unicorn answered with some effort. "Sorry about the surprise. But if I had warned you, you wouldn't have let me."

"But why?" Thimblerig said, still feeling his chest for any sort of puncture wounds. There were none.

"It was the only way I could take your shame," Tannier Isa replied with a weary grin. "Now, instead of carrying your shame, you carry some of my light. Now fix your grassy headdress, trust me, and go and do what you need to do."

Taking a deep breath, Thimblerig re-adjusted the now-soaked headdress that he'd forgotten he was wearing, and he scrambled up the slippery, craggy rock to the top. Breathing heavily, he stood in the rain at the top of the rock, regarding the dark shapes of the wild dogs sitting in a circle around his little company. He didn't know where the gerbil was, but he hoped he was ready.

But now he had a new problem. Had the gerbil already done it or had the little guy been caught? How much time had Thimblerig spent with Tannier Isa? If Nurlan was still waiting, how could he get the wild dogs' attention well enough to give the gerbil time to enact his plan? He thought back to the animals at the Rock, how some would scream and cry to be seen. He thought about Sheila's dance, which had also worked. Maybe he could a mixture of both?

"Hey! Hey! Wild dogs! Over here!" he yelled, hopping around, careful not to slip on the wet rock. But the darkness and rain was preventing anyone from noticing. He needed to do more if he was going to be noticed. He started screeching like an angry hawk and flapping his arms up and down, but the wild dogs below were oblivious, continuing sleeping and guarding with no indication that they noticed him at all. He was so frustrated! It was no use. He was as good as invisible.

"I could really use some help!" Thimblerig cried, and he immediately began to feel warmth building in his chest where the unicorn had driven his horn. He looked down and was shocked to see that his chest was glowing. What was this? What had the unicorn done? He began slapping his chest to try and extinguish the glow, but it refused to cooperate and continued to grow brighter and brighter. Suddenly, the energy flared and burst out from within him, followed by an ear-splitting crash. It illuminated the sky brighter than the brightest lightning, and the wild dogs below scattered in shock.

164

Quickly recovering from the surprise of becoming a groundhog firefly, Thimblerig did his best to channel every nutcase he'd ever seen on the Rock. He screamed like an angry feral cat, he jumped up and down, and he tore at the grass with which he'd covered himself. The wild dogs were up in an instant, all eyes on him, the crowd growl building as they assessed this new threat.

How long would it take for the gerbil to pass the message on to the company? He hoped it would be soon, as he was running out of insanity moves. The wild dogs were moving toward the rock, with the exception of a few who stayed dutifully by the elephant. Those would be the unfortunate ones, if everything went according to plan.

"Hey, wild dogs! My groundmother could track better than you!" Thimblerig shouted, jumping up and waving his arms above his head. When he landed, his back paw came down on a particularly slippery section of rock. He slipped, and before he knew it he fell from the rock and splashed into the muddy ground at the base.

"That wasn't a part of the plan," Thimblerig muttered as he tried to get up from the mud. Neither had it been part of the plan to be surrounded by the drooling mouths and gleaming razor-sharp teeth of a dozen wild dogs, but there they were. He closed his eyes to the inevitable, feeling sorry that he hadn't been able to help his friends, and then he heard the trumpeting call of a very angry bull elephant.

Thimblerig had been quickly forgotten by the wild dogs, who were now scattering in disarray to avoid being stomped by Pavel. The gerbil had done it!

Thimblerig glanced back across the area in front of the rock, and was angry to see that the rest of the company of animals had failed to follow behind the elephant as they were supposed to. In fact, the enforcer himself had cornered them. Mullins stood defensively in front of the others with a look of defiance clear on his face, even in spite of the rain and darkness. But the wild dog stood low to the ground, hair erect, growling a growl that was audible even from where Thimblerig stood.

Without taking time to decide if it was a good idea, Thimblerig dropped on all fours and charged across the field, aiming directly for the side of Kid Duffy, running as fast as his stubby little groundhog legs would carry him.

Mullins eyed the enforcer, angrier than he'd ever been. They'd been so close to escaping! As soon as the gerbil had passed on the news that Thimblerig was springing some scheme to free them, he'd steeled himself to make the dash. He'd been relieved that the groundhog had come around, but he was unsure what con he could concoct to get them out of this dire situation.

And then Thimblerig appeared on the rock, dressed like a bird of paradise, doing his crazy dance in the rain. It had not been at all what Mullins had been expecting! And then the pièce de résistance – that impressive light display - had sealed the deal. The wild dogs were confounded, the company made a break for it, and then Kid Duffy stood in their path, not caring that Pavel was decimating his ranks. The blood gushed down the side of the wild dog's rain-soaked head leading Mullins to conclude that he hadn't escaped the elephant's rampage.

"Out of our way," Mullins snarled as well as his gazelle throat would allow.

The wild dog grinned. Mullins gulped, frightened but resolute. These might be his last breaths, but Tabitha was standing right behind him, and if he could buy her even a couple of seconds, he would do it, no matter what it cost.

And then a crazed bird of paradise came flying out of the showers and darkness and smashed into Kid Duffy's side. The blow came as such a surprise that the wild dog went down like a sack of figs, the wind completely knocked from his lungs. Mullins and the rest of the company stared dumbly at the wild dog gasping on the muddy ground when the bird of paradise scrambled to his feet and screamed through the growing storm, "What are you waiting for? An invitation?"

"Thimblerig?" Soapy asked.

"Who else would it be? Asarata's root scrubber? Let's go!" Thimblerig pushed Mullins and Tabitha, grabbed Sheila by the paw, and slipping and sliding across the deepening mud, took off towards the Edge, glancing back to make sure the others were following.

CHAPTER 20
ESCAPE TO THE EDGE

Running full steam in the darkness during a torrential downpour was not easy. Thimblerig was pushing them hard because he knew that the wild dogs would be regrouping, and the enforcer would be angrier and more determined than ever. But more than that, he knew that the flood could happen at any moment, and he still wasn't sure where they were supposed to be going, except to the Edge. In his vision, he'd seen a trail, and he only hoped that the trail would be there in reality.

"Keep moving! We're not far!" he cried over his shoulder, but he needn't have bothered. The company hurried obediently, having accepted his leadership again without hesitation, without so much as a word of explanation. Thimblerig knew that it had little to do with him and everything to do with the unicorn.

Finally, he thought he understood their faith.

They topped a small rise on the treeless steppe and the Edge rose before them like a wall of blackness. With the wind and rain whipping around them, raising hair and feathers, the little company turned as one and looked at Thimblerig in expectation.

"What's next, 'Rig?" Big Bunco shouted to be heard over the crashing of the storm. "Where do we go?"

Staring at the dark walls, he was about to confess that he didn't know when he saw a beacon of light cutting through the rain and the darkness up ahead. "That way!" he cried, pointing ahead. The others looked and gasped. This time he was not the only one to see it. He glanced at Shi Lau, in his usual place on the top of Elbridge the camel. The duck's bill was hanging wide open.

"You see it, Shi?"

"Is that... it couldn't be..."

"It can be and it is."

"Don't get cocky, groundhog," the duck answered. "You're ruining the moment."

168

Thimblerig laughed, and then shouted, "What are we waiting for?" he led the company down the rain-drenched slope towards the unicorn's light.

It took about thirty minutes for the company of animals to navigate the slope in the darkness and make their way across the grassy field to the base of the Edge. All were keeping their eyes on the beacon of light as they ran, and Thimblerig noticed that the light was also moving as they approached. It was getting further away and then started moving up the side of the Edge, as if the unicorn was running up the wall vertically. It reminded Thimblerig of the wild dogs in his most recent vision, the way they scurried up the wall like spiders. He had no idea how they were supposed to do that.

If this also bothered the others, they were being remarkably quiet about it. On the one hand, this reassured the groundhog, because it could mean that they were all finally accepting his leadership without question. On the other hand, it could mean that they were biting their tongues in anticipation that he was going to screw up again, so they could really let him have it.

The walls of the Edge rose endlessly into the mists, making it impossible to see the tops of the mountains. They were grey, virtually lifeless, with tiny bits of scraggly vegetation intermittently interrupting the smooth rock wall. There were supposed to be forests beyond the Edge, but this was not a very cheerful place. It was cold and wet, a place an animal might come to die.

"Why isn't he here?" Manuel asked, panic in his eyes. "He should be here!"

"And the puddles are getting deeper," Nurlan said, looking nervously down from his perch on the top of Kuandyk's head at the waters gathering at the saiga's feet. "This can't be good."

"Soapy, run ahead and see if you can find anything," Thimblerig said.

169

"Right, boss," the ape answered, leaping into the darkness.

The smaller animals were shuffling around, trying to find a place to stand where the puddles weren't as deep. Elbridge and Shi Lau were both looking back where they'd come from, undoubtedly fearful that the pack would reappear out of nowhere. "We'll be alright," Sheila said confidently. She stepped over to Thimblerig and put her paw on his shoulder. "The unicorn brought us this far, and he's not going to let us down now. We have to keep trusting him, and Thimblerig."

The kangaroo's words swept through Thimblerig, making him stand taller, and instantly reminding him where his attention needed to be kept.

"Sheila's right," he said. "He's still showing us the way."

At these words, Soapy came lumbering back through the storm, a wide smile on his face. "There's a trail! Right where the light was! It's kind of tucked in a little crag in the rock face, but we should all fit!"

Kid Duffy was living in a world of complete darkness. He'd been living in this murky world forever. Time had no meaning. There was no emotion. There was only darkness.

But there was something else. If he listened very carefully, he could hear a muffled voice. He wanted to ignore the voice and enjoy the nothingness longer, but a smaller, irritating part of his consciousness demanded that he pay attention. Reluctantly, the wild dog strained his ears to try and understand. He heard words that didn't mean very much; "enforcer", "wake up", "Blonger"…

"Blonger"? That word was particularly unpleasant. He wanted to run from it, but he couldn't. He had to climb out of the night and face it.

The idea of climbing out of the blackness triggered a physiological response of fluttering eyelids and an awareness of haggard breathing. He was soaking wet. The wind and rain was blowing against his wet fur, and he was chilled. And as he tried to move, he felt pain, with every muscle and bone hurting.

170

Like a wall of water during the worst of the rainy season, it all came rushing back to him. He was Kid Duffy, the enforcer of the wild dogs. A feathered creature had knocked him flat on his back. Then a bull elephant had trampled him.

He opened his eyes to find that a half dozen wild dogs surrounded him, some bleeding profusely, others holding paws up to avoid putting down weight. It was a damaged, sorry pack that stood and lay before him.

But hadn't there been others? Hadn't they been guarding several animals when everything fell apart? They were believers that Blonger had personally ordered him to bring in. Even though it hurt, he glanced to the left and the right to see that the animals they had been guarding were nowhere in sight.

"Where are they?" he slurred. "What happened to the prisoners?"

"They went that way," the closest wild dog said, gesturing towards the big rock.

"Was the groundhog with them?"

"He was."

"We need to go," he said, painfully rising to stand on all fours, testing to see if anything was damaged beyond repair. It would be most painful later, but for now he appeared to be only sore and bruised. "We need to kill that groundhog and recapture the believers before word gets back to the leader."

"Word has already gotten back to the leader."

Kid Duffy turned to see Blonger materialize from the mist and the rain like a spirit, followed by the rest of the pack. How had he found them so quickly? It didn't really matter, because the results were inevitable. Kid Duffy had failed the leader, and Blonger hadn't gained a reputation for being merciful.

"It's been a spectacular hunt, Enforcer," Blonger said as he walked up to Kid Duffy, who had crouched down, tail tucked between his legs, averting his eyes. "We caught almost all of them, you know. The lynx especially gave us a run, but we

171

eventually cornered her, and I was able to deliver the final bite myself. Now we're just missing the elephant and your believers."

The leader's voice was calm and gentle, which made him seem more dangerous. Blonger stepped up close. "Enforcer, you have served me well this past year. You've done everything I've asked without question or hesitation. I have appreciated your loyalty and service."

"It's my honor to serve you, leader," Kid Duffy said, raising his head and licking the leader's face submissively, hopefully.

"Yes it is, I know," Blonger said, eyes closed, enjoying the attention. "That's why it's such a pity." Kid Duffy pulled his head back. "Yes, a pity," the leader said, standing. "Like the end of the festival of Asarata. We're always sorry when it's ended, but there's always hope, because soon there will be a new festival."

The leader of the wild dogs had a wicked gleam in his eye that Kid Duffy had seen many times before, but never directed at him. Instinctively, Kid Duffy had a primal urge to seize Blonger by the neck, driving his sharp teeth deep until all of the leader's life had bled out. But Kid Duffy, like all wild dogs, had been trained and conditioned since a cub to be unflinchingly loyal to the leader, and any ideas of self-defense died before they had the chance to make the transformation from thought to action. Kid Duffy had failed the leader, and he would stand by whatever verdict his master rendered.

"Yes, leader," he said quietly, resolved. "I understand."

Blonger nodded and raised himself to his full height. He turned to face the pack, and scanning the closest wild dogs, saw the hunger in their eyes. He smiled, pleased with once again holding the fate of an animal in his jaws.

"The position of Enforcer is now open."

For a few moments, the wild dogs did nothing but look back and forth at each other, waiting to see who would make the first move. Finally, the wild dog named Lupo stepped forward, eyes averted from his former boss at first, but then looking up to

172

stare defiantly at Kid Duffy. Behind him, two other wild dogs moved forward, and finally a fourth from across the circle. Teeth bared, low growls building from within, the small number of ambitious wild dogs slowly approached Kid Duffy, who closed his eyes and waited, his fate accepted.

The wind and rain had been relentless before the company of animals had started their ascent up the trail into the high cliffs of the Edge. They'd had to wade through water pouring down the cliff walls from higher elevations, but the trail had cut off up the mountainside, rising sharply. Before they knew it, they were several hundred feet higher, the rocky path narrowing to the point that the larger animals had to choose their steps carefully. The wind howled all around, and the rain was now blowing in from the sides of the cliff with such ferocity that it seemed to be trying to shove them off the trail down into the rocks below.

"This is unbearable!" Shi Lau quacked, holding tightly to the camel Elbridge's neck in an attempt to keep from being blown into the gale.

"You could have stayed below and taken your chances with the rising water," Mullins called back. "You're a water bird, after all."

"Doesn't keep the rain out of my eyes or you out of my business," the duck spat back.

"Quiet!" Big Bunco shouted, stopping suddenly in the front of the line. "Do you hear that?"

"All I hear is the storm," Shi Lau answered.

"Button your bill, Shi Lau," Thimblerig ordered. "What is it, Bunco?"

The little elephant stepped to the edge of the trail and stared down into the violent mists below. At first all she could hear was the sounds of the storm; the rain crashing, the wind wailing as it blew through the precipices and bluffs, the thunder booming and rolling through the chasms.

And then she heard it. The howling of wild dogs.

"The pack's down there," she cried, turning back to Thimblerig. "They found us!"

Thimblerig darted to the side of the trail and glanced down. He couldn't see or hear anything other than the storm, but he trusted Big Bunco's ears. He knew that they only had one choice, and it was reaffirmed in each of their eyes that they were far past the point of laying down and giving up. "Let's keep moving," he said, lowering his head and pushing forward into the rainy darkness.

Kid Duffy was still alive, but just barely. He had half-heartedly defended himself against the four wild dogs who had challenged him, but only because it was expected of him, and he had even managed to sink his teeth into Lupo's front leg before being brought down by the other three. They'd made quick work of him, and turned on each other, biting and scratching and clawing until only Lupo remained standing. This hadn't surprised Kid Duffy, as Lupo had already built a reputation for his brutality, which meant he would be a perfect subordinate for the leader.

Kid Duffy didn't feel remorse for losing his position and his place in the pack, and this surprised him. For the past year he had been enforcing Blonger's orders blindly, brutally putting down animal after animal for the smallest infraction, whether the animal had deserved it or not, and he was able to do this because of Blonger.

But something unexpected had happened during this encounter with Blonger that had changed him. For the briefest of moments, he'd seen the leader for who he really was, for what he stood for, and he hadn't liked it.

Now he would probably die soon. Kid Duffy didn't know how much blood he'd lost, but he was too lightheaded to stand or raise his head or care. He closed his eyes, surrendering to once again to the darkness.

A bothersome flash of lightning pulled him momentarily back from the edge of his desired rest. He opened his eyes when

174

the lightning flashed again, only this time it didn't flash and dim but kept lighting up the air, sizzling and popping like it was alive, dancing around the wild dog with energetic frenzy.

Kid Duffy's eyes grew wide as the energy coalesced into the shape of a large stallion made of the energy of lightning.

Then the stallion spoke.

"Kid Duffy, I think you might be ready to listen to me."

Kid Duffy watched, amazed, as the lightning travelled up the body of the stallion until it found its place, burning like a flame, in the shape of a single horn on the top of the stallion's head.

CHAPTER 21
UNEXPECTED HELP

"Look up there! The light's back!"

Thimblerig had been walking point with Big Bunco, head down to guard against the driving rain, lost in thought about the unicorn, when Sheila's voice roused him.

Sure enough, ahead of them about a hundred yards, the signal light burned through the darkness once more, beckoning them onward. It wasn't moving this time, which gave Thimblerig some hope that perhaps the unicorn was finally going to join them.

At the same time, Big Bunco turned away and looked back down the trail. "The pack's getting closer."

"We've got to make it to Tannier Isa!" Thimblerig called out. "He's waiting for us up there!"

Quickly closing the gap between where they'd stood and the light, the animals pushed forward, only to have the light vanish. "No!" Thimblerig cried out, running faster. He was the first to arrive at the point of the trail where the light had been, and found the dark, foreboding mouth of a cave.

"Did he go in there?" Sheila asked, hopping up beside Thimblerig, peering into the inky blackness.

"I don't know," Thimblerig answered. The light appeared to have gone in that direction, but now he couldn't see anything to suggest that it had. What were they supposed to do? If they continued down the trail, they were likely to be overtaken by the pack. If they chanced going into the cave, they could be trapped. Why would the unicorn want them to chance it?

"I see a glow!" Sheila shouted hopefully. "Look, you have to step into the cave, but light is coming from this passageway!"

Stepping in, Thimblerig saw a glow further in the cave. Was it Tannier Isa?

"They're coming, 'Rig! You need to decide!" Big Bunco said, agitated.

176

Thimblerig was much more comfortable with the idea of being in a cave then on a rain-washed trail, hundreds of feet up the side of a mountain. Besides, the caves in the Edge were said to be more like passages, and it could be that the unicorn was showing them a shortcut to escape. And if the wild dogs followed them in, Pavel could use the enclosed space to his advantage to help defend the company.

"We go in," he decided. "Follow me."

He entered the cave, and one by one, the members of the company followed him until a single animal remained outside. Pavel stood in the rain, staring at the mouth of the cave, unmoving.

"Hey fella, you coming?" Kuandyk called, being the first to notice that the bull elephant hadn't joined them.

"I can't do it," he answered. He was shaking now, and was breathing so hard that the saiga could feel his hot breath from inside the cave.

Somewhere back up the trail, the barks and howls of the pack were getting louder. "Pavel, we've got to get going! The wild dogs are coming!" Nurlan cried desperately.

Unhearing, Pavel stood still, continuing to shake.

"We got a problem, Kuandyk," Nurlan said, scurrying back to the top of Kuandyk's head. He stuck two fingers in his mouth and whistled loudly into the cave. "Hey, the elephant's freaking out back here!"

Hearing the gerbils panicked cry, Sheila reacted quickly, turning and hopping back up the passageway and outside to Pavel. She grasped him sturdily by the tusks and pulled his head down so that his eyes were level with her own.

"Pavel, you need to breathe," she said, her voice firm. "Deep breaths, Pavel. Take deep breaths."

The elephant pulled back involuntarily, dragging Sheila up off the ground as he raised his head. He stepped dangerously near the side of the trail, and Soapy and Thimblerig ran out to try and

177

help. Sheila held stubbornly onto Pavel's tusks and continued trying to calm him with her words.

"Pavel, listen to my voice. You need to breathe and calm down. You're safe with us, Pavel. You're with friends."

Thimblerig marveled at the kangaroo's skill with the bull elephant. Her voice was kind and soothing, the result being that the elephant's gasps began to subside. He fixed his eyes on Sheila and started to calm down.

"That's better," she continued quietly, stroking the side of his leathery face. "We're following the unicorn's footprints, Pavel. We can't go wrong."

"The unicorn's footprints," he repeated, his voice sounding stronger. His breathing was becoming more regular, and the wild look in his eyes had almost completely faded.

"That's right, Pavel. He's leading us every step. Didn't he come to you in the wild dog's cave? Well, this is his cave, and there's nothing to fear here. Just remember what it was like when he was there, with you."

How could he have forgotten what it felt like to be with the unicorn? The last of the panic slipped away and he took a deep breath. "I'm sorry, I don't know what happened," he stammered, embarrassed. "All I could think of was the dog's cave."

"It's Blonger's fault," Sheila interrupted. "You have nothing to be ashamed of. The wild dogs did this to you, but it doesn't mean you aren't strong. And just remember, this is Tannier Isa's cave, not Blonger's."

Pavel nodded, looking past Sheila to the others, who were watching him with concern. Thimblerig stepped up and regarded the bull elephant. He was still shaky, but under control. They didn't have time for a shaky elephant, and Thimblerig needed to get them all moving again before the wild dogs came. He and Sheila looked at one another and she nodded as unspoken words went between them. She released the elephant's tusks and took gentle hold of his trunk, draping it over her shoulder, holding it tightly. "We're ready," she said.

And so the company set off silently down the dark passageway, finally out of the rain. Thimblerig led the way, using senses honed from a lifetime of living in burrows. The others stumbled along behind him, not so confident in the dark confines of the underground corridor. The glow was still visible in the distance, close enough that they could follow, but far enough away that they couldn't see it directly.

"Why do you think he's doing it this way?" Big Bunco asked, walking along beside the groundhog.

"Doing what?" Thimblerig replied.

"Leading us from a distance. You've seen him and talked to him, and we all believe in him and are following you because we want to follow him. So why doesn't he just come and lead us himself?"

It was a good question, and one that Thimblerig had been wondering about as well. It really would make a lot more sense for the unicorn to just show them himself, and do it right the first time, to just help them avoid all the hardship and the struggle.

The struggle? What was it his groundmother had said?

"Sometimes we need the struggle," he muttered.

"What's that?" Big Bunco asked.

"What? Oh, nothing. Just something my groundmother told me when I was a cub."

"Tell us," Soapy said.

"Well, one day she and I were out gathering some greens for dinner when I came upon a cocoon hanging underneath a fern leaf. It was moving and shaking."

"Oh! I've seen this!" Ophelia said. "The butterfly was trying to get out!"

"Exactly," Thimblerig answered. "The cocoon was enormous, and I sat and watched as the butterfly worked and worked, and she finally broke through just a bit, but she couldn't

179

pull herself out of the hole. She finally stopped trying, exhausted."

"Poor thing," Sheila said. "Like a baby joey trying to grow old enough to get out of our pouch."

Thimblerig continued. "Well, groundhogs are experts at digging, and the cocoon was nothing for me, so I thought I'd help! So I did what I shouldn't have done and I dug out the opening so that it was big enough for the butterfly to pulled itself free."

"What's wrong with helping a butterfly out of their cocoon?" Mullins asked.

"I kept waiting for her to open her wings and fly away, but she tumbled out of the cocoon to the forest floor below. She couldn't fly! She could only drag herself along the ground, shriveled and helpless."

The company of animals walked silently through the dark cavern, listening to the groundhog tell more about himself than he'd told yet. They all recognized the significance of the moment.

"When my groundmother found me, I was sitting on the ground beside the butterfly bawling my eyes out. She picked me up and listened while I tried to explain what happened. She looked at the butterfly and the cocoon, and said, "She needed the struggle." I didn't understand, and I asked my groundmother what she meant. She said, "Sometimes we see someone struggling, and all we want to do is solve their problem for them. But sometimes it's the struggle they need to get the strength to face what they need to face."

Even in the darkness of the cave, Thimblerig could sense Big Bunco staring at him, and it made the groundhog feel uncomfortable.

"What?" he asked.

"Sometimes we need the struggle," she said with a smile. "That's deep, 'Rig."

All of the animals were looking at him, and Thimblerig didn't know what to say. He simply harrumphed and continued to make his way down the cavern passageway, trying to pretend like nothing had happened.

They'd been walking for about fifteen minutes when Thimblerig brought everyone to a halt. The passage forked to the right and the left, with the passageway to the right going up and the one on the left going down. The glow wasn't definite on either passageway, and could be coming from either.

"Why'd we stop?" Shi Lau called from the camel's back.

"There's a fork in road," Thimblerig called back. "I'm just making sure…"

Growling and barking echoed down the corridor from which they'd just come, interrupted his words.

The wild dogs had entered the cave.

"This way!" Thimblerig shooed the company up the corridor to the right, desperately hoping it was the right choice, thinking he'd seen light coming from that direction. For all he knew, he was sending them all to a dead end. Pavel and Sheila had just gone past when someone whispered his name.

"Thimblerig?"

He glanced around, but nobody was there. How many whispered voices would he hear on this journey?

"Of course it's him," a second whisper answered. "Who else would it be? Let's get to work!"

"Who's there?" Thimblerig called out, stepping back out and looking down the dark passageway to the left and the right.

"Bud, you best get back in here or you'll be left behind."

Thimblerig turned and found himself face to face with a black spider as big as his face, dangling down from the ceiling of the cavern by a strand of web.

"We got a job to do, and don't have much time," the spider said. She grabbed hold of another web that went off to the right and skipped off in that direction, joining the webs.

181

Thimblerig hopped back inside the passage and looked back to see whom this "we" was.

Thimblerig saw long-legged spiders, spiders with tiny legs, hairy spiders, all moving quickly, pirouetting back and forth from one side of the corridor to the other, building off each other's work, and fashioning a massive web across the entrance to their passageway.

Thimblerig had never seen spiders acting this way. It was like watching a dance as the spiders sailed back and forth, up and down across the corridor, crossing each other on their miniscule silk threads, moving with perfect timing, spinning their webs faster than he could watch.

"What's going on here?"

At the sound of Shi Lau's voice, Thimblerig turned to see that the company stood as a crowd, watching the spiders working their silky magic, covering the entrance to the passageway with a thick, impenetrable mess of webs from floor to ceiling. It wasn't pretty, looking like it had been there for ages. Dumbfounded, Thimblerig thought that it might just do the trick.

It was also finished in the nick of time as the sounds of the wild dogs grew suddenly louder as they came around a bend and ran into the fork, just as the company had several minutes earlier.

Thimblerig could just make out the wild dog's silhouettes through the web as they sniffed around the entrance to their corridor. He counted five or six, and assumed that there were others further back in the corridor. The rest of the pack was probably waiting at the entrance to the cave for some sort of signal.

"Their scent stops at the opening," one wild dog growled to the other.

"They couldn't have gone that way," the other replied, probably eyeing the web. "They must have figured out a way to mask their scent. Let's keep going or Blonger will have our heads."

The company sat still and quiet as the wild dogs took off down the left passageway, their barking and baying echoing down the cave as they ran. After a few moments they were far enough away that the animals could breathe again.

Thimblerig was about to make a comment about close calls when Big Bunco put her trunk up against his mouth. She pointed back at the webbed entrance and Thimblerig saw the shadow of a lone wild dog, apparently left behind as a precaution. The wild dogs were nothing if not cautious.

He was gesturing to the company to start moving further up the trail when he felt a tickle moving up his back. His heart leapt in his throat as he saw the long legs of a brown spider pulling itself up from his back onto his shoulder.

"The unicorn said you wouldn't mind if we hitched a ride," the spider said with a small raspy voice. Although Thimblerig would have traded every dried fig stored in his burrow to not have a spider clinging to his fur, after what the spider and his mates had just done for them, how could they refuse?

"Not a problem," he whispered, forcing down the impulse to fling his eight-legged passenger far away. He dropped down on all fours and made his way back up to the front of the company.

CHAPTER 22
THE ARK

The company continued hurrying along the passageway for another hour or so, being careful to avoid tumbling down as a group in the darkness. Fortunately, the tunnel was straight, and the glow continued to stay ahead of them, close enough to illuminate their path but far enough to remain just out of reach, until Thimblerig realized that the glow was getting brighter.

"It's the way out!" Shi Lau called excitedly, flapping his wings carefully, trying not to flick off any of the spiders sharing his spot on Elbridge's back. Now that they were nearly out of the tunnel, all of the animals were glad to feel the fresh breeze on their face. Thimblerig just hoped that they'd find an actual trail at the opening and not a sheer drop.

As it was, the cave opened up to a wide trail that appeared to be on the verge of washing away in the pouring rain. The storm had grown in intensity during their time in the mountain passage, but the dim brightness in the sky showed that morning was coming. The slight breeze they'd enjoyed down in the tunnel turned out to be stronger by a factor of ten when they were at the entrance to the cave. Still, they had no choice but continue out into the squall.

Their journey through the mountain had brought them to a very different landscape. There were trees here, even on the side of the mountain from which they emerged, and Thimblerig felt a little better knowing that they were coming back to a forest.

"What's that?" Soapy asked, pointing out into the storm.

At first, Thimblerig wasn't sure what the ape meant. All he could see was the driving rain and the mist rising from the ground. "I don't see anything," he said.

"Out there," Soapy continued gesturing, now with both hands. "At the bottom of the trail. I've never seen anything like it before."

184

"Why don't you hop down," Thimblerig said to the spider on his shoulder. The spider complied, shooting a web over to Mullins and sailing over. Thimblerig stepped out into the rain and focused out where Soapy pointed.

It was nearly impossible to see anything while being pelted by raindrops the size of figs and knocked about by gale force winds, but finally Thimblerig could barely make out a dark mass on the valley below. It was hard to tell, but it looked to be about as long as Victory Field, and was a dark brown color. It had to be the thing Tannier Isa had shown him in his vision! What had he called it?

"It's the ark," he remembered out loud. He felt such awe that the mysterious object from his vision was there in real life, just as the unicorn had shown him.

"What's an ark?" Shi Lau asked, flapping into the rain beside the groundhog. "What's it got to do with us?"

"It's our destination," he replied as patiently as he could. "It's the place of safety."

"We're with you, Thimblerig," Sheila said reassuring as usual, hopping out into the rain beside them. Grateful, Thimblerig smiled at the kangaroo. He'd so recently been certain that she was insane, but it turned out that she was the wisest of them all. Never wavering in her faith, either in him or the unicorn.

"Alright everyone, we're going to make a run for it," Thimblerig called out.

"What about the spiders?" Tabitha asked. "They'll be washed away in this mess."

"Under my ears," Pavel rumbled from the back. He stepped up and raised his palm-frond sized ears. "They'll be safe there."

Better you than me, Thimblerig thought as he watched the spiders climb off their current hosts and up the tree-trunk legs of the elephant. Pavel flinched as he watched them crawl up and across his chest on the way to the safety of his ears, but soon enough they settled in and the elephant nodded.

185

When they hit the wind and rain, the little animals hitching rides on the bigger animals had to grip their hosts with all their might to avoid being blown off. The trail, which led down towards the green valley, had streams of water running down, turning the flat rocks into slippery traps. Thimblerig kept one eye on the ark and the other on the trail to avoid slipping again. Once they reached level ground they looked to have a straight shot and he marveled that they were actually going to make it. What would they find when they got there? It was such a big ark that it couldn't just be for their small company of animals, so would there be other believers?

Other believers.

Somehow they'd become believers, all of them. Mullins, Soapy, Big Bunco, Thimblerig himself, they'd all started this journey thinking they were going to strike it rich. Now they had nothing, but they were going to escape the flood with everything, and it was all because of Tannier Isa.

Even so, he still couldn't figure out why they'd been chosen. It might have been understandable if they were the top cons of the forest, if they'd become notorious or gained reputations for cleverness or cunningness, but they were nothing special. Thimblerig, especially. The wild dogs had been right a few days ago. He was an utterly forgettable, low-ball grifter who – until now – could have stored all his life's winnings in the small hollow of a tiny tree.

But if there was one thing he'd come to understand about the unicorn, it was that he did things his own way and for his own reasons. Thimblerig was amazed that he'd gotten them this far, within sight of the vessel. It was too much to believe, and if he hadn't witnessed it with his own eyes…

Thimblerig slowed and came to a stop. Rising in front of them, stretching far to the left and to the right, was the ark. Greater and more imposing than in his dream, it was a giant wall of dark wood, made from the logs of trees, somehow fashioned and joined together in work more intricate and impressive than anything the apes – even with all of their building capabilities - could have managed. What kind of animal could build such a thing?

"Are we supposed to climb it?" Soapy yelled through the storm, gaping at the massive structure in front of him.

"I can't climb that thing," Pavel answered.

"I don't think any of us have to climb," Big Bunco replied, pointing to the left with her trunk. "Look!"

A hundred yards away a long wooden ramp led from the ground to an open doorway. To their surprise, animals of all kinds were moving up the ramp and entering the ark.

"It's what we were promised," Sheila said breathlessly. "It's the place of safety."

"And there are other animals!" said Tabitha.

"Lots of other animals," Mullins agreed, looking at the size of the ark.

"Including wild dogs," Thimblerig said, pointing out beyond the ramp.

The pack was there; dark smudges peppering the hillsides surrounding the ramp, watching. Even from this distance, their offensive posture was recognizable, and Thimblerig knew at once that the animals going up the ramp were in danger, and they didn't appear to know. There was no panic, no indication that anyone realized that the wild dogs were anywhere nearby. It wouldn't be a contest, and as soon as they made it into the ark, anyone inside would be massacred.

"We've got to do something," Thimblerig sighed.

Blonger was ecstatic. Here he'd been, hunting down a pawful of believers, getting angrier and more impatient with each passing moment as it appeared the believers had given him the slip, when they'd rounded a corner of the mountain passage to meet the shocking sight of hundreds of animals entering some sort of monstrous wooden structure.

187

If he had been the kind of animal to feel remorse, the leader might have been feeling that emotion now. After all, he had severely punished Kid Duffy for being wrong about the supposed "herds of believers" that were rendezvousing in the Edge, when it turned out he had been right. As it was, the leader was overwhelmed with the possibility of the prize that lay before him.

Glad that he had rallied all of the pack for the end of the hunt, Blonger stood and considered how they could quickly take control of the situation. Watching the animals making their way up the ramp he noticed a strange pattern; there were only two of each kind. He saw a pair of hippopotamuses, the flashing orange fur of a couple of foxes, two enormous lizards, and pairs of several other kinds of animals that he didn't recognize. Then a single particular animal caught his eye.

A large black and white striped tiger that Blonger didn't recognize stood statuesque in the pouring rain near the base of the ramp, eyeing the pairs of animals as they shuffled past, standing over them like some sort of protector. It was abnormal to see a predator acting in such a way, and the unnatural sight of it disgusted the wild dog.

"Enforcer!" he barked.

"I obey, dear leader," Lupo said, limping forward and bowing his head reverently. A bit too eager to please, perhaps? Blonger would teach him proper behavior after the battle, if his new enforcer survived.

"We're going to take the structure for the wild dogs. But first, we'll need to kill the tiger."

The rain fell all around them, lightning struck with increasingly frequency, the earth shook with the thunder that followed, and the leader of the wild dogs huddled together with his new enforcer and planned the attack that would end the unicorn believers once and for all.

CHAPTER 23
A SURPRISING ALLY

The company of animals was still too far away when the wild dogs attacked the animals near the ramp. All they could do was watch helplessly as a half dozen wild dogs leapt on the tiger at the same time. The black and white fur of the tiger disappeared behind the patch worked wild dogs, and the valley filled with the howls, barks, and roars of battle. The tiger managed to knock aside two and break the neck of another, squeezing the wild dog in its deadly jaws. But just as soon as one dog would be cleared away, two more would jump up to replace them.

A howl from Lupo brought in the second wave, and five more wild dogs jumped into the fray. The tiger crashed to the ground, overwhelmed by the number of wild dogs. Suddenly, Pavel burst into their midst, flinging dogs aside to the left and the right. Caught unaware, the wild dogs were quickly knocked aside, and so the bull elephant gingerly picked up the wounded tiger with his trunk and then lumbered up the ramp towards the entrance to the ark.

"Follow Pavel!" Thimblerig shouted to the others, taking advantage of the chaos. "To the ark!"

Following in the elephant's wake, the groundhog scurried, hopping over the writhing bodies of the downed wild dogs. The other members of the company were having an easier time of it than he was, but still they kept tight formation behind him. They just about made it to the base of the ramp when Thimblerig's paws hit a slippery patch of mud, and unable to avoid tripping over the leg of one of the downed wild dogs, he went airborne.

Thimblerig landed flat on his back and lay in the falling rain trying to get his breath back. Through the rain just to his right he could see the big shape of the elephant continuing up the ramp, but where were the others? Suddenly rough hands grabbed at him, and he was once more lifted back up to his feet.

Unable to speak, he gestured towards the ramp.

189

"You okay, 'Rig?" Soapy asked.

Thimblerig nodded in response, pointing impatiently back up at the ramp.

"Let's get moving!" Shi Lau cried. "What's the hold up?"

For once, Thimblerig agreed with the duck. He nodded, and was finally able to gasp out, "Move!"

They turned and started moving up the ramp, and had ascended halfway only to find the path blocked by a single wild dog. "Ah, you must be Kid Duffy's elusive, missing believers," Blonger said, with calm voice and burning eyes.

Time stood still, and Thimblerig's paws were trembling as he stood before the most powerful animal in the forest, the one who was to blame for all of the difficulties they'd been facing. This was the one who was answerable for the terror they'd experienced over the past couple of days, for the terror the forest had faced for years. And now as they stood just a few steps away from their goal, he stood in the way again? He was sick of the feelings the name brought up; the memories of dead animals who he'd liked and even loved, the anxiety of the wild dog's secret police, the humiliation of the extortion, bribes, and pay-offs. All because of the so-called leadership of the dog blocking their path, trying to keep them from being where Tannier Isa wanted them to be.

Tannier Isa.

Thimblerig felt a burst of new confidence at the thought of the unicorn, the one who had chosen *him* to save these animals. Not Blonger, the most powerful animal in the forest. The unicorn had chosen a no-name nothing con artist of a groundhog with no unique qualities, when he could have chosen the leader of the entire forest.

But why?

As he stared at the proud and arrogant leader of the wild dogs, the reason for the unicorn's choice became as clear as an untouched water hole in clear bright summer sun.

The one Tannier Isa had chosen was the one who would have no choice but to trust him.

But trust him with what? Had he been chosen for this very moment? He certainly hadn't shown any unique abilities leading the animals to this point. It made sense, that he would be able to do something different here. But what? Talk his way out of it, maybe? That was perhaps his only evident skill. And so as fearful as he was, he took a deep breath, prayed that the unicorn would be with him, and stepped forward with the confidence of a grifter playing long odds.

"Blonger! You need to let us pass!"

The leader of the wild dogs arched a single eyebrow before speaking. "A command? I usually get a lot of whimpering, begging, and crying. It's almost a refreshing tactic."

"That's the unicorn for you, doing the unexpected," Thimblerig answered, with more confidence than he felt. "Take this storm for instance. It's not just any storm."

"Is that so?" the leader asked, smiling joylessly.

"Thimblerig, we need to get onboard," Mullins said quietly, eyes on the clouds above. "There's not much time…"

"This place, the forest, everything is about to get washed away," Thimblerig continued. "I've seen it with my own eyes, and nothing will survive when the waters come. And I mean nothing. The ark behind you is the only thing that will save any of us, and that includes you and your pack."

"Thimblerig!" Big Bunco cried. "What are you doing?"

"Shush," Sheila whispered.

"'Everyone's welcome', remember, Bunco? That includes the pack, if they'll do things his way." Thimblerig answered, keeping his eyes on the leader.

"You're right about one thing, groundhog," Blonger said without emotion. "I am welcome to the structure behind me. My pack will see to it."

"Thimblerig?" Mullins said. "You need to see this."

191

Turning, Thimblerig saw that the pack had recovered from the elephant's assault and had regrouped behind the company of animals at the base of the ramp. Even in the downpour he could see that there were too many of them.

"Where you're wrong," Blonger continued. "Is thinking I have to agree to do things your way."

"Not my way," Thimblerig said, turning back to face the leader. "His way."

"Right. The unicorn king," Blonger replied, nodding. "Of course you are talking about the mythological protector of the forest, who you believe in so desperately, who hasn't been seen in the forest in several lifetimes."

"I've seen him, Blonger."

Thimblerig looked past the leader and was shocked by the animal he saw standing at the top of the ramp in the cold rain: Kid Duffy, the enforcer, tall and proud, not the least bit daunted by the leader of the wild dogs.

Even more caught off guard, it was all Blonger could do to sputter, "It's can't be…"

"Yeah, I know. Crazy, isn't it?" Kid Duffy replied, loping down the ramp at a relaxed pace. "Considering how you and the boys left me for dead back on the rock, and now here I am, fit as a fig. All thanks to Tannier Isa. He came to me after you nearly killed me and fixed me up with that horn of his. Said I should have been following the groundhog as my leader, and not you."

As Kid Duffy talked, the leader's breathing grew heavier and heavier. He was not taking the news well.

"The unicorn saved me and brought me here. This groundhog, the animals here, the ones in the ark, they're my pack now." The former enforcer walked past his former boss and stood behind Thimblerig.

"Duffy," the leader growled menacingly. "Listen carefully to me…"

"What's it going to be, boss?" the former enforcer interrupted once again, deep gravely voice dripping with danger and challenge. "Not that you were ever good at listening to anyone's advice, but I'd suggest you back down."

Through the pouring rain, Thimblerig looked past Blonger to the entrance of the ark where he saw the dim shapes of other animals starting to come out onto the ramp. How many were inside?

His thoughts were interrupted when a savagely barked order from Blonger came; an order that Thimblerig had been dreading, but expecting.

"Wild dogs! Attack!"

CHAPTER 24
THE BATTLE FOR THE ARK

Thimblerig jumped out of the way as the leader of the wild dogs lunged at Kid Duffy, a blur of sharp teeth and burning hatred. He twisted around to find his company surrounded by wild dogs, but the events of the past few days had changed this little group of animals much in the way that it had changed the groundhog, and rather than cower in fear, they quickly formed a circle facing outward towards the enemy.

With a fierce cry that shocked the groundhog, Sheila leapt up towards the closest wild dog, pummeling it with a steady stream of kicks from her right foot. This move emboldened the other animals, and Tabitha and Mullins charged another wild dog simultaneously, head down and horns out, forcing the wild dog over the side of the ramp to the wet ground below.

The other animals attacked in their own way, with Elbridge taking a bite out of a wild dog on one end while kicking another two with his powerful hind legs on the other. Shi Lau was helping create general pandemonium by finally flying, buzzing the wild dogs from the air and keeping them off balance while the llamas and the saiga antelope head-butted them, knocking them down or over the edge of the ramp.

"Sheila!" Thimblerig called out. "Get to the ark!" The kangaroo landed a final haymaker on a wild dog and then leapt higher than the groundhog dreamed she was able over the heads of several wild dogs to the other members of the company. They formed a cluster and began pushing and shoving their way up the wooden ramp towards the entrance.

Turning his attention to the conflict raging around him, Thimblerig was stunned by the range of animals having come out of the ark now fighting against the wild dogs. There were bigger animals, including pairs of hippopotamuses and hefty brown bears, and Pavel was in the mix as well, having dropped off the tiger inside the ark and come back out to join the fray. But there were also smaller animals fighting ferociously, including a couple of crocodiles, a vicious badger, and several sheep.

And the animals kept pouring from the ark, overwhelming the wild dogs by using their normal strategy against them. Wild dogs were being tossed over the ramp by apes, knocked off by charging bulls, and drenched and blown about by the rains and winds from above.

For the first time in a long time, Thimblerig started to feel hopeful that they might just make it out of this after all. Once the animals from the ark had cleaned the wild dogs from the ramp, they could all go inside, where they would be safe from enemies and the flood. He just hoped that this real ark was as good on the water as the one in his dream. Thimblerig was about to turn and make his own way up the ramp into the ark when the sound of a lone wild dog's howl cut through the uproar of the conflict.

Thimblerig stopped and turned back to see a brutal struggle going on between Kid Duffy and Blonger, with each dog lunging and snapping sharp teeth with the singular goal of ending the life of the other.

Out of the rainy mists, another wild dog appeared before Kid Duffy and drove him back to the ground. The distraction was what the leader needed to get the momentum and put Kid Duffy down.

The leader wasted no time howling the order for the rest of his army to join the fight. He wasn't a fool, and he'd held back the larger portion of the pack just in case they encountered too much resistance. The force on the ramp was being overwhelmed, but with the help of his reinforcements, he would take ramp, the doorway, and the ark.

In the darkness and rain and madness of the battle, the leader didn't notice the little ball of brown fur barreling toward him down the ramp. Using the angle of the descending ramp to help him build speed and momentum, Thimblerig ran square into the leader's side, just as he'd done to Kid Duffy before, and drove him off the ramp into the puddles and slop of the muddy ground in the rainy darkness below. Unfortunately, the groundhog's momentum carried him over the side as well, and the fall was great enough that Thimblerig should have broken something, but he was mercifully spared injury by the pool of water in which he landed.

The enraged leader recovered quickly and was up in an instant, yanking the groundhog out of the water by grabbing him in his clenched jaws and shoving him up against a rock above the pool just under the shelter of the ramp. "I've had enough of you, you filthy digger!" he screamed at the disoriented groundhog, dropping his typical controlled façade.

Thimblerig could hear the Blonger's voice but he couldn't connect the words. Had he done it? Finished the job? Had the others made it onboard? He'd done his best, and hoped that it was enough to seal the deal.

"Are you listening to me?" the leader growled, pushing his bloody, rain-drenched face close to the groundhog's, forcing Thimblerig to focus on him. "This is all your fault! Now I'm going to enjoy killing you, and eating your heart while you watch. Your worst nightmare is standing in front of you, groundhog."

It started out as a small chuckle that the leader mistook for sniveling, and while Thimblerig did his best to try and stifle it, he finally couldn't stop himself and he started laughing harder than he'd laughed in ages. "I'm sorry," Thimblerig said as he saw the look of disbelief on the wild dog's face, his tears of laughter mingling with the falling rain. "But you think you're my worst nightmare?"

Blonger's face contorted in such a way that he hardly looked like a dog any longer. He was obviously not used to being laughed at, or possibly not used to the sound of laughter at all. Having accepted that he would not survive this encounter, Thimblerig still chuckled as he sat in the mud waiting for the end.

The evil look washed off the wild dog's face as he glared at the groundhog and regained control. He nodded in understanding and waded out past the groundhog, out from under

196

the covering of the ramp into the pouring rain. The water was growing deeper with each passing moment, but the leader hardly noticed. He was looking out at the battle as he spoke.

"That *is* funny, groundhog. And it makes me realize that I need to put off killing you until after you've learned your place. First, I think I'll arrange for you to have a front row seat as I execute all of your friends in that monstrosity above us."

Thimblerig wondered what game the wild dog was playing now. He'd seen what was happening on the ramp, that the animals from within the ark were sweeping the wild dogs away like his groundmother used to sweep the dirt out of the burrow.

"Your pack's losing," he said. "The ark is safe."

"You mean what was just happening up there just now? That wasn't my pack. That was just the advance guard. My pack's arriving now. Come see."

Thimblerig's heart grew cold as he became aware of the bays and cries he could hear now coming from beyond the ramp. He stepped out into the waters beside the leader and saw a howling mass of black heading towards the ramp.

"There must be hundreds…" he muttered.

"Oh yes. That's my pack. They'll quickly overwhelm the pitiful force on the ramp then the animals inside will be mine."

Their conversation was interrupted by a wild dog slamming into the ground just to their left, hurled off the ramp above. Thimblerig looked up the side of the ramp above and could just see Pavel's as he fought against some wild dogs.

At the same time, the earth shook with a rumble that was louder and much more violent than the battle being waged above. Thimblerig had been through an actual earthquake once before, but it had lasted only a few seconds, while this shaking went on and on. The earth lunged violently beneath him, and then a massive column of water erupted vertically from the ground, not twenty feet from where he stood. Water and stone debris spewed from deep within the earth out into the rain-soaked sky. A heartbeat later, another explosion blew out a cliff wall above the

197

ark to the left, showering them with more debris, and releasing another violent column of water that gushed out horizontally, washing away everything in its path, including the left flank of the advancing pack of wild dogs.

Blonger watched the destruction intently, stunned by the unexpected loss of such a large portion of his forces so quickly. The groundhog dropped in the water to try and dart away, but the leader whipped around and grabbed him in his jaws, slammed him up against a rock outcrop and held him fast.

From where he was held, Thimblerig could see several of the animals staring wide-eyed at the destruction happening around them. Even at a distance of several feet in the darkness and the pouring rain Thimblerig could see Pavel, eyes open wide, and the groundhog knew exactly what Pavel was thinking, because he was thinking it too.

"Tannier Isa, help us," he muttered.

And then he was forced to watch helplessly as the remaining forces of the wild dog army reached the base of the ramp and the battle for the ark started once again.

CHAPTER 25
THE MOUND OF DRY BONES

Meanwhile, while the battle raged, over the mountains, across the steppe, and through the forest, Benny the wild dog patrolled the perimeter of Victory field more miserable than ever before. His mishap with Kid Duffy while chasing the trespassers had cost him dearly. Now he was cut out of the hunt, the only wild dog left behind. Even patrolling Asarata would have been better than this job tonight, what with the nonstop deluge of rain that had long ago washed away the last ounce of any sort of good mood that Benny might have been retaining.

'Patrolled' would be a fairly liberal description of Benny's current activity, which consisted of lying under the widest leaves he could find in an attempt to stay out of the rain. The problem was that puddles were everywhere, growing deeper every moment, and there was no high ground anywhere except the mound in the middle of the field.

Benny grumbled and cursed at Kid Duffy for forcing him to walk this beat again and miss out on the hunt. He was cold, wet, and hungry, and didn't even have a bone to gnaw on.

"A bone?" he said to the wind and the rain, as a crazy idea came to his mind. Just past the bushes and trees in which he lay was the mound of Victory Field. Why was it a mound? Because the wild dogs had completely annihilated a herd of unicorns on that very spot, leaving their bodies to decay as a monument.

Decayed bodies means bones, he thought, slowly rising to all four paws. *Bones are good for gnawing.*

Benny considered it for a moment, and then plopped back to the wet ground angrily. Was he so desperate that he would consider gnawing on bones that old? Not to mention that it was against Blonger's laws for anyone to be on the mound, even wild dogs. Hidden down deeply was a more frightening reason he didn't act on the impulse, and that was the rumors that the mound was haunted.

"But the mound is not going to be collecting water like this," he said as he splashed the water pooling around him, pushing the ridiculous idea of ghosts out of his mind. "How can I be expected to guard this place if I can hardly even walk through the water? If I was up on the mound, I could see the whole perimeter from one spot, and I could do a better job."

Besides, the pack would be gone until at least the morning. They would never try to return in a storm like this at night, not to mention that they'd be busy celebrating their victory over the prey. He immediately felt even more resentful as he considered the fresh meat that all of his brothers and sisters would be enjoying while he was out in the middle of this muck, starving to death, unappreciated and forgotten.

"It just makes good sense that I get a better view," he said to the rain and the leaves. "And if I happened to see a bone or two while I was up there, then what's the harm? We beat them, didn't we? They won't be needing those bones any more."

Having made up his mind, and before he could talk himself out of it, Benny stepped into the field and started trotting towards the center and the mound, his stomach growling at him to continue and to find something to chew on to help get through the night.

The field was filled with mist, which made it difficult for Benny to keep his bearings straight. Continually looking forward, Benny knew that he just needed to keep heading in a straight line and he'd eventually come across the...

Benny came to an abrupt halt. He'd seen something up ahead, hadn't he? It was light, but not lightning. If the mound were ahead, then the top of the mound would have been glowing.

"You've gone without food for too long," Benny said to himself. He started moving again until he reached the base of the mound, and he sniffed around to see if he could find a tibia or a fibula sticking out, but there was nothing. Of course there wouldn't be, because too much time had passed, and bones wouldn't just be lying around. He might have to dig a bit once he got up top. He began climbing the mound, picking his way carefully to avoid slipping and falling. Seeing water pouring down the sides of convinced him that he'd made the right choice to try and make it to the top. Even if he were still getting wet from the rain, at least up top he wouldn't have to lie in puddles. There were no more strange lights, nothing to prevent him from making it to the top of the mound where he could dig around and find a bone or two, and park it until morning. He'd be down at daybreak, and nobody would ever be the wiser.

Reaching the top, Benny started digging in the soaking wet grass and the sticky mud, Benny couldn't help but think that with ideas like this he should be higher up the chain in the pack. The other idiots would still be down below shivering and starving, but only someone with his ability to think creatively would have had this idea and the nerve to act upon it.

Striking something hard, he kept digging around, pulling out as much water as he pulled out dirt. The pouring rain made the job that much easier, eroding the dirt faster than he could dig it, and finally he saw something gleaming in the darkness. It took him a few moments to free his prize, and before he knew it he had a slightly decayed unicorn bone to gnaw upon.

Satisfied, he settled down in the wet grass at the top of the mound, and began chewing. Perhaps it was the relaxing sound of the rainfall, or the busy events of the day catching up with him mingled with the comforting sensation of having something to chew on, but Benny nodded off. He didn't even realize he'd fallen asleep until he woke up with someone tugging at the bone in his jaws. He opened his eyes and glanced around the mound top, but nobody was there. Who had been tugging on his prize?

The unicorn bone had slipped out of his mouth, and again he chomped on it and shifted around trying to get comfortable again. He'd just found a decent way to lie when the bone was yanked clear from his mouth, nearly taking out some of his more important teeth in the process.

In a flash the wild dog was on his feet, growling, looking for the animal responsible. There was still nobody there, and his prize lay on the ground in front of him.

And it was wiggling.

The memory of those old dog stories came rushing into his mind and even though he was soaking wet, the hairs on his back started standing up. The stories couldn't be true, because there were no such thing as ghosts. But the bone at his feet started pulling itself across the grass and down the lip of the mound top, where it disappeared from sight. He felt something bumping against his back foot and looked down to see another bone sticking halfway out of the ground, knocking against his foot as if he was in the way. He moved his leg and the bone pulled itself out of the ground and dragged in front of the wild dog and also disappeared down the hill.

Legs shaking, Benny carefully approached the edge of the mound top and looked over the side. It was difficult to see much in the darkness and pouring rain, but in the moments of vision granted by flashes of lightning the hill looked like it was alive. Bones were pulling themselves out from all the sides, digging their way out and dragging themselves down towards the field below, some tumbling down the hill as if trying to reach the ground.

Mouth open in horror, whining involuntarily, Benny was rooted to the spot as he watched bones of all sorts coming from everywhere now, passing him without notice on their way down to the level ground.

Suddenly even more uncomfortable, a sixth sense told the wild dog that he was being watched. But by who? Nobody from the ground could see on top of the mound in this weather. He turned to the right to find himself face to face with the intact skull of a unicorn. It was covered in mud as if having just pulled itself from the ground, it was sitting upright, with empty eye sockets that stared straight at him, and the sharp, pointed horn aimed right at his heart. The horn was glowing with an inner golden light and with such intensity and purity that it immediately hurt the wild dog's eyes to look at.

Benny began to whimper, and in response, the skull started to shake. It wrenched itself from the mud, and plunged straight towards the wild dog. Benny pushed back to avoid the killing blow from the skull's horn, and in the process tipped over the edge of the mound and tumbled down to the field below. He crashed into the bones that were moving from the mound and struggled to find a way to stand. Slipping and sliding over the wet muddy bones as they progressed across the field, he was carried along with them until he was finally dumped off to the side. He saw more skulls, all with glowing horns, and many that looked his way, but he was mostly ignored.

Jumping up and scurrying behind a tree at the edge of the field, Benny saw that the bones weren't moving randomly, but were arranging themselves across the field, joining together until they began to take the shapes of the bodies to which they'd belonged. Fully formed unicorn skeletons of all sizes came together bone by bone, one at a time, until dozens of skeletons stood together, pawing the ground, rearing up on hind legs, nuzzling one another as a living animal might to an old friend.

Benny was numb with fear. This was something no wild dog – no animal - had ever seen before, and it was something that he shouldn't be seeing now. Just when he thought that the sight couldn't be any more terrible, something started growing inside the skeletons. One moved close by, and he could see the animal's heart, lungs, intestines, growing inside the ribcage, sprouting out like flowers. At the same time, a thin membrane began to grow over the unicorn's body, starting at unicorn's feet and stretching out over the ribcage, up the spine, and around the skull. It was translucent at first, and Benny saw blood starting to flow from the heart, out through the veins and around the body, but the membrane quickly lost its transparency and became naked skin. White hair sprouted out of the unicorn's rump into a tail, and up along the neck into a mane, and finally across the entire body of the unicorn. Finally, the unicorn blinked, shook his head as if just waking up, and galloped off with a whiny to join the others.

Benny couldn't believe what he was seeing; a field now full of living and breathing unicorns of all sizes and colors. They were pawing around each other, continuing the nuzzling that they'd started when just skeletons. He was terrified, knowing that he would end up on the end of their horns if they knew that he was there, and so the wild dog sat hidden as still as he could, hoping that they would leave him be. The dark sky was suddenly and briefly illuminated, which quieted the unicorns. All of the unicorns were facing away from his location looking towards something bright in the distance, but the wild dog couldn't see the object of their attention. The unicorns were quite enthusiastic about whatever was happening, and they started snorting, pawing the earth, and whinnying with such volume that Benny wanted to stick his head down into the mud to avoid having to listen to it.

The horns of the unicorns all started to glimmer and crackle as if they each held bolts of lightning. Suddenly, with a rush of power and energy, the herd leapt away into the night leaving Benny huddling alone in the darkness and rain and mud.

Fearfully, the lone wild dog guard stepped out from behind the tree and watched the lights of the unicorns fade as they moved farther away, grateful for the first time that he'd been given this assignment, and relieved that he wasn't going to be wherever it was that the unicorn herd was headed.

And just when he started to relax, the earth began to shake.

CHAPTER 26
FLOOD

Mullins and the others were experiencing pure chaos as they made their way to the entrance of the ark. It hadn't been such a long way when they'd first stood at the bottom, and under normal circumstances, the walk would probably just take a matter of moments, but with wild dogs lunging at them from all sides, time stood still. It didn't help matters that the storm also exploded around them at the same time. With all kinds of animals dashing past them running down the ramp to engage in the battle, and the wild dogs trying to force their way up the ramp, reality had taken a holiday.

He wasn't sure how, but he and the others somehow managed to make it up to the entrance, which towered over them as they ran across the wooden threshold. Lamps were burning just inside the entrance, illuminating the interior, and an ostrich was barking orders to anyone who would listen.

"Marsupials and pachyderms to the left lower quarters, fowl and gazelles to the right…"

Ignoring her, the company of animals paused to make certain they'd all made it, doing their best to ignore the jostling as the occasional quake shifted the ark. Soapy took a head count, and realized someone besides Pavel was missing. They were looking back and forth, trying to re-count, when it hit Mullins who wasn't with them.

"Thimblerig!" he called. "Where's Thimblerig?"

The others looked around but in the crowded entrance it was impossible to tell if a small groundhog was skittering about in their midst.

"I'm sure he made it," Big Bunco said. "He always makes it."

"I'm not so sure," Kuandyk replied. "I saw him turn back towards the battle."

"We have to go back out and look for him," Mullins said.

205

"Back out into that?" Shi Lau squawked, gesturing outside where flashes of lightning illuminated the furious battle that continued to rage. "Are you insane?"

"He's our friend," the kangaroo said, stepping up beside Mullins. "I'm going to try, even if nobody else will."

"Let's go find him," Mullins said.

"Forget it! I'm not going back out there!" Shi Lau said stubbornly, the lone holdout. "What's the use of getting here if we just get killed going back out? No. I'm staying put."

"Oh be quiet, Shi Lau!" Elbridge shouted, shaking his hump forcefully so that the duck came flying off. The camel shoved the duck up against the ark wall with his head. "He could have left all of us to die and he came back for us. We're going to do the same for him. All of us."

Everyone was momentarily quiet and Shi Lau looked too stunned to speak, but finally finding his voice, he threw up his wings in defeat. "Hey! I was just playing devils advocate! Of course I'm going!"

"If we die, we die together," Tabitha agreed, stepping beside Mullins. "We're going after him."

Mullins turned and looked at the amazing creature standing beside him. He wanted to express all of his feelings to her, but his tongue swelled in his mouth, rendering him mute. He just needed one quiet moment to tell her…

Before anyone could say anything more, a she-lion rushed in through the open doorway, breathless and bleeding. "What are you all doing crowding here? The others are coming and we've got to get the door closed!"

Sure enough the doorway quickly filled with animals rushing in, and Mullins was pushed farther away from the doorway. "Wait!" He cried, trying to get anyone to pay attention. "We have to get out!"

"Get out?" the she-lion roared. "There's no time!"

"Nobody's going out," a hawk said, swooping in. "The unicorns are closing the doors."

Reaching to this news, Mullins and Tabitha squeezed their way through to the open doorway. They looked out into the storm and were stunned to see the dark stormy sky filled with golden lights darting to and fro, lighting up the storm much like the fireflies had lit up the darkness a couple of nights before. They were zipping around the ark, leaving tails of light behind, knocking the wild dogs away into the waters below the ramp. A wild dog emerged from the gloom, and charged the doorway. Immediately, one of the lights tore by, and Mullins saw the dim outline of a stallion slam into the wild dog, sending him careening off the ramp into the darkness below.

"Unicorns!" he exclaimed.

They were everywhere! Guarding the ramp, chasing the wild dogs away, standing in the open air on either side of the doorway...

On either side?

"They're going to close the doors," he said. "We've got to stop them!" The gazelle leaned out as far as he dared since the ramp had been pushed back, careful not to look down into the darkness below. "Wait! Don't close it yet! Thimblerig's still out there!"

But still the doors continued coming together, threatening to shut out the storm, the violence of the wild dogs, and Thimblerig.

"You can't just leave him! He saved us!" he cried at the unicorns, who paid him no mind. "Tannier Isa chose him! He has to save Thimblerig!"

"Mullins, look!" Tabitha cried. He glanced up and saw that the gazelle's attention was out in the storm. He followed her line of sight and saw all of the golden lights sailing together, converging on a single spot high above the ground. As they came together, the single light they made flashed brightly, nearly blinding the gazelle.

Then he heard a whisper.

"Gather your friends, Mullins, and follow me."

207

Several things happened at once to Thimblerig. First, Blonger let go of the groundhog's neck when the golden lights arrived. Second, the water rose so quickly that it threatened to overwhelm them both, and so he used the leader's loss of attention to pull away and grab at a tree that had been uprooted by the torrent. He clutched the biggest branch he could find, holding on as tight as he was able as he was swept away. At the same time, underground rivers burst through the walls of the mountain above, breaking it completely apart and sending it tumbling down below. Mammoth chunks of rock dumped into the waters and created a wave that drove straight towards the ark. The thundering wave slammed into Thimblerig's tree and holding on with every ounce of his strength, he rode as it swept along the side of the ark and finally out into the dark unknown.

Being caught in the raging, churning, heaving violence of the flood was beyond anything Thimblerig imagined he'd be able to endure. As he clung to the log with all his might, eyes shut tight in an effort to keep out the water; he understood that this was the way he was going to die. He could hear the trees smashing into each other, exploding into bits as they were slammed with the unbelievable force of the driving waves, and he wondered how long it would be until his own ride was pulverized. Then he heard growling.

Forcing one eye open to scan the immediate area, he instantly wished he had kept that one eye shut. The waves undulated angrily and the rain was falling so hard that it stung, leaving him no choice but to chance letting go of the tree with one paw and using it to shield against the rain so he could try and see what he'd heard.

And he saw him. Blonger was only a few feet away, somehow also hanging onto the same log that he was grasping. The leader was growling and glaring hatefully at the groundhog across the divide.

"This is your fault, groundhog!" the leader of the wild dogs screamed as their eyes met, and he began pulling himself over the branches towards Thimblerig.

The makeshift raft shifted with the wild dog's movement as it barreled along with the flooding rains, and this did nothing to help Thimblerig as the branch to which he was clinging was pulled up and over. He somehow managed to keep hold, but just barely. The shifting also nearly uprooted the wild dog, and he stopped moving momentarily.

"Don't move!" Thimblerig sputtered through the water. "You're going to kill us both!"

"Only you," Blonger responded, dragging himself forward again.

Thimblerig knew that his time was nearly over. If he let go, he'd be swept off into the maelstrom and never survive. If he held on, the wild dog would live up to his word and rip out his throat if they didn't crash into a huge rock and both die first. Strangely, the groundhog wasn't afraid, and he had an unexpected sense of peace. His job had been to get the company – his friends – safely there, and he'd done that. Now he had one more job to do to make sure they remained safe: Either talk the wild dog down or make sure he didn't survive the storm.

"It doesn't have to be this way," Thimblerig entreated, battling the wind and waves. "The unicorn," he sputtered. "He can still save you!"

Thimblerig couldn't fathom how the wild dog could possibly laugh in the middle of a world-ending flood, but laugh he did; a pathetic mocking laugh that was only cut off when the waves dunked them into the rushing water. The force nearly dragged Thimblerig from the branch and with the tree twisting and turning in the current he was barely able to pull his head back out of the water.

One thing was clear; he had to keep Blonger talking, as difficult as it was. The more he talked, the farther away the raging waters would carry them, and his friends would have more of a chance of staying alive. He had to run one last con, and give the wild dog what he wanted.

"Wait! No! It was all a lie!" he cried. "They paid me to bring them!"

The leader ignored Thimblerig's cries, continuing to drag himself across the branches, murder in his eyes.

"But I got greedy..." he continued. It was difficult to talk without filling his mouth with water, but Thimblerig persisted. "One thousand figs... back at Asarata... they're all yours if you don't kill me!"

Ignoring his pleas, Blonger lunged the final couple of feet, sinking his teeth deep into Thimblerig's shoulder, squeezing his jaws tighter and tighter. Thimblerig cried out, the pain unlike anything he had experienced, and the tears started to flow, once again mixing with the rain, his own blood, and the waters.

Blonger released him. "You offer me figs for your life? I don't need figs, groundhog. What I need is you, dead." And then he bit into Thimblerig's other shoulder, tearing into the groundhog's flesh down to the bone.

Thimblerig screamed out again, the pain threatening to overwhelm him, and things began to grow dark and numb.

In his numbness, Thimblerig saw the unicorn running through the fog, sensed his strength and power, felt the kindness and compassion reflected in those deep, black eyes. It was his imagination, but even the idea of the unicorn made him feel like he was covered with warm furs. In spite of the driving rain, the heaving waters, the violence of the wild dogs, the pain radiating from his shoulders, in spite of everything – he felt peace.

The tree shuddered as if it had become jammed in between some rocks, followed by a flash of brown screaming by. Blonger's hold on Thimblerig was released and the groundhog breathed deeply, wincing from the pain, fading into the welcome darkness. He thought he saw something standing over Blonger, thought he saw Blonger suddenly pulled away, but the rain

210

mixing with his tears made it hard to see. Was it Tannier Isa? Had he come to save him?

"Hang on, Thimblerig!"

A pair of strong arms locked around his waist and pulled him up out of the water. He looked up into the simian face of the last animal he expected to see in the middle of a flood while clinging to a tree.

"Soapy?" he stammered.

"Hang tight, bud. We'll get you out of here."

The ape looked back over his shoulder and shouted, "Pavel! You got it?"

Thimblerig glanced over and saw that the bull elephant was also standing in the water, grasping the tree with his trunk, keeping it from moving. This didn't seem strange to the groundhog until it occurred to him that they were all in the middle of a deep, raging, forest-ending flood.

"How is he - " he started, but he was interrupted by growls coming from Blonger on the other side. When he looked in that direction, he was surprised to see Mullins and Tabitha standing on the water at the other end of the tree. Blonger was below them, gripping with his front legs onto a branch helplessly as the pair of gazelles stood over him. They were quite oblivious to the fact that they should be sinking and drowning as the water rushed past them. What was going on?

"Alright then, 'Rig, just take it easy," Soapy said, gingerly pulled Thimblerig up, mindful of his injuries. "Sheila! You're up!"

There was the sound of rhythmic splashes, as if someone were skipping through a puddle of rain, then Thimblerig was lowered into a warm place. Sheila's pouch? He felt like he could lose himself in the warmth of it, but Shi Lau's voice brought him back.

"We've got to get going! The ship's sailing and we don't want to miss it!" And there was Shi Lau, flying circles around them all, looking back at something Thimblerig couldn't see. The

211

duck is flying? That seemed almost more unbelievable than the company of animals somehow walking on the water. This must be another dream, Thimblerig sighed contentedly as the duck glanced down at him and winked, then disappeared from view.

Things were quickly growing hazy and out of focus. He vaguely heard Soapy tell Pavel to let go of the tree, believed he heard Blonger crying out in anger and fear, had the distinct impression of a black stallion with a single flaming golden horn running along beside them all, and then he saw and heard nothing.

CHAPTER 27
THE THIN PLACE

It was dark. Not the kind of darkness you have when you sleep at night, where you can make out shapes, or where the ambient light helps you see bits and pieces of things. It was dark, so absolutely dark that Thimblerig couldn't tell up from down or left from right. Had he died, and this was what came after? Would he spend eternity in the darkness? As hard as he strained his eyes, it was useless, and he couldn't tell a thing about where he was.

"Hello?" he called. "Is anyone here?"

His words echoed in the silence.

"Are you serious?" he asked out loud, somewhat comforted by the sound of his own voice. "This is the forest beyond? I thought there was supposed to be trees and green rolling fields! But I'm alone with a whole bunch of dark nothing?"

As if being switched on one by one, his other senses began imputing information. It felt like he was sitting on a comfortable pile of grass. The air smelled earthy, and he noted the tangy scent of bran berry root. Fuzzy shapes started to materialize as his eyes adjusted to his new surroundings, and then he knew where he was. He was underground, in a burrow. It looked like his groundmother's burrow. But how could it be?

"When did you become so particular about being by yourself?" His groundmother's raspy voice said. "I thought you were proud of being a loner."

"It's a recent thing," he replied, smiling. And then there she was, just as he remembered her, eyes twinkling, gnawing on her branburry root, sitting cozily beside him on the bed of grasses.

His groundmother. The one who had raised him from a cub. The one who had been there in his time of greatest need, and never asked anything in return. The one he'd abandoned in her time of greatest need. He lowered his head.

213

"You done good, cub," she said, prodding his shoulder with the end of the root. He flinched involuntarily, the fuzzy memory of Blonger's attack coming back to him. But there was no pain. He touched his left shoulder, than his right, and saw that there were no wounds or scars.

"Oh, you're fine," she said. "Old wounds don't matter much here."

"Where are we?" he asked, looking around, amazed at how real it all was.

"Where does it look like we are? Go on, take a look around."

Standing cautiously, expecting pain or soreness but experiencing none, Thimblerig examined the room. Light streamed in from the three skylight tunnels like noon on a sunny day. There were rows of roots and nuts kept neatly on the rock shelves dug out by the entrance passageway. Beside the shelves, he noticed some simple drawings made on the wall. He bent over to examine them and saw that there was a picture of a stick figure groundhog cub holding hands with a bigger groundhog, another crude drawing of that cub and a bear, and finally a cub's drawing of unicorn.

"I drew these," he said.

"Mmm-hmm," she nodded. "You were so little you barely came up to my neck."

He glanced back over to the bed of grasses, on which his groundmother sat, smiling up at him.

"It's your burrow," he murmured. "How's that possible?"

"My burrow, eh?" she asked, glancing around. "Yes, I suppose it looks like it."

"Looks like it?"

"It is my burrow, but it's not. This is what they call a thin place," she said, trying to stand. Thimblerig scurried over and gave her a hand up. "It's not quite the forest you grew up in, and not quite the forest to come." She shuffled over to the root shelf as if looking for something, and then finally finding it, she put down her Burberry root and picked up a different one. She inspected it and smiled. "Mmm, ginger. I always loved ginger."

"How can you be here?" Thimblerig asked, stepping up to her. "You... I mean, you're..." he couldn't bring himself to say the word.

"Still as beautiful as the day I met your groundfather?" she asked playfully.

"No. I mean, yes, of course..." he stopped and took a deep breath. "No offense, groundmother, but you... died," he finally got out.

"How would that offend me? Everyone dies, you know," she laughed. "But to answer your bigger question, it was his idea." She shuffled back to her grassy bed, ginger in hand.

"Tannier Isa?"

She nodded, lowering herself back down on the grass. "He'd have met you himself, but he's a little busy right now, you understand. But he had some things he wanted you to know before you go back. He figured it might be a good idea if I had a little talk with you in a quiet spot. In the calm before the storm, so to speak."

Thimblerig collapsed on the bed beside his groundmother, unable to believe what he was hearing. "Go back?" he asked. "I'm not dead, too?"

She laughed, leaning back against the burrow wall. "You? Dead? No, cub, you're not dead. In fact, you've never been more alive, and the unicorn's not about to waste that."

He sat back, too. The walls of the burrow were cold and damp, and things had started to spin around. He felt dizzy and a little bit nauseous. How could he still be alive after everything that happened in the flood? What was he being sent back to? What could be left?

"You did well with the job he gave you, Thimblerig, even if you did have a rough start. Now, the unicorn has more for you to do."

"More to do?" Thimblerig asked. "Isn't everything gone?"

"Not everything," she answered, arching an eyebrow. "Don't you remember?"

It was like trying to remember a dream that had started to fade, but the dizziness was starting to wear off, and his mind was clearing. Had he really seen what he thought he'd seen? Had his friends really been standing and running and hopping on the water? Certainly he must have imagined it, or dreamt it as he was drowning in the flood.

"My friends…"

"That's right," she responded. "They still need you."

"But aren't they safe on the ark?"

Thimblerig's groundmother put the ginger to her mouth for a nibble, but scrunched her face terribly, and she quickly spit it out. "Help me up, cub," she said, struggling to stand. Thimblerig jumped up to give her a hand and she quickly shuffled back over to the rock shelf and replaced the root on which she'd been nibbling.

"Something wrong with the ginger?" Thimblerig asked.

"It wasn't ginger," she said, irritated. "It looked like ginger on the outside, but on the inside it was something else entirely." She turned to face Thimblerig. "It's an easy mistake to make with roots, and with animals. Even on the ark."

"Are you saying that there are animals on the ark that aren't what they seem?"

"Is that what you think I'm saying?" she asked mischievously.

"You and the unicorn," Thimblerig sighed, closing his eyes. "Is there a rule that once you die you can't just say things straight?"

A pair of surprisingly strong arms encircled Thimblerig, and he opened his eyes to find his groundmother hugging him. She looked up, smiling. "Sometimes we need the struggle, but take heart, Thimblerig. From now on you won't be struggling alone."

216

He smiled back, and let himself lean into the hug, enjoying the down-to-earth smell of his groundmother and the comforting feeling of her arms around his neck. It had been a long time since another animal had held him affectionately, and it occurred to him that he'd missed it.

Everything else could wait.

CHAPTER 28
HOME

"I think he's coming around…"

Thimblerig heard Mullins' voice, thick with concern, but it was coming from far away, as if the gazelle was standing on one side of the burrow, whispering. There were other voices whispering also, but the groundhog could only make out bits and pieces of what they were saying.

"…lost a lot of blood…"

"…thought he was a goner…"

A part of Thimblerig wanted to descend back into the darkness, back to his groundmother's burrow. It had to be a better place than this, where animals had problems and lost a lot of blood and were thought to be goners.

But he couldn't go back. At least not right now. His groundmother had made it clear that he still had work to do. He'd wanted to tell her that he was sorry for running away, for not being there when she was dying, but he hadn't gotten the chance.

"'Rig? Can you hear me? Can you give some sort of sign?" Another familiar yet muffled voice whispered through the dark haze that still surrounded him.

Big Bunco…

What is a Big Bunco?

It's a name. It came floating to him like a feather floating on a breeze. It's the name of someone whom he cared about, someone who cared about him.

He became aware of a new sensation; the fur on his head was being stroked gently, lovingly.

"It's alright, he'll come around when he's ready."

Sheila. It was Sheila's voice. Sheila who had carried him back from the flood in her warm pouch, like a child. He should have been insulted by the idea that anyone would carry him like a child. Instead, the intimacy of the act touched him.

218

And he then he knew where he was. He could smell the animals surrounding him and feel the rocking of the waves and the winds as they buffeted outside. He scratched a nail down on the ground beneath and felt firm wood.

He knew exactly where he was.

He'd escaped the flood. He'd escaped Blonger. He knew that the wild dogs were no longer a threat to him or anyone else, and he knew how he'd gotten where he was. He knew that his friends had risked everything to rescue him. He knew that together they'd confronted Blonger, they'd plucked him from the tree, and with the help of the unicorn, they'd run across the waters to save him and bring him back to the place of safety.

He opened his eyes to see that they were there. They were all there, looks of concern mixed with relief etched on their faces.

All of them.

His company of animals.

The suckers.

The believers.

His friends.

Sheila.

They were all there.

THE END

Thank you for taking time to read **Thimblerig's Ark**. If you enjoyed it, please consider telling your friends or posting a short review on Amazon, B&N, Lulu, or Goodreads. Word of mouth is an author's best friend and is much appreciated!

Meanwhile, be on the lookout for **Thimblerig's Ark: Forty Days and Nights**, coming out in 2015!

Nate Fleming
Chengdu, China